THE MISTRESS

VALERIE KEOGH

Boldwood

First published in Great Britain in 2024 by Boldwood Books Ltd.

Copyright © Valerie Keogh, 2024

Cover Design by Head Design Ltd

Cover Photography: Shutterstock

Every effort has been made to obtain the necessary permissions with reference to copyright material, both illustrative and quoted. We apologise for any omissions in this respect and will be pleased to make the appropriate acknowledgements in any future edition.

A CIP catalogue record for this book is available from the British Library.

Paperback ISBN 978-1-80549-422-5

Large Print ISBN 978-1-80549-420-1

Hardback ISBN 978-1-80549-421-8

Ebook ISBN 978-1-80549-424-9

Kindle ISBN 978-1-80549-423-2

Audio CD ISBN 978-1-80549-415-7

MP3 CD ISBN 978-1-80549-416-4

Digital audio download ISBN 978-1-80549-418-8

Boldwood Books Ltd
23 Bowerdean Street
London SW6 3TN
www.boldwoodbooks.com

For
Tony and Jen
With love.

PART I

HANNAH

I was brushing my hair when Ivan came into the bedroom. He said nothing, just stood there looking at me. I wasn't easily intimidated, but he was a big man and he had an air about him that said he could resort to violence if necessary. He operated in the shadier end of the world of finance. Shady but incredibly lucrative. Perhaps there, he needed to intimidate when necessary. I'd seen the way his lackeys bowed and scraped to him, the wary look in their eyes. I'd even heard the words they'd muttered behind his back when they thought nobody was listening.

But, although our relationship was coming apart like the seams on a cheap shirt, I was still his wife. Before we'd married, he'd treated me like a goddess. Afterwards, within a few months, I was relegated to a mere female.

He'd recently begun to cast aspersions, but he'd never been violent. Until now.

I was stunned and cried out when he knocked the brush from my hand, grabbed my hair and dragged me from the stool to the floor.

'How about telling me exactly what these are for,' he said,

pressing a card of tablets into my face, the foil scratching my skin.

It's hard to think sensibly when your hair is being pulled from your scalp so I jumped to the first lie I could squeeze out. 'They're for headaches. Remember, I get them now and then.' It might have worked. It was true that I suffered, although it was more frequently a convenient excuse.

He pulled me to my feet, ignoring my squeal of pain. 'I checked, bitch.' He crushed the card against my mouth. 'The contraceptive pill. You've been lying to me all these months.'

I might have explained to him then that I wasn't happy in the marriage, that it had been a mistake, and bringing a child into it wasn't going to make it any better – I would have if he hadn't drawn his hand back and walloped me across the face. His other hand was still wrapped in my hair so I wasn't knocked to the ground, but it felt as if my brain was rattling against the walls of my skull.

'Lies, every damn day. Milking me for every penny you can get your grubby little hands on. You'd never any intention of giving me a child, did you?'

Pain can make people say anything. It's why torture is so effective. 'No, I didn't.' It was a stupid time to choose to be honest, a crazy time to tell him, 'You're not fit to be a father.' Nor was I fit to be a mother, but there was no time to explore that as he drew his hand back for a second time. Held as I was, it was impossible to avoid the blow. This time, though, he released my hair as he hit and I was thrown against the wall. It seemed a good idea to slide to the floor, not that I had a choice; the blow had stunned me. Foolishly, I thought that was it, that he'd leave me there and take his anger downstairs to drown it in whisky. It took the toe of his shoes hitting my ribs to alert me to the danger I was in, but by then it was too late.

I don't know how long the assault lasted; I was out of it by the

third or fourth kick. When I came to, I was swaddled in the duvet pulled from our bed. I didn't know if he'd thrown it around me in a last kindly gesture before leaving me there, or whether I'd pulled it down in an attempt to protect myself from his blows. Whatever the reason, it was a soft surface to lie on until I could bring myself to move. I wasn't sure when that would be; it seemed that every part of my body hurt. I was still alive so consoled myself with the hope that he'd done no serious damage.

Shock can override pain, knocking you out to allow your body time to recover. I woke a few times, once for long enough to drag myself up onto the bed and rest my throbbing head on a pillow. Part of me expected Ivan to come and check on me, part of me afraid of what he'd do if he did. I looked around for my mobile. Unable to see it, I guessed he'd taken it with him. It didn't matter. There was nobody to ring. Ringing the police crossed my mind briefly but before I could decide, I fell asleep again, away from the pain.

When I awoke, I knew from the change in the light that it was a long time later. I uncurled and lifted my head a little to listen. If Ivan was around, he was staying remarkably quiet. Maybe he was embarrassed by his loss of temper. Not enough to come and apologise though. I turned, gasping in pain. Whereas earlier, various parts of me hurt individually, now it was a full, all-consuming blanket of pain. To add to my discomfort, I needed to wee.

I shuffled carefully, painfully, to the side of the bed, and attempted to get to my feet. When that appeared to be beyond my abilities, I crawled, slowly, hand, knee, hand, knee, stopping every few inches to catch my breath, gasping when that sent a dagger of pain through my chest. The cold tiles of the en suite bathroom were torture to cross and I peppered the floor with tears. And then there was the struggle to get onto the toilet, grasping the rim, pulling myself up, groaning in pain as I turned to sit, more pain

then, even more when I peed, unsurprised when I looked into the toilet bowl to see it streaked with blood.

I used the side of the bath to push to my feet rather than crawling again. It was a bad idea... standing... because now, I could see myself in the bathroom mirror. I gasped in shock and lifted a hand to my face. Nothing seemed broken, but my face was a mess. Red carpet burns across one cheek, purple bruising on both, my top lip bloody and swollen. Multiple marks of his ire dotted both arms and when I pulled up my T-shirt, I gulped to see the mass of bruising on both sides. 'Bastard,' I muttered.

I wasn't planning on ringing the police, but I needed to make him pay for what he'd done to me. For that, I needed my phone. A photo, after all, was worth a thousand words.

It took a long time to negotiate the stairs. I clung onto the banisters with both hands, gasping at each step downward, grunting as pain overwhelmed me, waiting till it eased before moving again. There were plenty of tears and moments when I was certain I couldn't go on before I made it to the hallway. The door to the kitchen seemed a million miles away. I was desperate enough by then to call out for Ivan, my voice a plaintive squeak that wouldn't have been heard on the other side of any of the closed doors. Trying again, I didn't manage much better, the sound fading quickly into a silence that suddenly struck me as unusual.

Normally, if he was home, Ivan would have the TV blasting. The bastard must have gone out.

It seemed I was on my own. I should be used to that.

Reaching the kitchen door, I pushed it open. Pain was slowing everything down, including my reactions, so it took a few seconds to understand what I was seeing. And a few more to realise that the body stretched out on the kitchen floor was my darling husband's.

2

Even if I'd been able, I wouldn't have rushed to his side. Instead, I stood in the doorway, trying to decide whether I could see the rise and fall of his chest to indicate he was alive, or whether I was in luck and the vicious bastard had popped his clogs.

But tears had blurred my eyesight and it wasn't until I had shuffled painfully across the room that I realised I was out of luck yet again. He was breathing. As I stood looking down at him, wondering what I should do, he opened his eyes and glared at me.

'Wurg da bla.'

Had the beating I'd suffered affected my hearing? 'What?'

He screwed up his face – no, half his face – then tried again. The strangled sounds made no sense. It took a while before clarity dawned on my pain wracked brain. A stroke... he'd had a stroke! He'd probably pushed his blood pressure up while he was beating the living crap out of me. Karma. The idea made me smile, then grimace and lift a finger to my burst lip.

'Wurg da bla.'

I looked down at him and sneered. 'Is that you saying sorry?' I would have liked to have kicked him where it hurt and would

have done if every movement didn't cause me agony. My phone was on the counter. It took me several minutes to take photographs of the bruises that streaked and coloured my body, reaching painfully to document as many as possible. Only when I was done did I press triple nine.

Perhaps it was the way I spoke, my voice barely above a whisper, rather than what I said that had both police and two ambulances arriving not many minutes later. I struggled to the door in anticipation and stood braced in the doorway as they pulled up one in front of the other. The posse to my rescue.

They were gentle with me, helping me onto a trolley, wrapping me in a blanket. I hadn't realised I was shivering till then, hadn't realised I was crying until one of the paramedics wiped a cool cloth over my face. 'Hush, don't cry, you're safe now.'

They must have given me something for the pain because next I knew, I was in a cubicle, surrounded on three sides by a white curtain, leads trailing from various parts of me to monitors that beeped reassuringly. There were voices but none I recognised, and none were directed my way.

When someone did come, a scrub-suited man who looked about sixteen and who introduced himself as Dr Peterson, the pain had returned. He checked my notes and peered knowledgeably at the monitors, as if to reassure himself, and perhaps me, that he knew what he was doing.

'Despite everything,' he said, 'you're probably concerned about your husband so I'll set your mind at rest by saying he's in a stable condition. The next twenty-four hours will be crucial.' His rather cherub-like countenance was marred by a sudden frown. 'Unfortunately, lying on that hard floor for the length of time he was, has resulted in some consequences for him.'

I could have told him that I didn't care about Ivan's condition, certainly wasn't interested in any consequences, that all I wanted

to do was get more of whatever drug they'd given me and drift off. When the doctor looked as if he was going to elaborate on my husband's plight, I moved slightly, then groaned. No acting skills were required; the pain was incredible.

'Okay,' Peterson said. 'Let's concentrate on getting you sorted.' He vanished, returning a moment later with a nurse in tow. There was some muttering, some fiddling with the intravenous line that was attached to my right arm, and then merciful relief.

Over the next few hours, as I drifted in and out of sleep, I was X-rayed, scanned, examined by people whose names and qualifications were heard in a drug-filled haze, suffered someone struggling to find a vein in my bruised arms from which they eventually drained what seemed like an awful lot of blood. Everything was explained to me in great detail that was forgotten as soon as heard. Finally, I was wheeled into a small, four-bedded room and helped across onto a bed.

A nurse bustled about, settling me, checking the monitors, asking me incessantly if there was anything I needed.

'No,' I said, not for the first time. 'I'm okay, thank you.' The buzz of whatever they'd given me earlier had worn off, but the vicious pain I'd experienced had eased to a dull ache. I needed to think; it was better to be alert.

The nurse fussed about a little longer, then apologetically said, 'There's a couple of coppers outside who want to have a word; do you think you're up to it?'

Definitely better to be alert if I was going to speak to them. Not that I'd anything to worry about, nothing to hide. I was blameless in this. For a change, I was the victim.

They didn't need to know that I planned to make Ivan pay for what he'd done to me. They didn't need to know that at all.

I'm not quite certain why I married Ivan. After I graduated from university, I took a position with a very exclusive public relations company. It had been my plan to work hard and make my way to the top. That was before I discovered what an incredibly vicious world it was. I'd thought I was tough, but compared to some of the barracudas I met, I was a helpless kitten.

So I did what women had done for centuries. I took the easy way out. I was beautiful, educated, charming if the situation required, any man's perfect other half. And there were plenty of men who'd happily pay for the option. Not *pay* pay, I wasn't a prostitute, although I suppose there are others who would argue that accepting accommodation, credit cards, spending money, whatever I needed, was akin to being paid. I considered I was making use of my natural talents.

So why did I marry Ivan?

Because I'd noticed two things when I hit thirty-nine. The first was that it took more time and money to keep looking as good as I did; the second was that I'd started to compare myself with the other women who crowded the pubs and clubs I frequented. The

equally beautiful, *younger* women. It became increasingly obvious that the men I was attracted to, were attracted to them.

Anyone who argued that it came down to personality was fooling themselves. In the busy nightlife that was upmarket London in the twenty twenties, it was appearance that counted.

It was around that time of self-doubt that Ivan wandered into my orbit. He was rich, handsome enough for a man pushing seventy, and flatteringly attentive. He courted me with weekends away in five-star hotels, a diamond bracelet I admired in Tiffany's on a weekend to New York, shopping trips to Harrods, everything a woman like me could desire.

'Marry me,' he'd said while we were out for dinner one night only a couple of months after meeting. He reached into his pocket, pulled out a ring box and flicked it open with his thumb.

The sparkle of the diamond under the restaurant lights almost took my breath away. It was a huge, almost vulgarly large solitaire.

I had always been against marriage or any kind of commitment. My father, who had walked out on us – on me – when I was only ten, had a lot to answer for. It was thanks to him that I was unwilling to put myself in the position of being abandoned again. But now that I was pushing forty, perhaps it was time to be clever and think of my future. I looked at Ivan in that upmarket restaurant, saw his shirt stretch across his paunch, the buttons straining to hold him in, and thought maybe this would be a good move for me. He was almost seventy, overweight, with a high colour in his cheeks. He drank too much, and smoked cigars where he could. He looked like a man who wouldn't make old bones. I didn't think there was any fear he might abandon me – dying was a different matter and his death would leave me more than comfortably off. 'Yes,' I said, sliding my hand across the table to allow him to slip the ring in place, 'I'll marry you.'

Marry in haste... who doesn't know the second part of that

annoying epigram? Ivan had mentioned a family home a few miles from Windsor. What he hadn't said was that this is where he expected us to live. All the bloody time. He had an office there, and still ran his financial business from it. He also made it more than clear that he'd expected to hear the pitter patter of tiny feet in the not-too-distant future.

I quickly became disillusioned with the turn my life had taken. I'd turned into a damn housewife. The most Ivan would countenance was a cleaner once a fortnight. And even then, he insisted they had to be supervised in every room for fear they might damage some of the tatty family heirlooms in his twee, chintzy country pile.

It didn't take me long to discover my beloved husband didn't love me. It shouldn't have come as a surprise. I didn't love him either. The big problem was in the level of our expectations. I'd got what I'd wanted, although being buried in the countryside wasn't exactly how I'd envisaged my life, but *he* didn't get what he wanted. A child. Ivan had waited till he was almost seventy before realising he wanted one and expected his wife to be a broodmare. He chose me because I was beautiful, and would, he assumed, have beautiful babies.

He also assumed I was far younger than I was, but what woman of a certain age doesn't lie and subtract a couple of years, or six in my case.

When there was no sign of a child appearing, the distance between us – already grand-canyon sized – grew deeper. I began to see dislike rather than possessiveness in his gaze, to feel a chilly reluctance in the press of his lips against my cheek. Until that final day, when the discovery of what he'd have seen as my treachery tipped him over the edge into vicious hatred.

* * *

I was kept a few days in hospital before being released with a warning to return if I suffered any headaches or if the blood in my wee returned.

It was another couple of weeks before Ivan was allowed home.

He was only home a couple of days when I knew I couldn't stay. It was something unbelievably simple that gave me that final push. I'd been searching through the bookshelves in our living room in search of a book to lift my mood, discounting ones I'd never read in favour of ones I'd read and knew would suit, where if they weren't quite happy ever after, the main female character always came out on top. I needed that story. To know that it existed somewhere. I was on my knees, searching through the lower shelves, pulling out each book, one by one, shoving it back in frustration when it wasn't what I needed. And then I came to a book I hadn't read in years. It perfectly suited the mood I was in and I lifted it out with a smile.

Struggling wearily to my feet, I crossed to the sofa, sat, and curled up. Ready to dive into the book, I flicked the pages to the start of chapter one, unsurprised when something fell from between the pages. I had a habit of using whatever came to hand as a bookmark and frequently found receipts, scraps of paper, old envelopes between the pages of books I'd read. Whatever this was, it fluttered once before landing face down on the carpet. It was slightly out of reach and moving still caused me some discomfort, but as I read, my eyes kept flicking towards it so that after only a few pages, I grunted in annoyance, put the book down on the back of the sofa and swung my legs slowly to the floor.

I reached for the small card and turned it over with little curiosity, my eyes widening when I realised it was a photograph of me and an old boyfriend.

Shuffling along the sofa, I held it closer to the lamp. I knew who it was, of course. Mark Shepherd. How could I forget a man

who'd loved me so desperately? I turned to look at the back. Nothing written there. It didn't matter; it took only seconds to remember when it was taken. Twenty years before. My last year in university. The knuckling-down year.

I brushed a finger over his face and reached for the memory. It came back like a caress from the past and, for the first time since Ivan's attack, I felt a lessening of the tension and fear that had gripped me.

Mark had made me feel loved.

I should never have let him go.

4

Mark Shepherd – I'd seen him that first week in university, when I was still buzzing with excitement to be in Bristol, away from home, everything, everybody oozing with potential. Like most women, I'd checked out every handsome, or near-handsome guy, marking them out of ten based only on appearance. We were young, self-obsessed, and superficial. Mark had a rather babyish, round face, his physique gangly and boyish, but he'd still warranted a second look and ticked a healthy seven on my personal hunkometer. I was reading public relations and psychology; he was reading psychology and law so we shared several modules but we never became friendly. He was always on the periphery of the crowd, pushed there by more vocal, active, assertive guys who were simply more fun to be with.

My first year in university, I lived on the campus. The accommodation was expensive, convenient, and came with a long list of rules and regulations. My mother was footing the bill so the cost didn't bother me. It was the grating rules and regulations that did.

When I told my mother that I wanted to move out, I could hear the edge of worry in her voice. Not for me, not for any fear of

my safety off campus; no, I knew exactly what she was afraid of. That if I were unhappy, I'd give up and return home permanently. I could feel my lips curl in a sneer. That wouldn't please her at all. Our relationship was one of filial and maternal duty, not of love. I wasn't sure she even liked me.

I knew she'd be happier too if I wasn't going home for the holidays. I tried to keep my voice carefully neutral as I explained how much easier it would be if I stayed in Bristol for the summer. 'I could have a look for a job when I get home, of course, see if I can find something in Thornbury. I don't want to be sitting around all summer, getting under your feet.'

'Could you get a job easily there?' This was quicker than I'd expected. Maybe I was being foolish and she'd already considered this. Maybe I'd underestimated her.

'Yes.' I drew out the word, as if I was thinking of this idea for the first time. 'It might be the best bet really. Stay here for the summer. As long as you're still happy to pay for my accommodation.'

There was the merest hesitation before she replied. 'I suppose it's worth looking for somewhere off campus. As long as it doesn't cost more.'

Luckily, I did find somewhere cheaper. I'd already become friendly with a few students who were in the same boat as me and together, we trawled websites to find somewhere suitable. We weren't fussy, cheap being the only stipulation any of us made.

The house we found was a ramshackle dump a fifteen-minute walk from the university campus. There were three bedrooms and a tired bathroom upstairs; downstairs, what had been a living room and dining room, made two more bedrooms, and a poorly built extension housed a second bathroom. This had been added to the main house so badly that if it rained heavily, rivulets ran down the inside wall. On a sunny day, if you leaned your head

back and peered upward, you could see a crack filled with celestial blue.

That first year together was wild. None of us five cared that the place was a dump. We could do what we liked – and frequently did. There were no restrictions on parties, or drinking, or drugs. So we did them all. And each other. Boyfriends came and went with blithe regularity in a series of mutual, easy-come, easy-go relationships, the men's faces almost interchangeable in their young, immature handsomeness, their bodies muscular and athletic. It was all so easy.

Of the five who lived in that grotty house, I was the only one who'd never taken an official part-time job to make ends meet. This was thanks in part to the largesse of my mother, but mostly to my unofficial part-time job... the *generosity* of some of the men I dated.

After all, what was the point in having a fabulous body if I wasn't going to use it for something more than ornamental? Anyway, it wasn't as if it was hard work. The men were always older. Sometimes very old. And pitiful. In fact, I'd often wondered if there was a direct correlation between how pitiful they were and how much they were willing to pay for my company.

It was the only amusement I had from the encounters.

But facing into the final year, I knew things had to change. I had already applied for a position with one of the bigger public relations firms in London. It didn't pay well at entry level but I intended to race up the corporate ladder.

Getting a first would almost guarantee me the position. I was clever, just unfocused, and easily distracted. I had no choice but to step away from my social circle. Difficult to do. Worse if I noticed how well they were partying without me, my absence of as little import as a glass of water taken from a pond. It was torture. I thought my friends would come looking for me, but when I met

them in the lecture halls, it was as if they hadn't even noticed my absence at whatever social event had taken place the previous night. That was the superficiality of our relationships. There was nobody I was close to, no bosom buddy to bend my ear and fill me in on what was happening. I didn't care. It made it easier to take a step back. To focus on the endgame.

It was at that point that I really noticed Mark. In the two years since I'd first spotted his potential, he'd filled out – more man than boy now. I saw him in the library, looking as if he belonged there, hunched over his books, one spread open in front of him, a notebook to one side as he took notes, his pen scribbling furiously. His concentration was total, intense.

His dogged concentration inspired me to attempt a semblance of the same. It kept me from getting bored. Before long, I found myself fascinated by him. I had often given psychology lectures a miss, but started to attend them, scanning the hall from the doorway, eyes scanning the tiered rows for his tousled head of dark hair. Over the next few weeks, I slowly moved closer to Mark in the lecture hall until finally, I was sitting almost directly in front of him. He was always one of the last to leave; I'd watched him as he checked over the notes he'd taken before packing everything carefully away as other students milled around, laughing and talking.

I waited for my moment, that slight lull when the noisiest of the students had left and the next influx of students hadn't yet begun.

'Good lecture, wasn't it?' I said, pushing my expensively high-lighted, blonde hair back all the better to peer up at him. I broadened my smile and fluttered my eyelashes. Oh yes, I could play the game when I wanted to. I let my hair fall and gestured towards the dais. 'This was such a great lecture that my head is spinning. I'm going to get some coffee and see if I can make sense of it all.' I nodded and moved on a few steps, turning with a frown. 'You

know the way they say two heads are better than one – d'you fancy joining me? Perhaps we could chat about what he said. It'd help make it clear, I think.' I laughed in feigned embarrassment. 'Sorry, forget it; it probably already is to you.' I was a firm believer that subtlety was wasted on men so my invitation was clear, pointed even. If he took it to mean that I wasn't very bright, or certainly less intelligent than he was, if we got to know each other better, he'd soon learn that was incorrect. I was, as the teachers in my school used to say with heavy sarcasm, *too clever for my own good*. But I could do dim like the best of them.

'Sure.' He nodded towards the exit. 'We'd better get out of here anyway, unless you want to stay to listen to a lecture in information technology.'

I wasn't sure if this was supposed to be a joke. Then he grinned and I laughed to cover my sigh of relief.

There were several cafés dotted around the university. We went to the closest and were soon seated at a small table near the back. It was a little airless but that worked in my favour. After a few minutes, sipping our drinks, I wiped a hand across my forehead. 'It's warm in here, isn't it?'

I slipped the jacket I was wearing off and let it drop to the back of my chair. I was wearing a long-sleeved, cotton T-shirt, the material worn thin by years of washing. It was a favourite of mine; I'd wear it till it fell apart, and probably for a while afterwards. I plucked at it, pulling at the V-neck, and huffing a breath down my cleavage. I saw him look. A quick flick of his eyes. Enough, I hoped, to show an interest. I'd have been pissed if I'd wasted all this time on a man who wasn't interested in women. And if he liked women, there was no reason he wouldn't be interested in me. I was the perfect package. Nature had given me an ample bosom, slim waist, and long legs, all of which I was more than content to show off given the opportunity. I was often described as

beautiful, sometimes exotic. Mind you, when people got to know me better, the word that was most often used to describe me was bitch. I had no illusions; it was much more appropriate.

I hooked one arm on the back of the chair, the better to show off my attributes, and reached for the glass of Coke with my free hand. 'So what did you think of the lecture?'

'It was good. The professor is an excellent lecturer. I like the way he backs up what he says by citing documented research.'

Mark had a low, melodic voice and a way with words that kept my attention even when the subject matter began to pall. He was knowledgeable about the subject, and it took no more than the odd *mmhm* of agreement from me to keep him talking.

He'd soon leave. I knew his timetable better than I knew my own and he had one of his law lectures next. Since, as far as I could gather, he never missed one, there was no point in trying to lure him away with promises of a quick tumble. He was still talking, using his hands to make a point, his face alive with enthusiasm I could never muster for any of my courses. His face, slightly cherubic two years before, had slimmed down. It was divided by an aquiline nose set over lips that were fuller than usual for a man. I imagined them locked to mine, then moving lower. Much lower. I shivered.

'You okay?' he asked with quick concern. He looked up to the air-conditioning unit set among the pipes that crossed the café ceiling. 'They can belt out cold air sometimes; you better be careful you don't catch a chill.'

We could go somewhere and you could warm me up. It's what I'd have said to any of the other men I knew, and we'd leave and head to my room or theirs, or to one of the shady, private places dotted around the university campus – the maintenance rooms on the ground floor of the main building, the groundsmen's huts which were supposed to be locked but rarely were, even to the shrubbery

by the north wall. I'd used them all over the last couple of years. But as I looked across the table and took in his genuinely concerned expression, I knew this guy was different. Or maybe I was. This studying lark, perhaps it had altered my brain chemistry.

I stood up so abruptly, he reared back, startled.

'Sorry.' I ran a hand through my hair. 'I forgot I have a tutorial. I better run.' I gathered my books, my bag, my coat, and with them threatening to fall from my arms at every stop, I hurried across the café. He called my name. I heard it drifting over the hubbub, humming there before dissipating and dying before I'd reached the exit.

I'd lied; I had no tutorial. There were lectures I should attend but even my new-found desire to succeed couldn't get me to attend any more that day. Instead, I dropped the books I'd borrowed back to the library and headed off to my digs. It was a relief to find nobody home. I needed silence to get my thoughts in order.

Mark – he'd shimmied under my skin.

It was that strange feeling that had sent me racing from the café.

It might have been love.

Love wasn't a concept I was familiar with. I had a more than passing acquaintance with lust. There were no strings, no need for chemistry or promises of everlasting devotion. A quick wham bam, thanks very much, and on to the next. It was what I was used to. It was what I wanted. A mutually enjoyable experience where it didn't bother me if they didn't call, didn't show up, didn't care. I was the same, every relationship a come-day, go-day one. I wasn't looking for more and certainly not in the year where I was supposed to be knuckling down to my studies.

But it was too late.

Mark was waiting in the entrance to the lecture hall the next time our schedules coincided. He didn't say anything as I joined him, he merely reached for my hand and held it in his as other students swirled past oblivious to the little drama being enacted.

For months, I was the perfect girlfriend. We studied together. Attended lectures together when we could. Discussed them afterwards, teasing out the ideas until they made sense to both of us. I even began to dress differently – less pseudo-goth, more pseudo-geek. If the new persona amused me, I'm not sure Mark ever

noticed. He was sloppily adoring, and I could have worn rags and he'd still have smiled in appreciation.

It was uplifting, almost overwhelming, utterly satisfying. He treated me as if I was made of fine porcelain, as if his fingers would bruise my flesh.

I brushed my finger over the photograph again, lingering on the curve of Mark's cheek. It had been good. I struggled to my feet and went to the kitchen for a glass of wine. If I was going to saunter down memory lane, I needed something to smooth the journey. It made sense to bring the bottle back with me. My past was a prickly place to visit; the balm of alcohol would be a necessity.

With a pillow behind me, and my legs curled under, I held the photograph of Mark in one hand while I sipped the nicely chilled Sauvignon and allowed myself to be swept back to a time when I really thought I was different.

Or was it merely the times that were different? For those months we were together, I was determined to get the first that would ensure I had a good start in London so was content to focus on my studies. When exams were over, when we had done as much as we could, and all we could do was wait for the outcome, that's when things changed.

I can even pinpoint the exact moment.

Mark and I had been together six months. Most of it had vanished in a haze of studying, both of us determined to do well, but there were also hours, days, where we held hands, walked, talked, just happy to be together.

He wasn't staying in Bristol for the summer, heading instead to his parents' home in Cheltenham.

'Come for a long weekend,' Mark had urged after we'd celebrated for a few days, losing hours to hangovers. 'You haven't got a job yet; make the most of it. My parents would love to meet you.'

His parents would love to meet me. I looked at his handsome face and knew that was it. The end of the idyll. I knew he loved me. He'd told me often enough. And I'd said the same. Meaningless words. I remembered my father saying the same as he'd tucked me into bed, pressing his scratchy face against my ten-year-old cheek, telling me how much he loved me. I remembered the words as if they were still echoing. The last words he'd ever said to me. The next morning, he was gone. Without an excuse or a good-bye. Never to be seen again. Thailand, my mother said, many days later when I'd dredged up the courage to ask.

In the pain of abandonment, I remember promising that nobody was ever going to hurt me again. Far better to keep the barricades in place. Mark had come so very close to breaching them but now they were re-enforced and it was time to end something that should never have begun.

In any case, if he, or his parents, knew how I'd planned to earn my living during the summer, they'd have cast me aside lickety-split.

'I have job interviews lined up,' I said and stuck to that lie over the next few days until he left, promising to ring, to think of me every minute, to miss me desperately.

Once he was gone, I convinced myself that those months were an aberration. It was as if I'd been in stasis for months and had suddenly woken up. I looked at my boring, nerdy clothes in horror and quickly dispatched them to the nearest charity shop before digging out my older, skimpier, trendier clothes and step-ping back into the life I had lived prior to meeting him.

It didn't take long to pick up the strings, old friends behaving as if I hadn't vanished for months, old men-friends delighted to take my calls, more than delighted to fall back into our very satis-fyingly lucrative arrangement.

Mark's calls to me went unanswered. His increasingly

desperate messages deleted unread. I supposed I hoped he'd get the hint without my having to say the words. Perhaps I should have anticipated his next step. If I had, I'd have warned my house-mates that Mark and I were over. I'd have told them to tell him, or anyone else who came looking, that I'd left, gone abroad, some-where, anywhere.

I climbed out of the taxi late one evening, one of my elderly friends sliding out behind me. His hands were all over me with insistent impatience, determined as he was to get value for the money he'd given me.

I was wearing one of my come-hither dresses. Not that this particular man needed any encouragement, but it was part of the service I gave, to look so fabulous that every man would lust after me, making the man I was with feel like a god to have me. The dress was short, low-cut, skintight.

We were laughing as the taxi pulled away. Mine was forced, my elderly companion's laugh lecherous and expectant. I was trying to get him indoors, not that I was prudish, but neigh-bours had already complained to the landlord about the behaviour of some of the tenants. My housemates were game to experiment and weren't averse to swopping partners or having a ménage à trois or quatre depending on who was willing or able to partake, but they weren't at all interested in entering into a business arrangement. They didn't say, but I knew they thought I was a slut to get paid for what they were all giving away for free.

Perhaps they'd have been more impressed if they knew just how much I did earn. Dimitri, the man whose hands were desper-ately trying to get their bony fingers around my nipples, was one of my better investments. A few hours laughing at his idiotic, misogynistic, racist jokes, a meal at one of Bristol's finest restau-rants, ten minutes or so while his little pecker poked away, a bit of

acting as I shouted my pleasure – not at what he was doing, but that it was almost over. Two hundred quid well earned.

I was thinking of the money when I saw a figure move from the shadow of one of the overgrown bushes in the small front garden, guilt vying with irritation when I saw who it was.

Mark.

I fumbled in my bag for my keys and opened the door. 'Go ahead up,' I said to Dimitri, giving him a gentle shove. I knew, of old, he could become belligerent after a few drinks. It usually resulted in sex that was rougher than I liked, but thankfully quicker too so it balanced out. Anyway, the bruises never lasted long. Drink also made him more than stupidly macho and possessive. I could see him looking at Mark with narrowed eyes and a sneer on his lips. I could almost see him thinking, *I could take him.*

He probably could too. Dimitri worked out every morning. He might be three times our age, but he was fit. And strong. Mark, who was always a little soft around the middle, hadn't improved in the weeks since I'd seen him. I guessed he'd been drowning his sorrows in beer at his local.

'I'll be up in a minute.' I gave Dimitri a wink and another firmer push through the door. 'He's an old friend. I'll just have a quick word.' I leaned closer, stretched up on the toes of my stilettos so that my mouth was level with his ear. 'Make sure you don't start without me, okay?' I sucked his earlobe into my mouth,

hard, before letting him go with a sultry grin and another push. This time, he didn't resist and crossed into the small, untidy hallway. I waited until he'd climbed the stairway and vanished from sight before turning to Mark.

'What are you doing here?'

He took a step forward into the circle of light that shone from the hallway. In the brighter light, I could see what the shadows had hidden. His cheeks were gaunt, dark smudges ringed his eyes, and to add to the picture of complete misery, his lower lip trembled. 'You haven't been answering your phone. I was worried. I thought something must have happened to you.'

It had. I'd come to my senses. I couldn't – wouldn't – allow myself to be close to anyone, to be that vulnerable, that open to pain.

He took a step nearer and reached a hand towards me. It stayed there between us, looking abandoned, disconnected. I watched as beads of sweat popped on his forehead and tried to ignore the whipped-puppy hope in his eyes, the stupid determination in that fucking hand.

'Nothing happened.' *Get the message, you stupid boy; don't make me have to spell it out for you because I really, really don't want to hurt you.* 'I've just moved on.'

'With him?' He looked at the window above where a light had come on, then back to my face, his expression battling disbelief, despair, heartbreak.

It didn't give me any pleasure to watch him suffer as reality hit him. I could almost hear the crack and ensuing rumble as the pedestal he'd put me on fell apart and brick by brick, tumbled to the ground.

'I'd heard rumours,' he said, 'but I hadn't believed them.'

Rumours? It wasn't surprising really. I sighed heavily. 'My life

before I met you was none of your business. When we were together, I was faithful.' It was only a little white lie to allow him to salvage his pride. I had been *almost* faithful.

'And now?'

'Now?' I shook my head. 'It was great while it lasted, Mark, but it's over.'

'Just like that!'

I was going to trot out a trite, *all good things come to an end*, but I suddenly felt a twinge of guilt for causing, however inadvertently, the pain I saw flickering in his eyes. 'I'm sorry. I'm not good at saying goodbye. I hoped you'd get the message when I didn't reply to your calls.'

He looked at me in disbelief. 'Get the message? I love you, I thought—'

'What? That we were going to be together forever? Get real. We had a great time, but it was always destined to end.' I knew that; it seemed he didn't.

There was a rattle as the window above was opened. Mark and I both glanced up to see Dimitri's bare shoulders leaning out. I lifted a hand to stop any remark he might make. 'I'm coming.'

'Not without me, doll.' He sniggered and pulled himself back inside, the window shutting with a bang that made the glass rattle in the frame.

'I have to go.' I half turned away.

'No, don't go, please, Hannah.' He grabbed my arm, his fingers biting into my skin.

'I bruise easily, you know.'

He let go and ran a hand over his face. 'I don't understand, I thought you loved me.'

'I did.' Love is such a transient emotion. You can love someone desperately one day, kiss her on the cheek, then disappear as my

father had done, never to be seen again. 'Now I don't. It's that simple.' I pushed open the door. 'I really have to go.'

'To him? He's old enough to be your father.'

My patience was beginning to wear threadbare. 'He's good to me. Now, that's it. No more excuses or explanations. It was good. It's over. Move on, Mark, and please,' I took a step into the hallway, kicking an abandoned shoe out of my way with more violence than was necessary, the shoe flying against the opposite wall and falling to the floor with a thump, 'don't come back.'

My last sight of him was him standing there with that whipped, abandoned-puppy expression on his face. He didn't leave immediately. I know because I peered through a gap in the broken letterbox flap, almost relenting when I heard, 'I'll always love you.' Only almost relenting. I knew I'd done the right thing. Men always wanted you when you didn't want them; if you wanted them, they vanished. Far better to be the one to do the vanishing.

Mark would learn that life was full of hardship and pain. I'd done him a favour.

Only when Dimitri appeared on the top of the stairway, naked, his erection pointing at his impatiently lustful face, did I abandon my post and head up the stairs to earn the money he'd already given me.

* * *

I dropped the photograph on the sofa beside me. Mark had loved me so much.

I sipped my wine, my thoughts returning insistently to those months we were together. Was that the last time I'd felt truly happy?

Maybe, I'd been wrong and we could have made it. Twenty years before, I was too young to realise that not all men were like my father. Not all men left.

I'll always love you.

Maybe it wasn't too late.

Maybe I'd been wrong and we could have made it. Twenty
years before, I was too young to realise that not all men were like
my father. Not all men left.

I'll imagine so ...

Maybe it wasn't too late.

PART II

HANNAH AND SUSAN

HANNAH AND SUSAN

7

SUSAN

It was their turn to host Christmas dinner and Susan had spent the last couple of weeks scribbling lists, hurrying to shops, dashing home laden with bags. Cleaning, cooking, wrapping. And now on the day before, she was almost done. The tree was up and decorated. Everywhere had a bauble or piece of tinsel hanging from something.

The space under the tree was filled with beautifully wrapped gifts. Some were for her husband, Mark. Some for her two sisters, their husbands, and their children. Something too for her mother and her husband. But most of the presents were for her son.

'You ruin the boy,' her mother had said more than once.

Susan was accused of mollycoddling him, of having her only child tied to her apron strings, of smothering the poor boy. Even her husband, a kind, sensitive man, thought she was too involved. 'You need to let go. You're strangling him, and he'll start to resent it.'

Perhaps if she'd had more children, she could have shared her love, but although they'd wanted them, and kept trying, it had

never happened, so all the love she had was given undiluted to Andrew.

But even the most critical of her detractors, and that would be her mother, would have to admit that Drew was a lovely boy. Polite, well-behaved, a credit to his parents. When she heard the praise, Susan felt the warm glow of satisfaction. *You see*, she wanted to tell them all, *wrapping him in love did no harm at all*. She would have done if hubris didn't scare her, the fear that she might be struck down for her pride in him.

A bright, intelligent boy, if he had one fault it was that, like his father, he had little ambition. It was Susan who'd encouraged him to think about university, she who painted a bright future for him once he was settled in a good career with a healthy income.

When he'd shown a vague interest in computer science, it had been enough for Susan. She spent every spare minute over the last few weeks doing research on which university would be best. There were seven in and around Bristol but she quickly narrowed it down to two that offered computer science. The University of Bristol and the University of West of England. She printed out information for both and put it into two different folders before gift-wrapping them and tying them together with a wide Christmas ribbon, a big, floppy bow adding an extra flourish. She propped the package under the Christmas tree and was still fussing with the position of it amongst all the other gifts when she sensed she was no longer alone in the room. With a final adjustment, she turned to see Mark standing there, one shoulder propped against the wall. She straightened and took a step back, casting a pleased eye over the display.

'Are you sure you know what you're doing?'

'Don't spoil it, please.' She reached a hand towards him, sighing when she felt his fingers close around it. There was no resistance as he pulled her towards him, and she moved into the

curve of his body where she fit like a perfectly engineered jigsaw piece, their individual strengths and weaknesses clicking into place. They complemented one another, had done from the very beginning, their love deepening with the years. 'He'll love it. You know what he's like; he's so laid-back.' *He is just like you*, she wanted to say, *intellectually brilliant, but useless at looking into the future.* Had it been left to Mark, they'd still be living in the tiny apartment they'd first bought, and he'd still be working for that going-nowhere company. It was she who'd pushed for the move to a small house, then a few years later, when funds allowed, to this bigger one. It was she who'd encouraged him to take risks, to apply for positions with better companies and to move on to even better when he'd a few years' experience. It was thanks to her that they had this lovely home and Mark was a senior partner in a successful and well-regarded law firm.

She pressed a kiss to his cheek. 'Now, if you want dinner, you'd better let me go.' She wasn't surprised when instead of doing as she'd asked, he tightened his hold on her.

'Drew's out till later; why don't we go upstairs and have a siesta?'

And they did. Susan could never resist him. With Drew living at home, and his friends calling around, often unannounced and sometimes staying in their spare room for days, the times for spontaneity were few, making them more precious when they came.

Perhaps she should have considered this the following day when Drew opened her carefully wrapped gift. The room was full of noise, the high-pitched squeals of her sisters' combined seven offspring, the low rumble of laughter from her brothers-in-law, her sisters running commentary on every gift that was opened, and her mother's voice trying to be heard over everyone else. They faded away as Drew opened the files and looked at her with the

determined expression he'd learned from his father. 'I'm going to the University of Glasgow; I've already looked into it.'

There was no thought then of the freedom she and Mark would have; all she could think of was how far away Glasgow was. It might as well be the other end of the earth. 'Glasgow!' She'd laughed, a forced, harsh sound, wanting to believe he was joking. 'Don't be silly. Why on earth would you go all the way to Glasgow?'

'They do a well-regarded computer science course.' Drew tossed the files she'd taken so much trouble over onto the sofa, where they teetered before sliding to the floor.

Susan stared at them. The information she'd so diligently sourced and printed out had slid free, the pages lying slumped against the bottom of the sofa. Discarded, like her dreams. *Her dreams*. She gulped back the lump of horror that had become lodged in her throat. Was that it? Was she living vicariously through her son to make up for the life she'd missed?

Ten years older than the eldest of her two younger sisters, her plans to go to university had been scuppered when her father, away in the US on a temporary secondment from his job, had rang her mother to say he'd met someone, had fallen completely and unexpectedly in love, and wasn't coming back. He'd sent money – he wasn't a total pig – but what he sent barely covered the mortgage when interest rates climbed through the roof. Her mother switched to a night job which saved childcare bills, but she began to depend more and more on her eldest daughter to close the gaping hole her husband's absence made in their lives and their finances.

When Susan finished school, with grades that would have got her into any university she'd wanted, she applied for a job in a local supermarket that allowed her to work flexi-hours. And if, now and then, she found it stultifyingly boring, if sometimes she

could hear her grey cells begin to rust, she'd tell herself that someday... someday... her life would improve.

Two things stopped her from growing bitter. She adored her sisters. Jan and Emma were adorable children who grew into charming, funny, entertaining, clever teens. Susan could have gone to university then as a mature student, could have grabbed her dreams back and made them come true. But her sisters were both so clever, and they had such plans. All of which needed funding. And so it was that Susan stayed working in the same supermarket where her loyalty had been rewarded by a management role, to watch with pride and an almost overwhelming envy as her siblings grasped their dreams.

After they'd graduated, both of them leaving Bristol to work in London, Susan had met Mark so the wrench of them leaving wasn't too traumatic. And when, a year later, her mother married a man she worked with and left to live in Spain, Susan clung to Mark for support. Perhaps it was the reason their relationship moved as fast as it had. She'd never been alone; couldn't handle the emptiness of the now-too-big house she'd lived in all her life. When her mother suggested it be sold, Susan hadn't the energy to be sad, abandoned, lost.

It was then that Mark threw her a lifeline. 'Will you marry me?'

They were in McDonald's, her teeth almost closed on the Big Mac she'd ordered. She'd sat there, unable to bite down, eventually opening her mouth to withdraw the burger, dropping it messily onto the bag she'd ripped open only seconds before. In a different life.

The question was so unexpected, the venue so incongruous, maybe she'd imagined it. She looked up from her contemplation of the suddenly unappetising meal and met Mark's eyes across the table. He was looking puzzled. 'Sorry, I'm daydreaming,' she said.

Of course, he hadn't proposed. They were in McDonald's, for goodness' sake, hardly a venue for a romantic proposal. 'Did you ask me something?'

'I asked you to marry me, Susan.'

She stared at him, wanting to say no, that there was a world she hadn't seen, a life she hadn't yet lived. But she was still feeling lost and so she reached for the lifeline he'd thrown her. 'Yes, I'll marry you.'

8

SUSAN

That was nineteen years before. Susan had never regretted saying 'yes' that day although she wasn't sure she'd loved him. Not then. That had come later, growing slowly as they'd made a life together. One that was made better when her sisters came to live nearby, making her feel whole again. Then, to glue it all together, she and Mark had a child.

And now Drew was leaving her.

Her eyes flitted over the information she'd so painstakingly put together. Both universities had an excellent computer science course. There was absolutely no need for Drew to traipse all the way to Scotland. But she wasn't stupid. To make an issue of it now would be to have him dig his heels in. He might have inherited his brains from his father, but his stubbornness had come undiluted from her.

It quickly became clear that everyone else – everyone – thought he'd made the right decision in choosing Glasgow. Even, to her annoyance, Mark.

'It'll do him good to live away from home for a few years. Let him learn some independence.'

Her mother, making her annual visit from Spain, was vocal in her praise for Drew's choice and took the first opportunity to have a quiet word with her daughter. 'I can see you're not happy with this—'

'Glasgow, Mum! Could he get further away?'

'It's a train ride. A short flight. He's not going to Australia.' Evelyn March put a gentle hand on her daughter's arm. 'You can't see it yet, but it'll be for the best. It's time to cut those apron strings. He'll be able to breathe, and you'll learn that he'll be perfectly safe outside your domain. You'll be able to get back to work. Get a life that doesn't revolve around your child.'

'Like you did?' The bitterness in the words surprised both of them, her mother pulling her hand away as if she'd been burnt, Susan reaching for her, a gesture that was destined to fail as her mother stepped back, nodded, and pushed through the door to where everyone else was enjoying pre-dinner drinks. Mark had been heavy handed with the measurements and already she could hear the noise level rising.

She hoped her mother would have another drink and forget to feel offended. If Susan didn't have to cook the damn dinner, she'd have had a few herself and drown her sorrows that her only child was choosing to go to university so far away.

Drew was good with his young cousins. He'd taken them up to the attic room where he had a den of sorts and would keep them there until it was time for dinner, by which time, the drinking members of the party would be immune to their noise. Jan and Emma, always the designated drivers, appeared not to hear the din their offspring made and certainly never made any attempt to quieten them. They followed a line of parenting that basically allowed their children to do what they wanted – and say what they wanted – usually at decibels that would normally come with a government health warning.

Susan loved her sisters but they'd developed into the kind of entitled mothers that tended to make women her age raise their eyes, and women of their mother's age either criticise bitterly or ignore by avoiding as much as possible.

Since criticism would have raised the hackles on both her sisters, Susan was almost relieved their mother chose to ignore. That she achieved this by downing glass after glass of whatever alcohol was poured for her didn't matter. Luckily, she was a cheerful drunk. As for her partner, Jacinto, the only indication he was inebriated was a deterioration in his already almost incomprehensible English so that by the end of the night nobody, not even his wife, could understand him.

Susan stood in the doorway of the living room. 'Everyone okay for drinks?' she said, although she knew they were, that Mark was taking good care of them. Everything was on schedule in the kitchen so she sat and joined in the conversations that were flowing. Like most women, her sisters and mother could carry on several at any one time without losing their train of thought, hopping from one topic to the next and then back with hardly a pause for breath.

Mark, like their husbands, usually gave up trying to follow after a while. In another twenty minutes or so, she'd find the three men ensconced in a corner, and her mother and sisters would gravitate together as the conversation became more personal.

They'd wait till Susan had gone to do the final preparations for dinner before putting their heads together and talking about her. Drew had thrown Glasgow into the mix before vanishing with his cousins. A deliberate ploy, he knew they'd work on her in his absence.

After dinner, she'd be at their mercy. The children would vanish with Drew again. Mark would take his brothers-in-law into his man-cave, the spare bedroom he used as an office where a

ridiculously over-large TV had pride of place, and they'd watch sport or some movie. Probably *Die Hard*. Again. Every year, they'd watch it at least once, and cheer every time as if they hadn't known how it was going to end, as if they believed that this time, it might end differently.

It didn't. It ended the same way every time. It was written in stone. Like Drew going to Glasgow. His future already cast.

Would he come home for Christmas next year? Or would he make his excuses and spend the holiday in Glasgow? She looked around the room at the animated faces of her family and wanted to scream at them. *Get out, all of you. Take your noisy brats and leave. If this is going to be our last Christmas with Drew, Mark and I would like to spend it with him. Just the three of us. The three fucking musketeers.*

But of course, she didn't say that. She didn't say anything, just kept smiling. Like she'd always done. Smiling and waiting for that interminable day to end.

There was no escape from it. Just as there wasn't from the inquisition her sisters and mother would put her through all in the interest of her welfare. *Concerned about her*. She predicted they'd start with those very words. She almost sneered at the inevitability of it all as she saw the conspiring glances as they'd finished tidying up after a meal she'd slaved over, the pleasure in it ruined by what was to come.

She'd polished off a couple of glasses of wine over dinner, and as the party divided as she'd predicted, she filled her glass again. It should have been the time to relax, a comfortable, post-prandial bliss where the women would sit and chat without fear of being interrupted for a while. Instead, the silence was heavy with anticipation.

They moved back into the living room. Susan took her usual

place at the end of the long sofa, the wine glass in her hand. Her mother sat on the other end. Jan and Emma hesitated before sitting in single chairs, Emma jumping up almost immediately to cross and take the seat between Susan and their mother. It was almost amusing to see how Susan had guessed correctly that it would be Emma, always the voice of reason, who'd be nominated to speak.

'We're concerned about you, Susan,' she said, leaning closer and resting a hand gently on her sister's thigh. She pulled it away, startled, when the response was a prolonged cackle of laughter.

Susan put her glass down on the side table as laughter threatened to spill the Merlot in a bloody splash down the cream damask of the sofa. 'I'm sorry.' It would have been easier to have controlled her laughter if her sister hadn't looked so offended, so fucking up her own arse. As it was, her laughter rolled on for longer, tears streaming down her face. It subsided to a chuckle before finally dying away. If the silence was uncomfortable before, it was ominous now.

'Well, you can see now why we're concerned!'

Emma turned to shoot a shushing glance at her mother before trying again. This time without the hand, as if afraid it was one step too far. 'As soon as Drew mentioned going to Glasgow, we knew there'd be trouble—'

'We?' It was better to know exactly what she was up against. Had they all ganged up on her. Even Mark?

Emma waved a hand around the room. 'The three of us. We knew how you'd feel.' She tried a smile. 'All being mothers, I suppose.'

Susan raised an eyebrow but didn't point out that their mother had been more than delighted when they'd moved out, how she'd departed for Spain without a backward glance or the slightest

regard for her eldest daughter. The daughter who'd brought her sisters up, who'd been there for them through exams, through the tough university years, the boyfriends, the ups and downs, who'd kept them all together while their mother worked.

She didn't resent them. Everyone left. It was the nature of life. Now Drew. It proved her point. 'I'm fine about Drew going to Glasgow. It's a good university. He's made a good choice.' She had no clue if it was a good university or not. It wasn't one she'd researched. She was sure it was perfectly acceptable. *If only it wasn't so far away.* Had she said that aloud? She was conscious of the worried glances that were being passed between her sisters and mother and turned to reach for her glass, giving herself time to come up with the correct reassuring words. 'I'm looking forward to having more time to myself. I'm thinking about getting back in the job market.'

'Good,' her mother nodded, as if it was done and dusted. 'You need to get a life.'

Susan had considered getting a part-time job years before when Drew had started school, but Mark wasn't keen on her returning to the only work she knew. 'I'm not sure it gives the right impression to have my wife working in the local co-op,' he'd said, laughing to show he'd meant no offence, that he wasn't really being a snob.

It was her fault. She'd pushed him to get to the top, and now that he was there, he liked the view.

She'd shrugged, stayed at home and contented herself with being the best wife and mother possible. The very thing that had chased Drew away. If he left, she was still a mother, wasn't she? And still a wife. Her life still had purpose. 'But he's going so far away.'

This time, she knew from the expressions on the faces

surrounding her that she'd spoken aloud, that they'd heard her plaintive cry. 'Listen to me!' She jumped to her feet, startling them. 'I'm being silly. It's only Glasgow. It'll be fine. Now,' she said, reaching for the remote control. 'I've recorded the King's speech; let's have a listen to what Charlie has to say.'

9

SUSAN

Bristol Temple Meads was always busy but it seemed to Susan that there was no space between the crowds, barely air to breathe, and certainly no room to release the grip she had on her son's arm despite his continued attempt to pull away.

Drew looked down at her with obvious impatience. 'I need to hurry, Ma, or I'll miss the train.'

He'd miss the train, then he'd have to stay with her. She clutched his arm more tightly. She was being stupid, of course she was, but the thought of him moving so far away made her heart ache and her head pound. Fear had dug sharp nails into her, and when she looked at him, at his young, innocent, boyish, darling face, they bit tighter and she was immediately dragged back to the delivery room and the agonising pain before he'd come blue and floppy into the world. Even now, eighteen years later, she could still remember the shock when she'd thought he'd died, that she'd done something wrong, that she'd killed her child. And then he'd screamed his way right into her heart, embedded himself so deeply, she'd never been able to let go.

The mass of people in the concourse didn't appear to be

moving, their necks all craning meerkat-like in the same direction. At first glance, Susan thought time had frozen, or maybe she just hoped it had. Her hand tightened on Drew's arm as she gasped. He looked at her, his expression part concern, part irritation.

She gave him a shaky smile that she hoped appeared reassuring. She wasn't going crazy. Time hadn't stood still. People were merely standing looking at the bright-yellow information displayed on the departure board. Others were moving, negotiating the gaps in between the unmoving figures. It was impossible to separate the noise into its individual components – the growl and scream of the train engines, security announcements, the blend of voices, shouts, laughter, the rumble of wheeled cases – it was almost overwhelming.

Or was it the impending loss that was sitting so heavily in her chest? Susan knew she was to blame for her son's decision to go to Glasgow. She'd held on too tight, and now she was going to lose him. Perhaps forever. She felt the tug on her arm as he moved forward, his eyes now fixed on the departure board, bright-yellow, determinedly cheerful figures telling the stark truth. The train was on time. It was going to Glasgow and taking Drew with it.

Don't leave me. The words a painful shriek in her head. She clamped her lips tightly together. She couldn't let them out.

'This is it,' Drew said, nodding toward the ticket barrier. He dropped his bulging holdall on the ground at his feet, the manoeuvre allowing him to remove his arm from her grasp. In the fuss over balancing his holdall on top of the wheelie suitcase Mark had been pulling, Susan was ignored. She stared at two people she loved most in the world. She was losing one. Luckily, she still had the other.

She'd have liked to have gone through with Drew, to have settled him into a seat, to make sure he got his luggage on board

safely, that he took out the sandwiches she'd made for him. She wanted to repeat the advice she'd already given him, about staying safe, making good friends, keeping out of bad company, eating well, not drinking too much. So much she'd have liked to say, but there he was, phone in his hand, ready to go through. A final hug. Her arms tight around him, holding on. His arms around her for a second, letting go, hands pulling her arms down. Pushing her away. 'I'll ring as soon as I get there,' he said, bending to plant a kiss against her cheek. 'Don't worry about me; I'll be fine and I'll be back before you get around to missing me.'

I miss you already. She shoved her hands in her pockets to stop herself reaching out to grab him for one more hug, for another chance to inhale the scent of him. Perhaps if she did, if she smelt the woody cologne he favoured as a young man, it would dispel the memory of him as a baby and it would be easier to let go.

'Bye, son.' Mark grabbed Drew in a hug, both holding on and letting go at the same time, their hands lingering on each other's arms, eyes meeting, a smile growing. 'You take care of yourself. If you get into trouble, unless it's serious, we don't want to know!' Mark gave a pantomime yelp when Susan punched him on the shoulder. 'I'm joking!'

But she knew he wasn't. To Mark, Drew was a man, venturing forth to find his feet in a changing world. To her, he was her boy, her son and, whatever cologne he wore, he was still her baby. He always would be.

Drew laughed, gave her another quick hug before manoeuvring through the ticket barrier with his luggage. On the far side, he stopped to give a last wave, before heaving the holdall over one shoulder, grabbing the handle of the case with his other hand, and joining the flow of people heading to the train.

Susan craned her neck to follow him. Drew was tall and for a while, she was able to keep him in sight, then suddenly, he

vanished and she cried out, as she had all those years ago when he'd finally made an appearance, wet and slippery, crumpled, and adorable.

'He's gone.'

'He'll be back, stop worrying.' Mark pulled her to him and kissed the top of her head. 'I swear you'd do anything for that boy.'

'I'd kill for him.'

Mark's laugh was loud, infectious, bringing a smile to her lips. She could feel it rumbling through him. He thought she was joking. That his rather reserved wife was being overly dramatic, that she wouldn't be in any way capable of such violence. He knew her well, but not that well. She'd kill for her son. Mark's arms tightened around her as his laughter died. 'How about we go for a drink, eh?'

He kept his arm around her as they negotiated the crowded station concourse, perhaps afraid she'd turn, jump over the ticket barrier, and run to hold on to her son.

She felt the weight of his arm on her shoulder, anchoring her, steadying her. He was a good man. She'd kill for him too.

10

HANNAH

I stood in the hallway, surrounded by my Louis Vuitton suitcases. My initials, a large HB, broke the stripe down the front of each. I'd been so sure our marriage would last, I'd even had the same two letters put on the handle. How stupid I'd been.

Leaving them there, I climbed the creaking, old stairway to the landing. Ivan's door was shut. I curled my fingers around the doorknob and, without knocking, pushed it open. 'I'm off,' I said, looking him straight in the eye. He didn't move or answer. I walked a couple of steps into the room, feeling tension tighten across my shoulders, resisting the temptation to turn and run. He couldn't hurt me now but fear doesn't let go that easily. 'I'm not sure of my plans. I might pop back.'

He didn't seem to care.

Ten minutes later, the suitcases were jammed into the boot and the back seats of my red BMW. Luckily, I'd been clever since we wed. To give Ivan his due, he'd never questioned the amount of money I appeared to need so my bank balance was exceedingly healthy.

There were sufficient funds to cover a few weeks stay in a

hotel. Longer if I could drop my expectations. But staying in a hotel didn't fit with my plan.

So it was I found myself a few hours later pulling up outside the epitome of suburbia, AKA my mother's house. I stared out the car window and sighed. A few days here and I'd be screaming. A week and I'd be tearing my eyes out. Two weeks, and I might be resorting to violence.

But I knew the role I needed to play and moving back home would help. It would give it an authenticity that I might struggle to pull off if I was living in a luxurious hotel.

I hadn't contacted her to say I was coming. I wasn't sure of the response so arriving unannounced was a safer bet. Present her with a fait accompli. She would be too conscious of the curtain-twitching neighbours on each side of the terraced house to turn me away from their doorstep. Much as she'd like to slam the door in my face.

Although she'd never been what you could term a loving mother, it wasn't until I was suspended from school when I was sixteen that our relationship really fell apart.

Mother was called to a meeting with the school head, a tall, angular woman with unusually long arms and fingers, named, rather appropriately, Crabtree. 'I'm horrified, appalled and disappointed to have to tell you, Mrs Parker that your daughter was caught...' she hesitated and swallowed before lowering her voice to a barely audible whisper. 'In flagrante delicto.'

My poor mother, she who had married her first-ever boyfriend, my father, and had I'm certain only slept with him, looked suitably horrified, but it was obvious she'd no idea what the head was talking about.

'They caught me and Simon shagging, Ma.' I raised my eyes to the ceiling when it still didn't sink in. 'Sex, Ma. Me and Simon were having sex.'

That word, of course, she did know.

'Both Simon and your daughter have been suspended for a week and will only be accepted back into the school if we are assured this...' Crabtree's face creased as she sought for an appropriate word, '...behaviour isn't repeated.'

'Of course.' I could see the cogs turning in my mother's head.

'We hope there will be no repercussions to further interfere with Hannah's education.'

'Repercussions?'

'She's afraid I'll be up the duff, Ma.' I shook my head. 'I shouldn't be; Simon used a condom. Although,' I tilted my head as if giving the situation careful consideration, 'he did have to pull out very quickly when we were disturbed. I hope that won't have any repercussions.'

'I'll take her to the GP. Make sure.' My mother hesitated, her hands gripping the handle of one of only two handbags she owned. It was worn around the edges, a bit like her. 'Hannah won't get into trouble for this, will she? With the police, I mean.'

Mrs Crabtree sniffed. 'Hannah and Simon are both lucky, Mrs Collins. They are over sixteen.'

So last year, I was committing a crime. It wouldn't have stopped me, but it was probably as well they didn't know. Or that the boys handed over their pocket money in return for fumbling between my legs or having a feel of my barely-there breasts.

Luckily, they didn't know any of this.

11

HANNAH

But that was then. I sat in my car and looked toward the terraced house and shivered. It wasn't the house where I'd spent the first ten years. We'd moved shortly after my father had left us, my mother's shame too hard for her to bear. In a different town, where nobody knew us, she became the Widow Parker. So much more socially acceptable to my mother to be a widow than an abandoned, discarded, unwanted wife.

And I – a gawky ten-year-old – was forced to join a new school mid-term where cliques had already formed and I was an outsider.

At home, Mother drummed into me the need to maintain the deception about my father with harsh words, and painful slaps.

No friends, no father. I did what I could to fit in. I did what I had to do. And if the attention, the affection I craved, were paid for with a pound of flesh, it wasn't harming anyone. Except myself.

It was Mother who opened the door when I finally climbed from the car and did that long walk up the short driveway, every footstep taking me reluctantly back to a different version of

myself. For my sanity, over the years, my visits had been defined by their brevity and the long gaps between. I was never sure why I bothered to visit really. She didn't love me, I didn't like her, yet I was drawn to my home, the way you're drawn to pick at a scab. Till it bleeds.

I frowned as I tried to remember the last time I'd come, shrugging when I couldn't. Two years, perhaps three.

'Five years since you were here last,' my mother said without a whisper of regret. 'The last time we spoke was a year ago; you'd just come back from Mexico where you got married. On a beach.'

The last three words were accompanied by a sniff of ridicule. She looked over my shoulder to the car. 'He didn't come with you then?'

Yes, he did, I married the invisible man. 'No, he's not coming.' And because I knew it would give her some satisfaction, some mean-spirited enjoyment, I told her, 'I've left him, if you must know. It didn't work out.'

For a microsecond, she looked smug. As if this was what she'd always expected. But her expression quickly changed, her mouth tightening as her eyes flickered over the suitcases I'd dropped on the ground either side of me. 'You're here to stay?'

'For a while.' I waved towards the car. 'The rest of my luggage is in the boot. You don't mind, do you?'

Of course, she did. My presence upset her fantasy of being the loving mother of an absent daughter.

I was there for a reason. To appear pathetic was part of my plan, and how more pathetic could it look than for a thirty-nine-year-old to be forced to move home? I picked up my cases and gave her a cheery smile. 'It'll be like old times, won't it?'

Mother stood in the doorway, one hand on the door, the other on the wall, blocking my entrance. I kept her gaze till she broke it and stepped back. She was a weak woman; she always had been.

I took my cases up the stairs to my room. Five years since I'd stayed last and then only for one night. But the memories of my childhood still hung heavily in the room. A musty, dirty smell of times gone by.

'Are you going to just stand there?' Mother was behind me. 'Just how long were you planning to stay?'

I turned to her with a forced smile. 'I'm not sure as yet. Does it matter?'

It did, I could see it on her face, in the tight lines around her mouth, the opening and closing of her hands as if she wanted to reach for my cases again and hurl them down the stairs. My last visit, all those years before, had been arranged weeks prior to my arrival. It had given her time to prepare, but even then, the lunch we'd shared had been a brief, uncomfortable hour where we'd made banal chitchat about nothing.

This time, without preparation, she was thrown. The end of my marriage might have afforded her the opportunity to offer comfort and sympathy, to show some form of maternal love, but that wasn't her way. It never had been. Instead, she glared at me from her hooded eyes, gave a jerky nod that might have indicated that it did indeed matter how long I was planning to stay but she didn't like to say so, and turned away on a muttered, 'I'll leave you to unpack.'

The single bed was where it always was, jutting out from the side wall, a small table on one side, a two-drawer locker on the other. The bed was draped in the same pink, candlewick bedspread that had covered it for as long as I could remember. I sat on the edge of the bed, then lay back, resting my head on the lumpy pillow, and shut my eyes.

Tiredness swooped in to claim me but it was memories that won over. Moving houses had never dimmed the memory of that last night, my father's bristly cheek as he gathered me into a hug,

his deep voice telling me how much he loved me. Holding me for such a long time that perhaps I should have guessed there was something wrong. Should have done something. *But I was only ten.*

It didn't matter. Nor did it matter that I wasn't to blame for him abandoning us. Guilt swamped me. Guilt and sorrow had been my playmates for years.

Sometimes, I was angry that the love he'd professed to have for me hadn't made him want to stay. Or to keep in touch. Or to try to contact me in all the years since.

Sometimes, I hated him but mostly, even to that day, I felt an absolute and wrenching sense of loss.

The house was so quiet, so empty. Even if Drew wasn't home, his presence was always felt. The piles of dirty clothes dropped on the floor of the utility room because he never could remember which front-loading machine was the washer and which the dryer; his trainers kicked off in whichever room he was relaxing in; half-empty mugs left in various places. She'd complained about it all, and now she'd be delighted to see a pile of stinky gym gear on the floor or a mug leaving a ring mark on the polished, walnut sideboard. Instead, she slouched around the house, feeling lost. Worse, she sat in his room, on his bed, clutching his pillow like a lovelorn teenager.

Drew had finally succeeded in escaping her over-enthusiastic mothering. He might return for the holidays, for the first year anyway, but he was never going to come home permanently.

'Why don't you look for a job?' Mark asked over dinner a week later. 'You're an intelligent woman; you could find something. Or perhaps volunteer in one of the charity shops in the town. They're always looking for staff. Now that you don't have to worry about Drew, you should find something for yourself.'

Don't have to worry about Drew! He had no clue. She dropped her cutlery on her plate and pushed it away. 'I'll never stop worrying about our son,' she said, getting to her feet. She scraped the uneaten food into the bin and dropped the plate into the dishwasher.

When she turned, Mark was also on his feet, a concerned expression twisting his face. 'You know what I mean, Sue. You were worrying about what he was going to do when he finished school, whether he'd settle down at university. Now he has, and he sounds like he's doing well.'

Drew had rung every night and she had to admit, he sounded happy. Relaxed. As if he wasn't missing home in the slightest. She tried to stop worry from colouring her words, to be subtle as she quizzed him about his accommodation, if he was eating properly... what he was eating, wanting an inventory of every morsel that passed his lips. The first few calls, she'd managed to sound unconcerned, but as his conversations became briefer, anxiety crept in, unbidden, unwanted, certainly by him, his responses getting shorter, the pauses longer. Once, he'd hung up on her as she was asking if he'd done his laundry at the right temperature.

It was a few seconds before she'd realised she'd been cut off and she'd looked at the phone in confusion before the truth slapped her so hard, it brought tears to her eyes. Already, he was changing from the polite boy she'd known to this stranger who would hang up on his mother. Not even the text message that pinged seconds later to explain that Drew had walked into a notorious signal black spot, did anything to assuage her grief, her belief that she was losing him.

When Mark arrived home to find her sitting at the kitchen table, the mobile clutched in one hand, her eyes red from crying, he rushed to her side, dropping to his knees on the floor beside her chair. 'My God, what's happened?'

She told him, blubbering her misery, ending on a wail, 'We've lost him.'

He got to his feet, pulled out a chair and sat, then scraped the feet of the chair on the tiled floor as he shuffled closer to her. 'You're being daft, Susan. He's just finding his feet, enjoying the taste of freedom. He'll soon be home for holidays and causing his particular blend of chaos, and you'll be back to complaining about him being under your feet.' He laid a hand on her knee and rocked it gently. 'You need to stop moping around the house. Get your life back.'

Her life? She wanted her son back. 'I need more time to adjust.' Brushing his hand away, she got to her feet and crossed the room to the window. The garden was her pride and joy; she should spend more time tending to it. She rested a hand on the window, the cool glass grounding her. When she heard movement behind, she wasn't surprised to feel Mark's arms wrapping around her, pulling her back against him.

'I just want you to be happy, that's all,' he said quietly.

'I am happy.' It was a lie, she wasn't but she should be; she had everything: a beautiful home, a loving, attentive husband, a son they'd raised so well that he was confidently going off to make a good life for himself. *Without her.* She should be happy for him, pleased that she and Mark had done such a marvellous job, but she just couldn't shake off the sense of loss. *Empty nest syndrome.* That there was a name for what she was feeling didn't help. She rested her head back, sighing as Mark rested his chin on it. 'It's a matter of adjusting,' she said. 'I'll be fine in a few days.'

'You should meet up more regularly with your sisters. Or your friends. You were always saying you would if you had the time. Now you do. Make the most of it.'

'I will.' She turned in his arms, planted a kiss on his cheek.

'I'm meeting Jan and Emma tomorrow, in fact. We're having lunch.'

'Perfect.' He kissed her on the lips, then stood back. 'Now, how about we go out for dinner?'

Although he wasn't being critical, Susan felt colour racing to her cheeks. He'd been at work all day, probably had a quick lunch at his desk, and here he was, home for dinner, and there was nothing ready. It wasn't the first time either. The night before, she'd managed to scramble something together from what she had in stock, but supplies had run low. Normally, she'd have done a big shop once a week on a Thursday afternoon. But when she'd gone to the supermarket the previous day, she'd walked the aisles seeing all the food that Drew had loved and had piled it into the trolley. When she got to the checkout, she'd looked down in horror and abandoned it there, leaving it for some poor, hard-working assistant to unpack. She'd walked unsteadily from the shop and sat in her car in the busy car park, her eyes fixed and staring ahead.

Unwilling to venture back into the store for the items she really did need, she left and stopped at a petrol station on the way home for bread and milk. Apart from that, the cupboards were bare.

'Dinner would be good,' she said. She nodded towards the kitchen. 'Tomorrow, I'll do a big shop and maybe I'll cook your favourite meal.'

* * *

Susan made an effort as they sat in their favourite local restaurant. Her best smile, her most cheerful voice as she babbled away. 'I'm looking forward to seeing Jan and Emma tomorrow.'

'Give them my love,' Mark said.

'I will.' She cut into her steak, wishing she'd ordered something else. 'I'm looking forward to meeting them.' The steak was good, tender. Drew would have liked it. She wondered what he was eating. Who he was eating with. She hoped he wasn't alone. No, she couldn't let her thoughts drift there. 'Hasn't the weather been so mild?' she said, wishing she could come up with something more interesting to say. *I'm so lost, Mark.*

'What did you say?'

Susan looked at him, horrified. Had she said that aloud? Surely not. But Mark looked vaguely puzzled, not irritated. For the first time, she realised how quiet he'd been all evening. As if his mind was elsewhere. 'I was just saying how mild it was,' she said with a smile.

'Oh right, yes. It is, isn't it?' He picked up his wine glass and swirled the contents around before gulping it down and reaching for the bottle to refill his glass and top up her almost untouched one.

He was drinking more than usual. And wasn't he unusually quiet? If she hadn't been hungry before, now even the pretence was too much for her and she lined her cutlery up side by side on the plate. She expected Mark to comment, wanted him to, suddenly very afraid what it meant if he didn't.

And when he didn't, she felt a slice of anguish cut through her.

If she was lost without her son, what would she be without her son and her husband?

She couldn't let that happen.

She wouldn't.

13

SUSAN

She made an effort for lunch with her sisters the following day, wearing navy trousers and a cream, silk shirt instead of the jeans and T-shirt she'd normally have chosen. Smarter than normal clothes, slightly heavier make-up. Trying to look the part. A mother who was happy with her lot. A wife whose husband loved her. *He still did, didn't he?*

She'd been so lost in her own woes recently she hadn't paid Mark much attention. Last night, he'd been distracted, but now that she was giving it more thought, hadn't he seemed a little distant the last couple of weeks?

As she made her way to the restaurant, the thought haunted her. It refused to budge even to allow Drew to take over. She was being silly she decided, pushing open the door and pasting a smile in place when she saw Emma and Jan already at the table, deep in conversation.

The eldest of the sisters, Susan had married far younger than they had and Drew was older than their children by several years. They'd been luckier than she too – more prolific, Jan with three children, Emma with four. Over the years, Susan had babysat

several times. She was a natural with children. Everyone said so. Her sisters especially.

'You're so good with them,' Jan said, every time Susan babysat. 'Honestly, we can relax and have a good night out knowing they're in good hands.'

Emma said much the same thing.

'Of course they say that,' Mark said with a shake of his head at her gullibility. 'They're only too delighted for you to babysit. It doesn't cost them anything. I've said it before, and I'll say it again: they take you for granted.'

Susan would shush him and smile. She loved to babysit. Loved it more when the children woke and she had to bring them downstairs. She'd sit with them in her lap and sing them the songs she'd sung to Drew before he got to be a big boy who didn't need his mummy to sing him to sleep.

They too were past that stage now. It didn't matter; she wasn't asked to babysit anymore. The eldest in each family was old enough to take on that role and she rarely saw the children these days. With Jan and Emma's children a similar age, it made sense for them to spend more time together and they frequently went on joint family holidays.

'You're welcome to come,' they'd said to her. And she would have done, but Mark's 'no' was quick and emphatic.

'Spend a whole week with all seven kids screaming their heads off? No thank you.'

Even Drew shook his head. 'I know what'll happen if I go,' he said. 'I'll be left looking after them while all you "adults"–' he curled his forefingers in the air and wriggled them around that word as if to explain how little like adults they behaved '–will vanish, leaving me to it.'

So they hadn't gone, and eventually, the invitations stopped coming. Now, they only met at Christmas and at family gatherings

and even those were growing more infrequent. She couldn't remember when she'd last been asked to one of the children's birthday parties.

And now, here in the restaurant, dressed up like a fool, she was sitting silently while her sister's discussed their children. Had she talked about Drew as much? Probably not. Her sisters' eyes would have glazed over. They'd oohed and aahed over him, but they weren't interested in the minutiae of a baby's growth, and by the time they had children of their own and eager to share, it was too late for Susan.

Anyway, they had each other; they didn't need her.

She sipped the white wine they'd insisted on ordering although she wasn't wild about drinking in the middle of the day. It tended to leave her muggy headed and she was bad enough recently without that. She wondered what Drew was doing. If he'd made some nice friends. Perhaps she and Mark should go up for a weekend. They both liked Glasgow and hadn't been for many years. She might suggest it to him that night, over the nice dinner she'd planned to cook for him. Perhaps she'd make it an extra special meal, get him in a good mood.

Get him in a good mood. A frown creased her brow as her earlier fear came barrelling back. This distance between them – had it been there a long time and she was only noticing it now that Drew had left? Or was it simply that Mark was feeling the departure of their son as much as she, but keeping it to himself? Yes, that made sense. He was a sensitive man. Perhaps she'd forgotten that. She brushed her fingers over her forehead. When had she become so self-centred? She took another sip of her wine, then put her glass down and poked a fork into the lasagne she'd ordered. It wasn't very good, and she was struggling to eat it.

'What do you think, Susan?'

It was Jan who asked, her head tilted bird-like as she waited

for an answer. There was a time when her sisters had valued her opinion, when they'd arrive home from school troubled about this or that and she'd sit and listen, comfort them, give them advice. Not any more. She didn't have the faintest idea what they'd been discussing but it didn't matter; the question had simply been for form. They no longer cared what she thought and it had been a long time since they'd paid any attention to her advice. 'I think it's a great idea,' she said, hoping it was the appropriate answer.

'See!' Jan said turning to Emma with a smug look in her eye. 'I told you she wasn't listening to us.' They turned as one to look at Susan, eyes narrowed in accusation. 'Honestly, have you heard a word we've said?'

Susan reached for her wine and downed it in a couple of gulps. Reaching for the bottle, she refilled her glass and picked it up. Then she shook her head and put it down again. Gently. Refusing to spill a drop. Refusing to make a mess. *Not her, she was the careful type. The good mother, good wife.* 'I'm sorry. I'm a bit preoccupied.'

'A bit!' Jan sniffed. She reached for the bottle and divided what was left between her glass and Emma's. 'It's Drew, I suppose. It's always bloody Drew. Let the lad go, for goodness' sake.'

'So that I can sit and listen to you two talking about your children ad nauseam the way you always do, on and on and bloody on.'

She saw the startled, horrified faces of her sisters, realised she'd spoken aloud and lifted a hand in apology. 'I'm sorry. I didn't mean that.' But her sisters were quick to take offence and slow to forgive. Like their mother, they sulked like children. They'd inherited her full bottom lip, and when they sulked as they were doing now, it stuck out prominently. Susan's thinner lips and brown eyes were courtesy of their father. Thankfully, it was all she'd inherited from him, not his capacity to abandon people.

It was tempting to pick up her glass and drain it. Maybe that's what she should do, turn into a lush. The thought made her smile. Luckily, she turned it into a grimace in time. 'I'm having a tough time adjusting, that's all.' She supposed she was hoping for sympathy, a little understanding.

Emma's sigh was neither. It was irritated. 'He's only gone to Glasgow. He'll be back in a couple of months for Christmas, then it'll be Easter, and the long summer. You'll hardly have time to miss him.'

Susan did reach for her glass then and took a mouthful of wine. Her sisters glanced at one another, Emma giving the slightest of shrugs. Susan rarely drank more than a half a glass; perhaps they thought she was becoming a lush. 'I know I'm being silly.' She put the glass down again, eager to reassure them, as she always had done. 'Anyway,' she shook her head. 'Enough about me, tell me what I've missed.'

'We don't want to be going on and on about our children, do we?' Jan wasn't being easily placated.

Emma, always more forgiving, nudged her sister with her elbow. 'Don't mind her, Susan; she's in bad form because Oliver got into a fight in school yesterday and she had to go and talk to the head this morning. It's left her in a sour mood.'

'Well, why wouldn't it?' Jan's voice was sharp. 'The money we pay for that damn school, they should be able to handle things themselves without having to drag parents in for a "meaningful discussion".' She reached for her glass and emptied half. 'A meaningful discussion, for fuck's sake! It was worse than being back in school myself.'

The rest of the lunch passed in discussion of schools, teachers, and how better behaved their children were than the rest.

Susan threw in a 'really?' 'yes' or 'no' when it was appropriate. It did cross her mind that since neither Jan nor Emma's children

were at all well-behaved, the other children must be monsters. It brought her thoughts back to Drew.

She'd done a good job with him, hadn't she? It was healthy that he was coping well without her, that he didn't feel the need to come home for a weekend or spend time chatting to her on the phone.

She switched her thoughts back to Mark. It was time to give him more attention. Perhaps it was her fault he appeared to have drifted recently.

Drifted – nothing more than that.

Their marriage was solid.

Solid.

She had no doubts at all.

None.

14

HANNAH

My plan was simple. I'd learnt over the years that simplicity is the key to most things. That and appearing to be far less intelligent than I am.

I'd kept tabs on a lot of my ex-boyfriends over the years. No other reason apart from natural curiosity to see what happened to men I'd left behind. It was easy; the world I lived in was full of people who knew someone who knew someone. As a result, I knew a little about Mark's life since we'd been together. The law firm he worked for was small but prestigious with a very classy website where I was able to look at his headshot and read his profile. There were no personal details, of course, but I read where he'd made partner several years before. The few personal details, that he was married and had one child, I'd acquired over the years from old friends and acquaintances.

I was amused when I'd heard he'd moved, several years before, into a new-build, detached house a mere mile from where my mother lived. I'd looked at it online. A small, exclusive development, the house screamed new money and whispered trying too hard.

It had always struck me as more than a coincidence that he'd moved there. Although we'd never visited my mother when we were together, he'd known my home address. Had he hoped to catch a glimpse of me? My ego wasn't so huge that I believed he still loved me despite those last desperate words of his, but the subconscious is extremely powerful and perhaps it had guided him towards the place where the woman he'd adored had lived.

I don't think he still loved me, but I'm sure he hadn't forgotten me. Did he sometimes look back and see our relationship in rose-toned hues and wish things had turned out differently?

I hoped so. Because that was my plan. To convince him I'd made a mistake all those years before, and that we should be together. I could make him love me. Care for me. Make me happy again.

That day, I was going to walk to Mark's house, scout out the terrain, see if I could peer in the windows, perhaps catch a glimpse of him, his wife, or their child. Any snippet of information would help add form to the rather nebulous plan bouncing around my head.

I especially hoped to get a look at his wife. It was always good to put a face on the competition. There wasn't the slightest doubt in my head that I could get rid of her.

I knew my worth.

Even better, I knew men.

* * *

It would have made more sense to have headed off sooner but to my surprise, I'd slept solidly and only woke when I heard the hum of the electric shower that told me Mother was in the bathroom. I slipped back between the covers to wait till she was done, my

hands behind my head, my eyes travelling over the swirls of the hideous Artex ceiling. Around and around.

It was easy to be dragged down a wormhole of memories. Throwing back the covers, I slipped from the bed again and spent the time waiting for the bathroom to be free in deciding what to wear. With most of my clothes still packed away, it didn't take me long.

The bathroom wasn't a room conducive to lingering. The same avocado-green bathroom suite. The same opaque glass on the small window. A shower was set into the bath, a plastic curtain on a rail above. It flapped against my skin as I showered, the cold fabric making me squirm away, the cheeks of my backside hitting the tiles on the wall, water and soapy bubbles flying everywhere. Definitely not a place to spend time and within minutes, I was out and grating my skin dry with the towels.

When I arrived downstairs, almost begrudgingly, Mother offered me breakfast. 'There's eggs. I could do you some fried or scrambled. Or there's cereal if you'd prefer.'

'Just coffee, thanks,' I said, and stood in the doorway of the cramped galley kitchen while she flicked the switch on the kettle, spooned discount supermarket coffee into a mug, and stood with her hand on the handle of the kettle as if begging it to come to a boil.

'Here,' she said, handing me the mug. 'There's milk in the fridge if you want. I assume you still don't take sugar.'

'No, nor milk.' I blew gently on the hot drink, then took a sip, it was as ghastly as I'd expected but it was caffeine and I couldn't function without. 'I'll eat out. You don't need to worry about cooking for me.'

There was no argument. *No, you must let me cook a meal for you.* Just relief that she wasn't expected to provide for me and wouldn't have to suffer meals with guilt as an aperitif.

I didn't finish the coffee; there was only so much crap I was willing to ingest on an empty stomach. 'Thanks,' I said, tossing the remainder into the sink. 'I'll be home later.'

She didn't ask where I was going, and I didn't volunteer the information. 'You still have your key, don't you?' When I nodded, she turned away. 'Don't make noise when you come in.'

I grabbed my bag from where I'd slung it around the newel post and headed out. It had been warm recently. An Indian summer, the weather people were calling it. It suited me, allowing me to wear ankle-grazing, navy trousers and a tight-fitting, white T-shirt. A stylish, smart combination that made me look good.

Looking good was the key. People rarely looked beyond the façade. Very wise too because sometimes, there were monsters below the surface. Sometimes, when I shut my eyes, I could still see Ivan's face twisted in anger as he rained blows down on me.

Only thinking of Mark chased the fear away.

15

HANNAH

I could have taken the car but it was a nice morning and only about a mile to Mark's house. Walking might give me more opportunities. Who knows, maybe he was having a late start and he'd pass me by on the way to the train station. We'd catch each other's eyes and we'd look bemused before yelling in delight, hugging one another. He'd kiss me on both cheeks, his lips lingering against my skin, inhaling the perfume I'd sprayed on that morning, one I'd worn back then, certain he'd remember.

We'd stand looking at each other, silly smiles on our faces. Then he'd ask what I was doing back in Bristol and I'd shake my head, tell him it was a long story, then tilt my head and ask if we could meet for a drink and I'd tell him my sad news. I'd put a heavy emphasis on the word *sad*, let my lower lip tremble, perhaps even conjure up a tear. How could he resist?

That was the way it should work out if there was any justice in the world. It made me smile though as I walked on, lost in my imagination.

It was important, when scouting, not to look as if you were doing so. I'd not planned to make that rookie mistake and had

looked at the Street View option on Google Maps to find exactly where Mark's house was. When I arrived at the entrance to the smart cul-de-sac of identical houses, I crossed over the road and peered into the enclave as far as I could. The houses were large and separated by expansive gardens. Ten years old, they still looked new, boxy, rather ugly and bland. It was Dullsville.

I walked a little further along the main road, then turned and walked back and into the cul-de-sac. The mobile held to my ear was the perfect excuse for walking slowly, for staring wherever I wanted. If anyone came from one of the houses, I'd start to speak.

Nobody did though. It was possibly good timing. Office workers would have already left and the school run completed. Most of the driveways had cars parked in them, some had two. The train station was a little over a mile away, so most people probably walked.

Mark's house was number six in the crescent of ten houses. I walked slowly, stopping now and then, and gesticulating wildly as I babbled random words into the phone in case any curtain twitchers were on the lookout.

Number six was identical to the other houses. The only difference I could see was their choice of plants for the matching pots that sat next to each side of the uPVC front door. Colourful fuchsia rather than the bay or box that some of the others had.

The garden to the front was only a few feet of pristine grass. Too pristine: on closer inspection, I realised why. It was fake. Who had Mark married? I could picture her. Fake nails, dyed hair, false eyelashes, breast implants. I'd had some cosmetic surgery in the years since we'd been together, what woman hadn't, but my breasts were the real thing and I rarely bothered with false eyelashes.

I walked slowly, trying to catch a glimpse through the window on either side of the front door. All I managed to get

was the vague impression of paintings on the far walls in each room. Nothing else. The curtains were draped from the centre; I imagined them held in place with twee tiebacks. There was nothing else to give any indication of the type of people who lived there. Only the fakery outside. Perhaps that was enough for me to know what I was up against in the fight to get Mark back.

It seemed pointless to hang around. I could hardly knock on the door and explain that I'd made a mistake twenty years before. That I was the woman Mark should be with.

But it seemed a shame to be leaving with nothing. I could knock on the door and ask her if she knew where Mrs... I sought for a suitable suburban name... Fox. I smiled, dropped my phone into my pocket and sauntered to the front door. 'Please be home, please me home,' I muttered under my breath, a mantra that was unlikely to make the woman materialise.

I was about to give up when the door was opened and I was looking at her. Mark's wife. I had to hide my smile then. This badly dressed, dull-eyed woman with slumped shoulders as if she carried the weight of the world on her back, and narrow, unpainted lips that looked as if they never smiled, would be no competition. 'Goodness,' I said, 'I'm so sorry, I think I have the wrong address. I was looking for an elderly friend of my mother's... Muriel Fox... I don't suppose you know her, do you?'

Of course she didn't, and I apologised again, shook my head and walked away. She shut the door immediately. No suspicious glances following me down the street. She'd have run after me with a scythe if she'd known that my plan was to lure her husband away. And now that I saw where he was living, and who with, I was more determined. I could almost view it as a rescue, couldn't I?

Buoyed by my success, I headed home to get my car. I knew

where Mark worked; I could hang about around lunch time, see if he came out. He had to eat. He can't have changed that much.

Bristol hadn't altered too much either. Perhaps a little more run-down than I remembered but the car park I'd always used was still there and convenient for Queen Square where Mark's company had their offices.

The Grove car park wasn't large and was often full but luck was with me that day; a woman walking briskly with her keys already in her hand was just ahead of me. I slowed and waited while she climbed in and thankfully without a lot of faffing about, pulled out.

It was too early for Mark to be thinking about lunch, but I walked around the square, found his office, lingered outside. Then I walked around Queen Square till I was bored. I was also hungry. I was crossing Queen Square Avenue when I saw exactly what I needed. A Spicer+Cole coffee kitchen which would have both good food and excellent coffee.

Unfortunately, I couldn't see the front of Mark's office from inside. Not even from the bar stool I managed to grab at the window. It didn't matter. I hadn't expected everything to work out so easily. Coffee, and the avocado on toast I'd chosen, would re-energise me, maybe give my brain a jump-start.

I could hang around day after day, lingering outside his office in the hopes of bumping into Mark. If this were one of those chick-lit stories, that was exactly the way it would go. Unfortunately, life tended to require more effort.

Perhaps it was the second cup of the very good coffee that got the brain cells swirling, because by the time I'd finished it, I was staring through the window to where I could see a green slice of Queen Square. No point in waiting for things to happen when I could make them happen myself.

Five minutes later, I was standing in the reception of the

offices of Bandon and Partners.

It was a lavishly decorated space with several comfortable chairs dotted about, a coffee machine gurgling nearby, and a stunningly beautiful man sitting behind a long desk that seemed to guard the corridor and door behind.

A sign on the desk had *Office Manager* in large, bold print, and underneath this, in more elaborate type, it said *Clifford*. He looked up as I approached, a friendly, professional smile that did nothing to warm the cold, assessing eyes. 'Can I help you?'

A few years ago, I'd have gone down the flirtation route – fluttered my eyelashes, stuck my chest out a little so that my nipples were visible through the fine cotton of my T-shirt, adopted a breathy, dumb-as-shit voice. But what might have had a chance of working at twenty-five or thereabouts wasn't going to cut it at thirty-nine.

But I had other personas I could use. My damsel in distress one had got me out of some very tight corners over the years. And it was age-proof. Luckily for me, I had a wonderful knack of being able to cry on demand. I dragged that particular trick out now and my eyes filled as I leaned closer to speak to him.

'I was hoping to speak to Mark Shepherd.' I swallowed and held a hand up as if to say this was so difficult for me. 'I don't have an appointment but we're old friends so I was hoping...'

There was no thawing in the hard eyes, but neither did he tell me to get lost, nor any polite equivalent of that.

I drew a ragged breath, hoping I wasn't overdoing it. He'd have made a good poker player; I'd no idea what he was thinking.

'If you'd give me your name, I'll see if Mr Shepherd is free.'

'Hannah Parker.'

'Take a seat, Ms Parker.' He indicated the chairs behind me and waited till I'd crossed to one and sat before picking up the phone.

The chairs were too far away to allow me to eavesdrop on whatever he said, and his expression was giving nothing away. Dammit, the man didn't as much as frown. Perhaps like me, he couldn't. The downside of Botox; it made reading faces slightly more difficult.

Unless Mark was in a meeting, I was in no doubt that he'd speak to me. Curiosity, if nothing else, would impel him to come down. I felt a frisson of excitement fizz through my veins. It was hard to sit still and I shuffled in the chair, my eyes fixed on the elevator door. Would it be better to jump to my feet and run to meet him, or sit elegantly and wait for him to come over?

I still hadn't decided when a movement behind made me jerk around. I'd been so fixated on the lift door, that I hadn't heard the footsteps approach. Caught unawares, I gasped to see Mark standing there. Perhaps it was the perfect outcome. The earlier tears were still shimmering in my eyes. From my seated position, my neck was arched, my breasts pushing against the fabric of my T-shirt. A subservient position to his towering maleness. After my gasp, neither of us spoke, or moved. It was bizarrely moving the way we simply stared at one other as the years peeled away to bring us back to those halcyon days when we'd been together, then as quickly back to the reality of the present day.

He'd changed. No longer the boy I remembered, his dark hair was threaded with grey, the six-pack I remembered running my fingers over had morphed into a belly that stretched the fabric of his shirt, his features had softened, his jawline sagging. Then he smiled, and he was the boy once more. 'Hannah!'

I got to my feet, and it was natural to drift into his arms as if the intervening years hadn't existed.

It was Mark who moved from our embrace first, his hands grasping my upper arms to move me away. He threw a glance towards the desk, an unattractive, ruddy red creeping over his

cheeks. Releasing his grip, he took a step away. 'Come up to my office,' he said, nodding towards the lift.

I picked up my bag and followed him.

'You're looking good,' he said when the lift door had swished shut.

Good? Maybe his eyesight had deteriorated. 'It's been twenty years. I've got older.' I lifted a hand to my cheek. 'Gravity hits us all after a certain age.' It was his cue to say I looked amazing, that I hadn't aged a day since he'd last seen me. I'd paid a small fortune to stay looking this young; the least he could do was appreciate it.

'You look exactly as I remember,' he said.

Since I had a clear memory of him telling me that I was stunningly beautiful back then, this should have pleased me, and it might have done if he'd been regarding me in admiration instead of puzzlement. Exactly as he remembered – perhaps he was thinking of the very last time he'd seen me. On the doorstep with that sugar daddy whose name was lost in time as with a lot of the men I'd known back then.

The lift stopped, the door opening into an eerily quiet corridor. I wasn't nervous by nature but it suddenly struck me that twenty years was a long time. I hadn't changed. The years may have spread layers of sophistication on the damaged young woman I'd been but they hadn't made me much wiser. I'd never have married Ivan if that had been the case.

Was I being foolish now? Mark had been a naïve boy when I'd known him. The intervening years, his successful career, marriage and fatherhood would have changed him. How much, remained to be seen. Not enough surely to make me slightly nervous of being here alone with him, or to be suddenly glad that Clifford knew I'd come up and would be on the alert for my departure.

I was being silly. Mark was no danger to me.

He was the one who should be afraid, after all.

16

HANNAH

If the size of an office was an indication of how successful he was, then Mark was doing very well indeed. Double sash windows looked out over Queen Square and filled the large office with light. The furniture was classy. Masculine. *Expensive*.

'Have a seat.' Mark waved to a chair and rounded the desk to the other side. He waited until I'd sat before pulling his chair out, the wheels rumbling loudly on the wooden floor the only sound breaking a silence that was almost overpowering.

I was waiting for him to say something, afraid of jumping in before I knew where I stood. So far, his expression had been as guarded as Clifford's. Maybe it was something they were trained to do when they started working for the company, how to learn a poker face.

'It's been what... nineteen, twenty years?'

'Twenty.' I smiled briefly, then pressed my lips together, allowing them to tremble slightly as my eyes filled in what I hoped would appear as a refined, upset woman act. It wasn't me; I was more the screeching, tearing your eyes out sort. 'You must wonder why I've appeared after all this time.'

He sat back, the chair rocking gently. 'A little.'

This wasn't working out exactly as I'd hoped. He used to be much more garrulous. I reached into my handbag for a tissue and blew my nose gently. 'Sorry, tears seem to come easily these days.' I could feel his eyes on me, appraising. Something else he'd learned over the years. No doubt a necessary part of his job. I kept my head bent, my eyes on the tissue I held between my fingers, pulling it apart. 'I've moved back home.'

'Back to Thornbury? Your parents still live there?'

'My mother,' I corrected. 'Yes, she's still there. I've been up and down frequently over the years. She's delighted to have me home although upset for me as well, of course.' I swallowed and dabbed my eyes with the mutilated tissue. 'Sorry.'

'Can I get you something? Tea or coffee?'

'Thank you, no.' I shoved the tissue back into my bag and got to my feet. 'This was a crazy idea. I'm sorry, Mark, I should never have come.' I made it to the door, about to admit defeat, when I heard the wheels of his chair roll noisily and his footsteps hurry after me. I opened the door, relieved when his hand landed on it to push it shut.

'Don't go,' he said, his mouth near my ear, his breath brushing my cheek. 'It looks like you need a friend. I'm glad you came to me. We were good friends once upon a time.'

'Before I ruined it.' My hand was on the door handle. He was so close behind me that I could feel the heat of his body, smell his woody cologne, hear his deep, ragged breaths. 'It's something I've always regretted.' I turned then. He stepped away immediately, shoved both hands into the pockets of his trousers then took one out and ran it through his hair. It made me smile. In twenty years, his mannerisms hadn't changed. He was nervous. He was right to be.

'Why have you come?' He smoothed his ruffled hair, fiddled

with the edges of his jacket. 'Not to tell me you've regrets after all these years, surely. There's been a lot of water under many bridges since then.'

I shrugged and turned the corners of my lips down. 'I hadn't planned to come, but I wanted to get away from my mother's smothering attention for the day so came into Bristol.' I leaned back against the door and sighed. 'I wandered, remembering happier times. I didn't consciously come to Queen Square but I'd heard you were in a law firm here so maybe my subconscious was trying to tell me something.' Pushing away from the door, I passed him and walked to the window to stare out. 'I found myself outside this building and knew I had to see you.' I turned then and gave him my best smile. 'For old times' sake.'

'You need legal help?' He stopped fiddling with his jacket and returned to his seat at the desk. 'I have an appointment in five minutes, but perhaps tomorrow...'

'No.' I turned and held my hands out. 'I just need to talk to you about back then. Why I was so cruel to you. You were always a good listener. I should have told you then but...' I let my hands drop and my shoulders slump to depict a picture of gorgeous misery.

He looked confused. Torn. He checked his watch again. 'I really can't cancel my appointment at this late stage but perhaps we could meet afterwards?'

I let my breath out in a puff and held my hand over my heart. I had a tendency to over-dramatise. I move my hand to flick my hair back. 'That would be so incredibly kind.'

'I'm not sure how long this meeting is going to take—'

I held up a hand to stop him. 'I'm happy to wait until you're free. To be honest, my tale would be easier to tell in less formal surroundings.' I sighed. 'It'd also be much easier to tell with a drink. How about I go to the Small Bar on King Street? I can sit

and have a coffee until you arrive.' I could sense him weakening, knew he wanted to meet me, out of curiosity, for old times' sake, or maybe because he'd never managed to completely forget me.

'It'll be at least an hour, maybe a little more.' There was an edge to his voice, as if he was trying to convince himself that it was a bad idea to meet.

It was, of course. A very bad idea. But the poor man had no idea he was jiggling on the hook I'd cast and had little chance of escaping now. 'I've nothing to hurry away for, Mark.' It struck me that I hadn't had to force the words to sound sad because they were true. I had absolutely nothing and nobody to rush away for. I turned for the door, looking back when I reached it. 'It is so good to see you. Oddly, I already feel a little less worried about everything.'

That he looked decidedly more worried than he had ten minutes before was immaterial. I'd soon iron those worries away. Making men happy was something I was good at, after all, Ivan being a sad exception.

Back on the street, I skirted around the perimeter of Queen Square and crossed down to King Street. There were other more salubrious places along the street but I'd chosen the Small Bar deliberately for its casual vibe. The interior walls were part wood-cladded; rough, bench-like tables were surrounded by simple chairs. It was young, trendy, unthreatening. Mark would have one of their beers and relax as he listened to my story. I'd sob into my G&T before downing it in a few mouthfuls and he'd suggest getting me another. And have another beer himself. Then I'd suggest we should have something to eat. The Small Bar did great chicken wings, perfect food for picking up and eating with your fingers. Was there anything more erotic than pulling slivers of meat off a bone with your teeth, dribbling grease down your chin, licking it off with a sweep of your tongue? It was foolproof stuff.

The Small Bar was always busy but this early, there were a couple of tables free and I snagged a corner one for convenience. It allowed me to rest against the wall behind and keep an eye on the doorway. I didn't really want a coffee and sat for a while twiddling my thumbs until the other tables filled up and the bar staff began to eye me suspiciously. Staking my claim to the table my placing my handbag dead centre, I crossed to the bar. 'Can I have an alcohol-free G&T, please,' I said to the bartender. There was time enough to have alcohol when Mark arrived but I wanted to stay sharp and focused; the tale I planned to tell him needed a certain amount of finesse.

It was a little over an hour before he came through the door, his eyes scanning the crowd. When they landed on me, his smile was automatic. 'I got away as fast as I could,' he said, pulling out the chair opposite me and dropping into it with a sigh that was part exhaustion, part *what the hell am I doing here.*

'You look tired. Let me get you a drink. Beer? I remember you always liked craft beers and this place does some of the best.'

'Beer would be good.' He looked towards the bar and shrugged. 'I'll let you choose.'

I wasn't a beer drinker so it made sense to ask the staff for a recommendation. I half listened while I observed Mark's profile. 'That one,' I said, stopping the staff member mid-diatribe. He didn't see anything amiss with my abruptness, merely nodding and reaching for a pint glass. 'And a G&T too, please.' I glanced towards Mark as I waited, pleased to see him immediately look away as if embarrassed to have been caught staring.

'Here you go,' I said, placing the brimming glass in front of him a moment later.

He took a tentative sip, nodded, and took a longer, deeper gulp. 'It's been a manic day,' he said in explanation.

I didn't believe him. I saw the way his eyes avoided mine, the

way he continued to sneak a glance at me when he thought I wasn't looking. I had no idea about the state of his marriage, but I knew men, and this wasn't one with a happy home life; this was a man ripe for plucking.

'It's been a manic few days for me too,' I said, taking my seat opposite. I took a genteel sip of my drink. Pacing myself. Get my sad story out first, then I could knock back a few.

'Tell me.' He put his glass down and slid his hand across the table, holding it there till I slipped mine into it, his fingers closing over, warm, strong and comforting.

The story I was going to tell him... it wasn't precisely a lie... it just wasn't the truth.

17

SUSAN

The lunch seemed to be endless, the conversation with her sisters more trying, more difficult than usual to pretend an interest in. Her sisters were the ones who'd gone to university, the ones who'd had bright, exciting lives before they married. Why was it that she found them dull? Or was it her? Yes, of course, it was her. She was dull. The childless mother, the stay-at-home wife whose husband had lost interest.

That was the truth, wasn't it? Nothing to do with Drew. Mark had simply lost interest in her. Not surprising since she was so dull.

'Goodness, is that the time,' she said, shoving her sleeve back and glaring at her watch as if it had cheated her out of minutes. 'I have to go.' She grabbed her mobile and dropped it into the opening of her bag. 'Sorry to rush, girls. There's someone coming at two.'

'Someone?' Jan looked bemused.

As well she might, these lunches were organised weeks in advance; they never booked anything to clash with them. 'An elec-

trician. Impossible to get hold of a good one so I had to grab him when I could.'

'Right.'

'If you have to go, you have to go,' Emma said.

As if she didn't care whether Susan stayed or not. In fact, she'd probably be relieved to see the back of her. She and Jan could settle down to the kind of nitty-gritty chat they preferred. They'd no doubt rip Susan to shreds before moving on to gossip about mutual friends: who was having an affair with whom, who was getting divorced, gambling, drinking too much. The tawdry underbelly of the circle they mixed in.

Luckily, neither asked why they needed an electrician; she wasn't sure she could have conjured up a suitable answer. She could have shopped for the things she needed for dinner in the shopping centre but that would risk bumping into her sisters, requiring more explanations. Instead, she drove to a supermarket she didn't normally use which meant she had to search the aisles for what she wanted. She felt frustration, irritation, sadness; it oozed over her, great waves of emotion that almost swamped her before receding into the empty hole that seemed to be at her core.

In her attempt to shake it off, to prove to herself how damn lucky she was, she went overboard with the spending, buying more expensive steak for the beef bourguignon than was necessary, plump scallops for the starter she'd not planned on doing, late British strawberries, expensive vanilla ice cream and a selection of cheeses from the delicatessen counter, getting carried away with herself as she pointed and pointed.

'You having a party?' the server said.

He took his time, cutting a segment, then wrapping each piece individually until it seemed to Susan there was a mountain of packages. What on earth was she going to do with it all? 'Yes,' she

said, conscious the man was waiting for her answer. 'Just a small one. But they like cheese; it'll all be eaten.'

If it was a small party of mice, perhaps. She piled the cheese into the trolley and went in search of wine. She took her time, picking up bottles, reading the labels, finally deciding on a Merlot that sounded like it would be a perfect match. It was more expensive than she'd normally pay for wine. A lot more. She dropped it into the trolley, then hesitated before adding a second. Normally, she'd buy a cheaper wine to make the beef bourguignon. But it didn't need a full bottle; she could have a glass while it was cooking and why shouldn't she have a glass of decent stuff? Anyway, the meat was so expensive, it seemed silly not to keep the quality of the wine equally good.

Packing all her purchases into the boot of the car, she felt a little better, calmer. She had to stop letting things get to her. She was being silly. She and Mark were fine. 'Fine,' she said firmly, driving from the car park too fast and forced to slam on the brakes when she reached the road.

By late afternoon, the beef was cooking on the hob, the aroma making her mouth water. The scallops would be cooked when Mark arrived. The cheese was in the fridge, taking up almost a whole shelf. The strawberries were in a bowl, hulled and ready to go.

When Drew had been home, she insisted they had dinner together in the dining room. If it was just her and Mark, they'd often have it on a tray in front of the TV. But she wanted that night to be special. A new start, she supposed. A romantic dinner *à deux* would be the first step in reclaiming her life. Because she'd lost the way. Just for a while. But she'd get it back. She'd *grab* it back.

The conservatory off the dining room was often too hot in the summer and too cold in the winter. But with the recent mild days and evenings, it would be the perfect place.

With the decision made, she scurried around to arrange every-thing. There were three chairs around the conservatory table, a fourth sitting in the far corner. With a sigh, she took the third chair and put it beside the other, arranging a small table between them, satisfied when it looked like a cosy reading spot. Perhaps they could read the Sunday papers there. It was a thought. For the future.

From the dining-room sideboard, she took a selection of candles and placed them on the windowsills and set a large one in the centre of the table. Mark was usually home just after six. She'd light them a few minutes before, set the room glowing.

With all the preparations done, she ran upstairs, had a quick shower, and searched for something suitable to wear. The built-in wardrobe stretched the length of the wall. The interior was well designed with hanging space and multiple shelves. She knew what she wanted, how she wanted to look: sexy, desirable, interesting.

There were a couple of formal dresses she'd worn to events thrown by Mark's firm. She pulled them out. They'd been expen-sive. She'd felt good in them. They were smart though, not sexy. Conservative, not desirable, not even particularly interesting. Dull, housewifely garments, she hung them back in the wardrobe. She should have gone shopping, bought something new. Too late now.

With time ticking by, she opted for skinny, black jeans. There was a black chiffon blouse she hadn't worn for a while; she pulled it out and held it up. The material was so fine, she needed to wear a camisole underneath. With a smile, she slipped on a black bra, and pulled the blouse on over it. She left her hair loose. It was long enough to curl onto her shoulders. Looking in the mirror, her smile widened. Hell, she looked good!

A glance at her watch told her time was running out. Leaving her feet bare, she hurried downstairs, grabbed the box of matches, and lit the candles. The scene was set; let the play begin.

I left my hand resting in Mark's and lifted my glass with the other, taking a few mouthfuls as if I was priming myself for my big exposé.

'I married a little over a year ago.' I shook my head, my mouth turned down in patent regret. 'Ivan is a lovely man; I should never have agreed to marry him.' Another mouthful of my drink. 'We're divorcing. That's why I'm home.'

She felt Mark's hand tense over hers and saw lines of disappointment creasing his forehead. 'I'm not a divorce lawyer, but I can recommend someone for you.'

'You think that's why I'm here?' Putting her glass down, she covered his hand with hers. 'The divorce isn't going to be a problem. Ivan is devastated. I hurt him so badly but he accepts that it's over.'

'You left the family home?'

I was pleased to see concern in his eyes. 'The house has been in his family for generations. Don't worry, though; there's a water-tight prenup and I'll get enough to buy something small somewhere.' To be a successful liar, you need to have three skills –

keeping the lie simple, remembering which ones you've told, and to whom. Consistency was the key. Mark was looking puzzled. I guessed what the next question would be and had my answer waiting.

He sat back using the movement to withdraw his hand from where it still sat nestled between mine. I felt suddenly bereft and wanted to stretch across the table, grab it back, hang on to it tightly, the way I should have hung on to him all those years before.

He lifted his glass and tilted it to his mouth to drain the last drop before putting it down with a determined smack on the wood of the table. Maybe I was wrong; the thought made me shiver. Maybe he was going to stand up, say goodbye and leave me, the way I'd left him. Payback. But instead of getting to his feet, he sat back, sliding his hands into the pockets of his trousers. 'So, if you don't need legal advice...?'

'I've always felt guilty about the way I treated you. And being back in Bristol...' I shrugged, reached for my glass, frowning as much as I could when I saw it was empty. As a hint, it wasn't particularly subtle but it was my experience that subtlety was wasted on men. I saw Mark look towards the bar, then back to my glass. 'Another?'

'It might help tell the rest of my story.' I huffed a loud sigh. 'I'll have a Prosecco this time, please.' I was half afraid he'd switch to something soft and was relieved to see him return with another pint for himself and my requested drink.

'I need to go home after this,' he said.

'Home to the wife and kids?'

'Just the wife. Our son, Drew, has gone off to university. In Glasgow.'

I'd known he had a son. It made it easier that he was out of the picture. Glasgow? The boy had gone a long way, I wondered if

there was a reason. Family friction, perhaps. Interesting. 'He didn't want to go to uni here in Bristol?'

The answer was such a bald, abrupt no that I knew things weren't all sunny in the Shepherd world and mentally rubbed my sticky little hands in glee.

Mark took a long drink and flicked his wrist to see the time on his watch. I picked up my glass and raised it towards him. 'Let's drink to old memories.'

With obvious reluctance, he touched his glass to mine.

'I never meant to hurt you,' I said, bringing the Prosecco to my lips. I took too big a mouthful, the bubbles hitting the back of my throat and making me cough. I put the glass down and held a hand over my mouth. 'Sorry,' I said. 'I'm so very, very sorry. I should have explained back then but I wasn't sure you'd understand so I took the easy way out and made you hate me.' I moved my hand up to cover my eyes, waiting for them to fill before taking it away.

Mark was staring into his beer. 'I never hated you.'

'You had reason to; I treated you badly.' I took a tissue from my bag and blew my nose softly. 'I never used to be such a cry-baby.' Not until I learned the skill and how effective it could be. 'It's the alcohol on an empty stomach. I haven't eaten much today.' I looked to where people at the table beside us were tucking into chicken wings and chips. 'I will explain...' I hesitated. 'I don't suppose you'd fancy having something to eat, would you?' Then I quickly shook my head, put on my sad girl face. 'No, I'm sorry, of course you don't.'

He checked his watch again. 'Maybe something quick.'

I jumped up before he'd time to reconsider. 'I'll go; I've already had a look at the menu while I was waiting so I know exactly what to get.' Of course, I did. Enough food to nibble on, more drinks to wash it down as I finally told him my sad tale.

I brought the drinks back with me. Another pint for him, another Prosecco for me. He raised an eyebrow when I put his drink down but didn't remonstrate. Instead, he picked up his almost finished pint, drank the remainder, then almost immediately picked up the fresh drink. 'It's good beer this,' he said, as if that was the reason we were sitting there. To drink pint after pint of craft beer. Or perhaps he was nervous about what he was going to hear. My explanation for having dumped him so abruptly. Maybe it had been haunting him for the last twenty years.

The food arrived. I'd gone overboard. Chicken wings, a double portion of fries, fried chicken and a peanut dip. If Mark was surprised at the amount I'd ordered, he didn't say.

'Always a danger when you order when hungry,' I said by way of explanation. 'We don't need to eat it all; I know you're pushed for time.'

'No, it's fine.' He reached for a chicken wing and proceeded to gnaw away at it, giving it his full concentration.

I ate a few fries, then wiped my fingers on a serviette. 'I often wondered... if I'd explained back then... if I'd been brave enough... would we have stayed together, maybe even still be together.'

The older Mark was more considered in his manner than his younger self had been. He'd learned to listen, to say nothing until needed. It probably served him well in his job, but it was extremely irritating in a social setting. Or perhaps I was dragging it out a bit.

'I'm sorry. I should just come out with it, but even after all these years, it's difficult to put into words.' I reached for a chicken wing, pulled it apart with my teeth, conscious of his eyes on me, watching every move. I sucked the small bones clean, giving it all my attention. I didn't have to look at him to know he was remembering how it was back then, how good I was with my mouth. I

tossed the bones onto my plate and reached for a serviette to wipe the grease from my fingers.

'You've been very patient,' I said. 'I remember that about you. Always patient, always kind.' I was screwing the paper serviette between my fingers. With a grunt, I threw it aside. 'Sometimes, it's easier just to say it. No trimmings, no qualifications.' I took a deep breath. 'I adored my father. I was the original daddy's girl, I suppose. We did everything together. Then when I was ten, I got up one morning and he was gone.'

Mark froze, a chicken wing poised mid-flight to his partially open mouth. He dropped it before shutting his mouth, as if my story had rendered him incapable of doing two actions at the same time. 'Gone? He left?'

'It might have been easier if he'd died.'

'No!' Mark looked horrified.

'Yes, because death often isn't a choice. I could have grieved for him if he'd died, wouldn't have spent the following years devastated because he'd abandoned me.'

He reached for me with his chicken-greasy fingers, gripping my hand so tightly it hurt. 'How terribly sad.'

'He didn't say goodbye to me or leave a note. It was my mother who had to break the news to me. It seemed he was bored with his life and wanted a new start elsewhere. He went to Thailand and, as far as I'm aware, he's still there.'

'You never tried to find him?'

I shook my head. 'I thought about it once. But I was still so angry with him, that I think if I'd found him, I'd have killed him.' I smiled to show I hadn't really meant it. I had, of course; I remember wondering if I could get away with it. 'My mother isn't a very loving woman, never was even when I was younger, so when he left, I sought other ways of getting affection.' All those boys I'd been with, trading sex for an embrace.

'I don't tend to tell people about my father; it makes me too emotional, even after years.' I reached for my drink and took a mouthful. 'Even now, I can't speak about him without getting teary.'

Mark was frowning. I wondered what he was thinking.

'I don't think I ever really got over that feeling of abandonment. Even though I was angry with him for leaving, I missed him so terribly. I think that's why I was so attracted to older men. To replace him and the security he gave me.' I swirled my glass. 'Sometimes, their attention cost.' I met Mark's eyes. 'I slept with them.'

'You...' He picked up his pint, drained it in a few gulps, then tipped it towards the bar. 'Another?'

This was going better than I'd hoped. 'Please.'

With fresh drinks in front of us, Mark once again reached for my hand and held it, gently this time. 'Why didn't you tell me? More importantly, why didn't you get help? You obviously had never dealt with the loss of your father. Latching onto these older men was your way of dealing with it.'

Everyone was a wannabe psychology student. 'Yes, I guess you're right.'

'A father complex, isn't that what it's called?' He nodded as if agreeing with his diagnosis. 'I'm sorry you didn't feel you could tell me. I'd have understood; maybe I might have been able to help.' His thumb swept over the back of my hand.

'You have no idea how many times I've said the same to myself.' Even in the noisy pub, my sigh was loud. It was filled with genuine regret. If I had chosen a different path back then, *would he have made of me a saint, or I of him a sinner?*

I shook off the stupid nostalgia for a time long past to face the future I wanted. It needed careful baby steps.

'We can't go back, but we have now,' I said. I twisted the hand

he held and curled my fingers around his. 'I've felt more alive in the last couple of hours than I have in such a long time. I don't want it to end.'

He had the grace to be discreet this time as he checked his watch. Perhaps he was frequently late home. Business meetings, corporate clients, etc. Other women? Perhaps. I wouldn't have thought him the cheating type, but what did I know really? The man in front of me may have different morals to the boy I'd known. It was in my interest that he did.

'I can stay a little longer,' he said.

Little did he know it, but he was already on that slippery step and I was going to help him fall off.

19

SUSAN

It was two hours before Susan gave up. Two hours where she'd fretted, checked her phone, checked the meal she'd slaved over, checked her make-up in the mirror, wiped away the smudged mascara, touched up her lipstick. Her messages to Mark had been read so she knew he wasn't lying dead somewhere, a victim of a random act of violence.

Finally, after two hours, ten minutes and thirty seconds of waiting, a message pinged.

> Sorry. First chance I've had to message. Stuck with a very needy client. Be home much later.

Susan read it through twice. It wasn't unheard of for Mark to be delayed in meetings with clients, nor was it unheard of for him to be out late entertaining them, but normally she'd have had advance notice of it. It wouldn't simply come out of the blue. What kind of a needy client was it?

She trusted him. He had never given more than a healthy admiring glance at another woman in all their years together. It

was simply a coincidence that he'd been delayed by a client when she was worried that he'd lost interest in her. A coincidence. They happened.

A candle flickered in a draught from a badly fitting window. She looked around the room, at her sad attempt to create a romantic atmosphere, to prove to herself, and to Mark, that their relationship was solid. She loved him. He loved her. They simply needed to find their feet. Or perhaps it would be more honest to admit that she did.

This wasn't the best start.

She'd used most of one bottle of wine making the beef bourguignon. What was left, she poured into her glass. It was gone in a couple of mouthfuls. The second bottle was open. Breathing. To be perfect for Mark's enjoyment. Fuck him, she thought, reaching for it and filling her glass. It was good wine. Too good to drink like lemonade, but she gulped it back without any effort at enjoyment, going for effect rather than pleasure. If the effect was to make her more miserable, it was doing the job.

Her sigh sent the flame of the big candle she'd positioned in the centre of the table flickering. She watched it for a moment, then licked her thumb and first finger and reached out to quench the flame. The wine, it seemed, had gone straight to her legs and she wobbled precariously as she got to her feet. Drunk in charge of a candle. The thought made her giggle, the sound rippling the silence and sounding a little manic. She held a hand over her mouth till it stopped, then went from candle to candle, red wine-coloured spit on her fingers as she put out every one until she was standing in the darkness. Just her and the glass of wine.

Perhaps she should relight them all and sit there at the table until Mark came home. Maybe slip on the only negligee she possessed, a relic of a romantic weekend away in the dim and

distant past. She could sit in the candlelight and pose. Like some kind of sad, pathetic Miss Havisham.

But she may be a lot of things... stupid, a little lost... perhaps a bit depressed, but she refused to be pathetic.

Leaving her glass on the table, she went through to the kitchen. There was no point in letting good food go to waste. She debated eating some, then shook her head. Whatever appetite she'd had was gone. The beef would be just as good, if not better, in a couple of days. She put clingfilm over the top of the container and slid it into the fridge. The scallops were on another shelf, waiting to be flash fried. They could have them the following day. And the strawberries. And the stupidly expensive ice cream.

'Stupid, stupid, stupid.' She hadn't shouted but the words seemed to echo noisily around the room. Or perhaps she had shouted. Perhaps she'd screamed her fucking head off.

With the kitchen sorted, she took a refuse sack from a roll, snapped it open and went back to the conservatory. The night-lights she'd lit with such enthusiasm only a few hours before were scooped unceremoniously into the bag, the big candle from the table thrown on top. Tying a knot in the plastic, she tossed it to one side to be disposed of in the morning. Then she cleared the table, put everything back as it was, picked up her wine glass and the almost full bottle and went through to the sitting room.

She sat in the dark, in the silence, sipping the wine until it was all gone. She didn't usually drink much, the wine was strong and she'd had little to eat all day so she was feeling more than a little woozy.

There were no further messages from Mark. She reread the older one. She'd assumed *much later* would be ten, maybe eleven, but it was almost midnight and there was still no sign of him. It was tempting to send another message, ask if he'd be home soon, if he was okay. *If he was with another woman.* Perhaps he was and

that was why he'd been so distracted recently. Maybe, like her, Mark had become unsettled with their slightly worn and stale life, but unlike her, he had looked outside their marriage for something new to aim for. Something new and exciting.

The thought curled in her belly. She'd lost Drew; she couldn't lose Mark.

She wouldn't. She'd fight for him.

On that thought, she put the empty wine glass down. In the hallway, being a dutiful, caring, loving wife... *he couldn't be with someone else, could he?...* she switched on a table lamp so that Mark wouldn't come home to a dark house. Then she gripped the banister and pulled herself up the stairs.

It seemed like a lifetime ago that she'd agonised over what to wear for the romantic evening she'd planned. She avoided looking at her reflection in the en suite bathroom mirror, unwilling to face the sadness she knew she'd see in her eyes. Blindly, she removed her make-up and slathered on some moisturiser with little care. Normally careful with her clothes, she wrenched them off and tossed them onto a chair before slipping naked between the sheets.

When Mark returned, she'd wrap her arms around him. Show him what he'd missed.

It was either that thought or the wine she'd consumed that sent her into a deep sleep. She was convinced it was the wine that was humming in her head when she woke some time later. Putting a hand to her head, she twisted around to see the time. Three. And it wasn't her head that was humming. It was the electric shower in the main bathroom.

Never in all the years they'd been married, not even in the days when he'd come home from a business meeting stinking of second-hand cigarette smoke, did he have a shower before going to bed.

There was only one logical reason he would do so now.

When silence returned, she turned back on her side. Shutting her eyes, she concentrated on breathing slowly and deeply as she heard the sound of the bedroom door being opened, the soft shuffle of bare feet on the laminate floor, the squeak of the bed as he slid in beside her.

And then the silence as they both lay side by side, suddenly miles and miles apart.

HANNAH

It had worked out far better than I'd expected. I stretched my arms over my head and wriggled my bare bottom on the fine cotton sheets. We'd been lucky to get a room in this boutique hotel only a stone's throw from the Small Bar. A smile hovered as I remembered the receptionist's sniffy expression when Mark and I had rolled in the evening before, slightly the worse for the drink we'd consumed and obviously desperate to get a room.

I'd almost expected Ms Prim and Proper to say it wasn't *that* kind of hotel, but instead, she'd taken Mark's credit card when he'd passed it over and handed him a key card. She'd thrown me a critically dismissive look as she did so. Just me, not Mark. Some things never changed.

One thing that had, was Mark's skill in the bedroom department. He'd learned a few tricks over the years and whereas I still faked an orgasm, I appreciated the dexterity he'd shown in attempting to get me there.

'I'd forgotten how beautiful you were,' he said as he'd rolled off me.

Were? It was a figure of speech but it still riled a little. 'You

mean I'm not now?' I leaned on one elbow and rested a hand on his chest. Post-coital inertia combined with an excess of alcohol seemed to have made Mark a bit dull-witted because he didn't immediately fire back with an *of course you are*. Instead, he looked at me blearily, eyelids drooping, his breathing growing deeper and more stertorous. If he started to snore, if he dared, I wasn't sure I'd be able to stop myself from punching him. 'Well?' My voice up a notch, creeping towards a place that was more screeching harlot than elegant seductress.

Luckily for us both, Mark stirred. He ran a hand along my flank and opened his eyes wide. 'You're the most beautiful woman I've ever known. For a long time, every woman I met, I compared to you. Even when I met...' He stopped suddenly.

Perhaps he hadn't wanted to betray his wife. I swallowed the snort of amusement. That boat had sailed. Twice, actually. Maybe a third time would convince him. I ran a hand down his belly, lingering before dipping further, then pulling away as if I'd changed my mind. Then again, and again, until I hadn't needed to move my hand quite so far down. Then I shimmied over and onto him and moved in a dance I'd learned long before, and I stared down at him, saw his face twist in pleasure, and thought how foolish he looked, how stupid it all was, how sad that it meant nothing to me. Less than nothing.

'I'd forgotten what an absolutely amazing lover you are,' I said a few minutes later, laying heavy emphasis on the *are*. I'd have liked to have rolled off him but an arm around my waist kept me clamped to his warm, sweaty body. But I was used to putting my needs and wants to one side to get what I wanted. It was usually worth it in the end. It would be this time. 'It feels like the last twenty years have never happened, that we're back there in my tiny, dingy room and all our future is there waiting for us. I'm just sorry I messed things up.'

His arm tightened around me, squeezing until I could barely breathe. I'd done a few rounds with erotic asphyxiation in the past. 'It'll heighten the orgasmic experience,' they'd said each time. Refusing to confess I'd never had an orgasm, yet alone a heightened one, I'd gone along with it and screamed loudly at the appropriate time. Then I'd reciprocated, wondering at man's capability for stupidity as I tightened scarves or ties around various men's throats until they went blue. It would have been so easy to have kept the tension tight and to watch them die. I didn't because I'd nothing to gain.

I'd nothing to gain from dying in this hotel room either. That definitely wasn't in my plan. 'I can't breathe,' I managed, pushing at his chest with my hand.

He released me with a muttered. 'Sorry.'

I kissed him lightly then rolled off, snuggled my head into the soft pillow and waited. I could have almost predicted what he'd say. The same variation on a theme I'd heard from so many men over the years.

'You know this can't happen again, don't you?'

Almost exactly the words I'd expected. 'I know.' I waited a beat. 'If I'd only been brave enough to have told you the truth back then, maybe things would have turned out differently.'

I felt his hand search for mine, and close around it gently. 'You going to be okay?'

'I don't know.' The most honest I'd been all night. I didn't know. It all depended on Mark and being dependant wasn't a comfortable place for me. Ivan had done more than hurt my body; he'd dented my self-belief. 'Meeting you again,' I said quietly, 'it's been overwhelming. The regrets seem heavier somehow.'

'I hate to think of you being so sad.'

'I hate to think of never seeing you again.' I took a shaky

breath. 'Perhaps we could meet tomorrow for lunch, or a coffee even, just to... you know... ease me back to a life without you more slowly.' I held my breath, listening to the cogs turning in the head of the man lying beside me. I knew he'd say yes, just as I knew we'd end up back in this hotel, or some other one the following night, or perhaps the night after. Soon though, I could feel it in the silence that cloaked us, he wanted this.

He still hadn't answered when he shuffled from the bed a few minutes later. 'I have to go,' he said, grabbing his clothes and pulling them on. He shoved his tie into his jacket pocket, then sat on the corner of the bed to tie his shoelaces.

I knew better than to ask him again, knew better than to nag. Anyway, I guessed what his answer would be.

'Just coffee,' he said, turning to look at me.

'Just coffee.'

'Okay, three o'clock in...' He frowned, trying to think of somewhere suitable.

'How about Spicer+Cole? It's not far from the office; you could nip out for half an hour and no one would be any the wiser.'

My remark made his frown deepen. Perhaps harping on about the clandestine nature of our meeting was making him reconsider. I stretched a hand towards him and softened my voice, adding a hint of pleading. 'It'll mean so much to me, you know.'

I thought he was going to change his mind and was ready to argue my case when he got to his feet and nodded. 'Okay, tomorrow at three for coffee.' He took his mobile out. 'You'd better give me your number, in case something comes up.'

I rattled it off, threw the sheet back and got to my feet to press my naked body against him. 'I miss you already.' Then I pushed him away with a whispered, 'Go, please.' Turning away, I held my hands over my face, staying in that dramatic over-the-top pose

until I heard the door click shut behind him. Then I took them away and whooped softly.

He was caught in my web; he would struggle, but he was never going to break away.

He was mine.

She didn't get back to sleep again. Instead, she lay there, listening to Mark's snuffling and occasional snore. Once, she turned over and pressed her nose to his back. He smelled the same as usual, maybe a little citrusy from the shower gel in the main bathroom. He didn't stink of betrayal.

If she went in search of his clothes, if she stuck her nose in them, would she find the sweet smell of another woman's perfume, the acrid smell of sex, the stench of infidelity? And if she did... if she did... could she bear it?

She lay there. No comfort in the darkness, none in the light that started to creep into the room around the edges of the heavy curtains. Even when the room was filled with daylight, she stayed unmoving as fear shot through her. Without Drew, without Mark, who would she be?

It was ridiculous. She'd had a life before either of them. Hadn't she? Or had that one belonged to her sisters, her mother? There'd always been someone who'd needed her and although she'd frequently railed at her mother and sisters' demands on her time, she'd felt useful, needed. Now, she felt lost, redundant. She

didn't even have a career to return to and the thought of sitting at a till in the local supermarket, subject to the stares of curious neighbours, filled her with dread.

Mark snored beside her. She turned, rose onto her elbow, and stared down at him. The years had been good to him. Laughter lines around his eyes and frown lines that cut into the skin above his nose had added character to a face which had been almost too boyishly handsome. The sprinkle of grey through his dark hair made him look so damn sexy. She wanted to reach out and brush it from his forehead. More, she wanted to wake him, make love with a passion they seemed to have lost in the last couple of years.

Make love, brand him with her smell, her sex, so that she'd be the one he'd be thinking of as he headed off to work. And in the afterglow, she'd ask him if he still loved her, and she'd believe him when he said yes, because he never lied to her. Honesty and trust. It was the core of their relationship, always had been. So why was she doubting him now?

She flopped back and covered her eyes with her arm. Maybe she was being foolish. Imagining things. Searching for something to worry about now that Drew was making a life of his own. Yes, that's all it was. Foolishness. When he woke, Mark would explain, and things would return to the way they were.

It was another hour before she felt him stir beside her, sixty minutes of swinging one way, then the other, from believing he'd cheated and lied, to being sure he wouldn't do such a thing.

As was usual for him when he woke, he immediately threw back the covers and swung his feet to the floor.

'Hi,' she said.

'Hey, you're awake early.' He rested one knee on the bed and leaned forward to give her a kiss. On her forehead. Not on her lips. 'I hope I didn't disturb you last night.' He smiled, before turning and moving to the window. 'Looks like it's going to be

another nice day,' he said, peering through the crack he'd made between the curtains.

'What time did you get in?' Trying to sound casual, not accusatory.

'Far later than I'd expected.' He stretched then rubbed his belly. 'We ended up back in his apartment where he smoked one fat cigar after the other. I stank and had to have a shower when I got home.' He collected fresh clothes from the dresser and wardrobe. 'Try and get back to sleep for a bit.'

'Yes, I'll try.' She was smiling as he opened the door into the en suite. How stupid she'd been. She'd let her worries escalate out of proportion and given herself a hideous night. Curling on her side, she shut her eyes and reached for sleep. It didn't come. What did sneak into her head was a laughing gremlin that whispered she was a fool, that Mark was lying to her and had come up with an excuse to shower away the scent of deceit; that he thought she was stupid enough, trusting enough, to believe every lying word he'd told her.

She heard the gurgle of water. He'd be having a shave. It would be a couple of minutes before he was done. She scrambled from the bed.

He'd hung yesterday's clothes, the trousers and jacket, on the back of a chair in the corner of the spare bedroom he sometimes used to dress in when he was up very early. The bedroom window had been opened. If his clothes had stunk of cigar smoke, or anything else, they didn't now. There was nothing in the jacket pockets apart from a few coins and a receipt for coffee dated a month before. She was ridiculously relieved to see it was for one coffee. His wallet and mobile were in the inside pocket. The mobile was of no use to her. It was password protected and she'd no idea what that was. The wallet held a photo taken of the three of them a few years before. A holiday they'd taken in Dubai. It

had been magical. She stared at it for far too long, reliving the memory, then flicked through the rest of the contents. Credit cards. A couple of business cards. Petrol receipts.

Replacing wallet and phone, she was about to scarper back to bed before Mark came out when she decided to check his trouser pockets. One of those last minute, in for a penny in for a pound things, really not expecting to find anything. Her fingers had closed around a crumpled piece of paper when she heard Mark's voice calling her.

Clutching the scrap, she hurried across the landing to the bathroom. Inside, she pulled Drew's abandoned, raggedy dressing gown from the back of the door, slipped it on and tied the belt. When she opened the door, Mark was across in the bedroom. 'I'm here,' she said. 'I couldn't get back to sleep and needed a wee.' She shoved her hands into the pockets of the dressing gown. The crackle of the paper seemed so loud, she wondered that he didn't hear it but he was yawning, reaching for his suit trousers.

'I'll go and make some coffee,' she said, trying to sound casual. 'It looks like you could do with some.'

'I'm going to be mainlining it all day, I'm guessing.'

'Right.' She left him to finish dressing and headed downstairs to make the promised coffee. The machine was gurgling, the room quickly filling with the aroma of the strong coffee he preferred in the morning. With maybe a minute before he arrived down, she sat at the table and took out the piece of paper.

It was a receipt. *Small Bar* was written across the top. *King Street, Bristol*, in smaller typeface underneath. It wasn't a place she knew, but King Street wasn't far from Mark's office. Maybe he'd taken the client there for a drink. She looked at the two items on it. Mark had said the client had smoked fat cigars. That didn't sound like the kind of man who would drink Prosecco by the

glass. And she knew her beloved husband hated the stuff. His drink would have been the beer.

So who was drinking the Prosecco?

A woman. It had to be. Which meant Mark had lied to her.

Susan's life had been a little empty recently. She knew how she was going to fill it. Find out what bitch was trying to lure Mark away. Find her and get rid of her.

She'd lost Drew; she had no intention of losing her husband.

22

HANNAH

I stayed in the hotel room till the very last moment, enjoying the generous breakfast I'd ordered from room service before indulging myself with a long soak in the bath, topping up the hot water as needed.

It was a few minutes after the eleven o'clock checkout time when I sauntered up to the reception desk in the lobby and handed the same snotty-nosed receptionist the key card. 'I had such an amazing night,' I said to her. 'Probably the best ever, if you catch my meaning.' I gave her a wink – just in case she was as thick as she looked – and sashayed from the lobby with my jacket slung over my shoulder, feeling better than I'd felt in a long time.

Everything was going so well.

There was nobody home when I returned to my mother's house. I hadn't bothered to let her know I wasn't going to be home the night before. Maybe she'd have been worried and was out searching for me. I gave that thought the loud laugh it deserved and went up to my bedroom to change my clothes.

When I was done, I sat on the edge of the bed and contemplated

the pile of dirty laundry that was piling up on the room's only chair. I could take it down and use the washing machine while Mother was out. But she didn't possess a tumble dryer. Winter or summer, everything got hung out on the line that crossed the small back garden. I pictured my silk and lace knickers and bras dangling there and her caustic comments on my finery. No, that wasn't happening.

I thought of the top of the range washing machine and a separate tumble dryer in the utility room of Ivan's house. It was this side of Windsor but still an hour and a half's drive away. A long way to go to do some laundry. But I could stay overnight, pick up a few things I realise I'd forgotten. Ivan wouldn't mind. He wouldn't even care.

Not today, though. Not when I had Mark dangling so precariously on that string. I needed to make the attachment more secure, needed him to be so desperate for me that he wouldn't think twice about leaving his wife.

With the weather still unseasonably balmy, I looked for something suitable in the suitcases I hadn't bothered to unpack. I wanted sexy but subtle – Mark was much more likely to swallow the bait if it didn't resemble a worm – so I settled on a mid-length, cotton dress that would have been almost demure if it weren't for the curve of my breasts clearly visible in the deep V of the neckline.

Mother hadn't made an appearance by the time I left the house. I wondered, vaguely, what she did with herself all day then dismissed her from my mind.

I opted to take the bus rather than drive. It wasn't busy, neither was the traffic, and it seemed only minutes before I was walking along Victoria Street and crossing over Bristol Bridge. It was only a ten-minute walk, and even though I walked slowly, I still arrived in Spicer+Cole too early. The café was always busy but the

lunchtime crush had eased and when I'd ordered my coffee, I found a table at the window with little trouble.

I liked to be early. It had several advantages. The best choice of seat, for one. From where I sat, I'd be able to see Mark walk along the street and see his expression before he'd adjusted it for our meeting. Would he be looking excited, or apprehensive? Being early too, allowed me to settle down, relax, look totally unconcerned with anything life might throw at me. It gave me control – and I liked that most of all.

It was even better when Mark was a few minutes late. It put him at a major disadvantage. He arrived looking slightly frazzled, his tie askew, jacket flapping behind him as he all but threw himself through the door. As he'd walked towards the café, his face had been creased in anxiety – had he been afraid I might have left, or was he more afraid I would have stayed?

Whichever it was, when he saw me, it was relief, excitement, and a frisson of desire that I saw flit across his face. He crossed the café to my side, hesitating only a second before leaning down to kiss my cheek. 'I'm so sorry I'm late; I needed to finish up a few things before I left.'

Did that mean he wasn't going back? 'You're worth waiting for, Mark.' My younger self would have stuck two fingers in her mouth and mimed puking at such a twee comment. But she had the advantage of youth, and a lifetime ahead of her, a lifetime of mistakes still to be made. I didn't have that luxury. Anyway, he didn't appear to think it nauseatingly twee because he leaned down once more and this time planted a lingering kiss on my lips. Straightening, he tilted his head towards the service counter. 'I'll go and get myself a coffee. Would you like another?'

I nodded. 'Another cappuccino would be great.'

In the queue, he ran a hand over his hair and straightened his tie. He glanced my way frequently. Perhaps he was hoping I'd be

looking at him rather than staring out the window. I wondered, was he disappointed that I didn't glance his way even once? I'd no need to, of course; I could see him perfectly well in the reflection in the window.

'Here you go,' he said, putting a brimming cup on the table in front of me.

'Thank you.' I picked it up, took a sip. 'They do very good coffee here.'

'Yes.' He added sugar to his, stirring slowly, looking distracted. He finally put the spoon down on the saucer and gave a weak smile. 'I'm feeling a bit...'

When he didn't seem able to find the correct word, I tilted my head and said, 'Discombobulated?'

It made him smile. His shoulders relaxed and he sat back in the chair. 'A good word for how I'm feeling, if I'm honest.'

'Me too.' A lie, of course, I wasn't the slightest bit confused; I knew exactly what I wanted, exactly what I was doing. I needed to be careful. I didn't want Mark to feel he was being swept along, that he had no control over what was happening. He didn't, but there was no reason for him to know that his destiny was firmly in my hands. Not until it was anyway.

For a few minutes, we sat in silence. I waited for him to break it, giving him power when it didn't matter.

'About last night,' he said, 'it shouldn't have happened. It can't happen again.'

It took only seconds to have my eyes fill with tears. 'I know.' I pushed my cup to one side and slid my hand across the table. 'I lost my chance with you twenty years ago.'

He looked at my hand for several seconds before reaching for it. 'I wish you'd told me about your father back then.'

'I wish I had too; who knows how our lives would have turned out.' Mine could only have been better. His hand was warm, dry,

strong, and comforting. I needed this. 'Last night was special. I'll treasure it.'

'As I will.' He pulled his hand away and shoved it into his jacket pocket. 'It was amazing, you've no idea...' He clamped his mouth shut, swallowing whatever it was he'd planned to say.

I searched for words that would be sympathetic without being critical. 'When we were together, all those years ago, I could always tell when you weren't happy.' I smiled. 'You haven't changed that much.'

He looked embarrassed to be so transparent. 'It's not that I'm unhappy as such. And I feel bad to be talking about my wife to...'

I lifted an eyebrow when he stopped. Had he been going to say mistress, or lover? Colour had flared in his cheeks. I needed to get him back on board. 'Sometimes, it helps to talk. And if you remember, I was always a good listener.' I hadn't been, but in the mist of twenty years, he was unlikely to remember whether I had been or not.

'It's just that since Drew moved out, Susan has been going through a difficult time adjusting.'

'Empty nest syndrome.' I bunched my hair in my free hand, held it on top of my head to allow the breeze from the air conditioning to cool my skin. The action showed off the arch of my neck and increased the amount of cleavage visible in the V-neck of my dress. I could see Mark's eyes drift from my face and shimmy over the exposed flesh before bouncing upward like a naughty schoolboy. He fixed his eyes on mine then with such forced concentration that I almost laughed. 'It's not something I'm going to have to worry about,' I said.

'What?'

I crooked one eyebrow. 'Empty nests. It's one advantage to being child free.'

'You've never considered having children?'

'Motherhood never appealed.' I could have explained why. Could have told him that my experience of being at the receiving end of it hadn't led me to think it was a good move. 'I think it's overrated, if I'm honest.' Perhaps my tone had been a little sharp, caustic, because he blinked and looked confused. I dropped my hair and, fixing my voice into Barbie-doll sweet, said, 'Or maybe it was as simple as never having met the right man, or rather, in having let the right man get away.'

He was incredibly easy to manipulate. I saw his confusion melt away to be replaced with blatant lust.

It was time to test the water. 'You probably need to get back to work. Thank you for meeting me, I truly appreciate it. Today, and especially last night, have been special.'

His hand tightened on mine. 'Don't go, not yet.'

I held his gaze and saw exactly what I wanted to see. 'I don't have to.'

Once she'd decided to find out the truth, Susan didn't delay. It took less than a minute on her laptop to find a private investigator service that seemed, according to the several reviews posted, to be both reputable and professional. Deciding to ring rather than email, she dialled the number.

'Global PI services, can I help you?'

A deep breath in, and the words came with the exhale. 'I think my husband is having an affair. I want to know if I'm right and, if so, who the other woman is.' Susan felt a lessening of the tension once she had the words out. This was the first step; she'd get this sorted, get her life back on track. *Back into the same worn groove it'd been in for a while.* That thought, striking her out of the blue, made her grip the phone more tightly. The voice on the other end of the phone was speaking and she hadn't heard a word. 'Sorry, what did you say?'

The voice was kind, sympathetic. Susan supposed they were used to dealing with all sorts of distraught, overwhelmed, sad women.

'My name is Cailey. I'll need a few details in order to direct

your case to the right agent. Is that okay?'

Susan thought she'd given her the details already. Mark was cheating on her. She wanted to know who the bitch was so she could... do something. 'Yes, that's okay. Fire ahead.'

The questions she was asked were initially mundane, the usual name, address, credit card details. 'We'll take nothing from your account until we send you a quotation and you send back a signed copy,' Cailey explained. 'Our fees are from thirty-five pounds an hour, plus expenses if tracking devices, etc. are required. This will all be explained by your allocated agent. Okay?'

'Yes, okay.'

'Is this the first time you've suspected that your husband might be having an affair?'

'Yes.'

'And you've no idea who she might be?'

'No.' If she did, she wouldn't need a bloody private investigator. All she'd need was a sharp knife. She pushed a hand through her hair. It was tangled. She hadn't brushed it this morning. Hadn't had it cut for a while either and it was longer than she normally wore it. Was Mark looking elsewhere because she'd let herself go, or had she let herself go because he was cheating on her? A chicken-and-egg scenario she'd consider some day when her head stopped spinning.

She answered a few more questions before the ever-patient Cailey told her she was going to analyse the information and decide which agent would be the best bet for her. 'I'll ring you back within the hour,' she said. 'All right?'

'I suppose.' I sounded like a rude, petulant brat. 'I'm sorry.' Sorry for being rude, for needing to hire a private investigator, for being suspicious, for having reason to be. Sorry for every fucking thing. 'Yes, that's fine; I'll wait for your call.'

Hanging up, she tossed the phone onto the table and rested her face in her cupped hands. Weariness stooped her shoulders, pushed her down. She folded her arms on the table and rested her head on them. A few minutes' sleep might do her good. Put everything into perspective. She'd ask Mark about the receipt that evening. There was probably a very good explanation. Perhaps the cigar-smoking, difficult client did indeed like a glass of Prosecco. Perhaps the moon was made from blue cheese.

Exhaustion led her into a deep, uneasy sleep where raincoated men hid behind pillars and rolled out in regular intervals like figures in cuckoo clocks. She heard the sound when the clock hit the hour, a tinny *cuckoo cuckoo*. On and on it went, till she wanted to grab the clock, smash it to pieces, tear the little figures to bits. She even reached for it in her sleep, the solid feel of the phone in her hand waking her with a start. Not a clock chiming: her phone ringing.

'Hello, hello!'

'Mrs Shepherd?'

'Yes, sorry.' There she was apologising again. 'I'd fallen asleep.' Apologising *and* explaining.

'A stressful time for you, obviously.'

'Yes, it is a bit.'

'Understandable. Let's see if we in Global PI can help you. My name is Ethan and I find it better, easier, and more efficient to meet a client face to face. Are you free to meet now? I can come to your home or we could meet on neutral territory if you'd prefer.'

Neutral territory? Suddenly, this all sounded crazy. She was a housewife, a stay-at-home mother: normal, dull, boring. Women like her didn't hire private investigators. 'I think this is a mistake.'

'Why don't you talk to me, no commitment. Sometimes talking to a stranger helps.'

She had nothing to lose. 'Our only child moved out recently.

He's gone to Glasgow. To university. I've been finding the adjustment difficult, I suppose. I noticed that Mark was being a bit distant but assumed that he too was missing our son. Then, last night, he didn't come home after work. He finally sent me a message to say he'd got stuck with a difficult client. He didn't get home till nearly three and when he did, he had a shower. This morning, he said the client had insisted on going back to his hotel room and smoked fat cigars one after the other. That's why he'd had a shower.'

'But you don't believe him.'

'I wanted to.' How she'd wanted to. She pressed her lips together to prevent the tears. 'He has been different recently. Distant. Staring off into space. It's hard to explain, but I know him so well and something has changed. I don't usually search his pockets, but I did this morning and found a receipt for beer and Prosecco.'

'And you're guessing the cigar-smoking client wasn't a Prosecco drinker?'

'I think it's unlikely, don't you?'

'Hmmm.'

The noncommittal, non-answer annoyed her. 'I think I'm wasting your time.'

'I think you're going to be suspicious until you prove it one way or another.'

He was right. Already she could feel the tendrils of doubt wrapping around her gut. 'Yes, okay. Let's do this.' She didn't like the thought of meeting in some neutral territory like someone in a bad spy novel. 'You could come here if that suits.'

'It'd be perfect. I'll see you in an hour.' He hung up without a further word, leaving Susan staring at the phone in dismay. Too late now to change her mind; James Bond was on his way.

The thought made her giggle stupidly, the sound falling with a

clunk into the silence of the room. She looked around the big, airy space and for the first time admitted something she'd never done before. She hated this house. No matter what she did to it, it was cold and clinical. She hadn't wanted to buy a new build; she'd wanted a character property: lots of old stone, cosy rooms, beams. It had been Mark's idea to go for new, persuading her it would be best for schools, for the clatter of kids they were going to have.

Breakfast dishes were stacked up, waiting to be dealt with, and crumbs speckled the countertop. She got to her feet and tidied up, wanting to put on a good show for this man she didn't know. Ethan – no surname, she noted. She wanted him to look at her, at their home, and wonder how Mark could have cheated on her, not the opposite: not understand why he did, not take his side. Susan desperately wanted someone to take her side.

Once the kitchen was restored to order, she hurried upstairs, had a shower, and changed into black jeans and a white, cotton shirt. Normally, she'd have stayed barefooted but she slipped her feet into a pair of shoes to give an air of authority. She was back downstairs and pacing the floor for the final twenty minutes, checking her watch every minute, grunting with frustration when time seemed to have stood still.

Finally, the doorbell chimed. And with it, the doubts escalated. Perhaps she should just ignore it. He'd eventually give up and go away. It probably happened all the time. Calling them had been a stupid thing to do. It seemed a long time before the bell chimed again, startling Susan into a step forward. Then another. Until she was at the front door, pulling it open. Ethan had been right. If she didn't find out, she'd always be suspicious. It would eat away at her. Unravel her completely.

Or had that already happened?

24

SUSAN

The man on the doorstep wasn't what she expected. Younger, skinnier, dressed in camouflage trousers and a tatty-looking T-shirt that might have been white sometime in a previous life. 'Ethan?'

'Not what you expected, eh?' he said as if he'd read her mind. He grinned, exposing the kind of dazzlingly white teeth possessed by contestants in reality TV shows. She presumed he kept his mouth shut when doing undercover work. 'I can do a mean James Bond, if necessary; unfortunately, it rarely is.' He pointed to the space behind her. 'Is it okay if I come in?'

'Yes, of course.' She stood back to allow him to pass. It gave her a certain amount of relief to notice that, despite his rather worn appearance, he smelt fresh. Like lemons. 'If you'd go through to the kitchen, I can made coffee or tea if you'd prefer.'

'Coffee'd be good, thanks.'

He sat while she made it, making no attempt to hide his curiosity as he looked around the room. 'You lived here long?'

'Years. We bought it new.'

'Still seems new.'

It wasn't a compliment, but since she agreed with him, she didn't take offence. 'It's all the glossy white; it makes it seem like a laboratory.' It hadn't been her choice. Mark had seen it in an interior-design magazine and had persuaded her it would suit the modern house far better than the pale-blue, shaker-style kitchen she'd had her heart set on. He'd probably been right; it did suit the house. The problem was... the house didn't suit her.

She put two mugs of coffee on the table, sugar and milk, teaspoons, a packet of biscuits. Drew's favourite. She wasn't sure why she'd bought them; neither she nor Mark were inclined to eat biscuits. 'Help yourself,' she said, amused despite herself to see he didn't need to be told twice, reaching for the packet and tearing it open.

'I missed breakfast,' he explained, demolishing three biscuits in rapid succession. He brushed crumbs from his fingers and pulled a small notebook from one trouser pocket, a pen from another. 'Right. I have a lot of info, so I just need some more details.' He flicked open the notebook, bent it back on itself, and put it on the table beside his coffee. 'What time does your husband normally arrive home?'

'Usually just after six. If he's been delayed, he phones or sends a message.' Apart from the previous night when she'd sat like a fool, candles flickering their contempt for her. 'He didn't last night, or at least not till much later.'

'Right.'

Susan sipped her coffee and began to relax as she answered question after question, revealing the minutiae of their daily life, realising as she did, how boring it was, how mundane, how lacking in excitement. 'We sound so dull,' she said finally when the questions stopped.

Ethan shook the last couple of biscuits from the packet. 'Not dull, just ordinary. Like most people.'

Like most people. She sighed, then stood to make more coffee. While the kettle boiled, she looked at him with curiosity and finally asked, 'Did you always want to be a private investigator?'

He was scribbling in his notebook and looked up with a smile. 'No, I wanted to be a police officer. I was for a while, but I quickly discovered I wasn't cut out for it. Too many rules and regulations. But then I did some undercover work and discovered I loved that.' He tapped his pen on the table. 'It's more my scene. Following trails, finding the pieces of the jigsaw, fitting them together. It didn't take me long to discover I could do it better in the private sector. The police are constrained by the need to make sure a case can stand up in court, we're not hindered in the same way although we're obviously not allowed to break the law.'

'Good,' she said because it seemed the correct thing to say. If she'd given it any thought, she'd have assumed private investigators broke the law with impunity. 'So when will you start?'

'Might as well be this evening. I'll check out his office, watch till he leaves. Go from there.' He returned the notebook to the trousers' capacious pockets. 'You're sure he's in work today?'

'Yes, of course.' Where else would he be? With the woman he was with last night? That was the problem with doubt; it had sharp, little claws that tugged painfully to remind you that you really knew nothing. 'That's where he's supposed to be, anyway.'

'Could you ring his office, find out if he's there? Save my time, and your money.'

She reached for her mobile. The office number was saved, although she rarely had cause to ring, contacting Mark on his mobile if necessary. She recognised the voice of the receptionist who answered. 'Hi, Millie, it's Susan Shepherd, could you put me through to Mark, please?'

'I'm sorry, Mrs Shepherd, he's not here. He left a short while ago; said he wouldn't be back today.'

'Oh right,' Susan tried to keep her voice steady. 'Has he gone to a meeting? I don't want to interrupt something important by ringing him on his mobile.'

'No, at least I don't think so; let me check his diary.'

Susan refused to meet Ethan's eyes as she waited.

'No, I've nothing down for him this afternoon,' Millie said. 'He did look a bit agitated when he passed the desk on his way out. I hope there's nothing wrong.'

Susan laughed. A false, forced sound that gave her the needed seconds to come up with something remotely plausible to say. 'No, nothing's wrong. We've been trying to decide what to do for our wedding anniversary, that's all. I bet he's gone to organise a surprise. That's so like him.' She laughed again, wondering if she sounded slightly manic, cutting the sound off abruptly. 'Don't tell him I called; I'd hate to spoil whatever it is that he's planning.'

'No, of course not.'

Susan knew she wouldn't; she also knew that Millie would discuss the call with the other administrative staff. Discuss it, examine it, possibly see it for the lie it was. She put her mobile down. 'He's not in the office. Should I ring him on his mobile?'

'Give it a go.'

'What should I say?'

'That you're checking that his troublesome client wasn't going to drag him out again... something like that. Keep it light, casual.'

'Right.' She picked up the phone again, feeling her blood pressure rise as it rang, then the sudden relief, or disappointment, when it went to voicemail. 'Hi, just me, checking to make sure you'll be home this evening at your usual time, okay? Ring me and let me know if you're going to be late. Or send a message. Right, love you.' She hung up, dropped her phone on the table and her head in her hand. 'Fuck, I sounded like an idiot. He'll know there's something up. I never sound so... so stupid!'

Ethan was munching on the last biscuit. 'Does it matter? Within a few days, I'll have all the information you need to confront him about his affair.' He took a mouthful of coffee then wiped crumbs from his mouth with the back of his hand. 'That is your intention, isn't it?'

Was it? Confront Mark with proof of his infidelity. Perhaps force him to decide. Stay with Susan or leave her to start a new life with this unknown woman who was probably younger, beautiful, who hadn't let life and circumstances wear her down as Susan had done.

Mark liked to give the impression he was tough, strong-willed. He wasn't really. He was easily swayed, easily pushed. She ought to know. It was she who'd encouraged him to apply for new jobs when his career appeared to stagnate, she who'd pushed him to apply for promotion in the new company, who'd convinced him it was the next step to being a partner.

It had been hard work. She loved him, but she knew his flaws. If she'd pushed too hard, he'd have felt cornered, and would have taken the easier option – he'd have stayed in the dead-end job, and watched others being promoted over him. Susan had tread a careful, fine line of encouragement, ego-pumping, support, backing away when necessary, taking a careful step forward when she could.

That was for a job. This was for her life. 'I'm not exactly sure what I'm going to do as yet,' she said as Ethan waited for a reply. 'I'll wait to see what you find out.'

'That's up to you,' he said, his tone of voice saying clearly that he didn't give a toss what she did, didn't care that whatever he discovered might destroy her. He got to his feet. 'I'll report back to you on Monday and we can go from there, okay?'

Monday. Susan nodded acceptance. In a few days she'd know exactly what she was up against. How beautiful was this woman

who'd captured Mark's attention? Was she a fleeting fixation, a sexual siren with obvious attractions, or would she be something more dangerous: an attractive, intelligent woman who'd give him everything he thought he needed?

Once Susan had all the information, she'd decide what to do.

She might be ordinary, she might even be dull, but she'd do whatever it took to save her marriage and keep the man she loved.

25

HANNAH

'I'm going to look for an apartment in Bristol. My mother is great, and she loves having me, but I can't stay with her forever.' Hannah wasn't sure why she lied. An ingrained habit she'd acquired in the years after her father had left. Years when she'd show up to school with bruises and tell the teachers that she'd tripped over the unruly dog they didn't possess rather than tell the truth for fear her mother would be taken away and Hannah would be doubly abandoned.

'I'm surprised you moved in with her at all.'

'I didn't want to be on my own and there wasn't anyone else I could go to.' *And I wanted to appear desperate and vulnerable.*

They were lying naked on the bed. The bedlinen had been cast aside, as had their clothes as soon as they'd pushed through the door in a tangle of hands, lips, and hot breath. The same hotel with the same receptionist who'd been on the desk the first evening, shooting critical daggers in Hannah's direction as they'd checked in.

'The divorce must have been tough.'

'It was. Ivan is a nice guy but we were never suited and, in the end, we were making each other miserable.'

I curled into Mark's arm, feeling warm and content. I heard his breathing slow and knew he'd fallen into a post-orgasmic sleep. Lying was such second nature to me that I did it even when it didn't matter. And it certainly didn't matter that I'd lied about Ivan, who didn't count any more.

What he'd done to me that day, the violence of it, it seemed to have reached deep inside me and hit a reset button to make me re-evaluate my life. The one I had lived, the remainder I hoped to have. That's what he did to me that day. He made me see my life in all its tawdriness.

I'd spent all of my adult life trying to find what I'd lost when I was ten, seeking out older men, trading my body to feel loved. The older men I'd gravitated towards when I'd been younger were less kind now that I was older. Less kind. Or downright violent. Like Ivan.

Seeing my life with new eyes had sent me spiralling in despair until the day I'd found Mark's photo. He had saved me and he hadn't even known I was in danger.

The last twenty years meant nothing. Neither did his wife. She wasn't making him happy and I knew I could. He loved me; he'd just forgotten he did. I'd keep reminding him until he remembered, until he'd put the twenty years we'd lost behind him.

I ran my hand over his belly, pulling gently on the hairs that grew thicker the lower I went and my tugging became more demanding until he groaned and caught my hand.

We were so good together.

And I was happy again.

26

SUSAN

During the following days, Susan watched as her marriage disintegrated minute by minute, hour by hour. It wasn't anything obvious. Mark never stayed out as late as he had that first day. He was home on time; in fact, he was even early a couple of days. And he was his usual, pleasant self, chatting about work, the weather, the weeds in the garden, the speed at which they grew, how he'd deal with them when he had time. Dismal mundanities. The sum of their life together.

Nor had he fallen into the classic crime of over-compensating – he didn't buy her bunches of flowers or boxes of chocolates, didn't compliment her more than usual.

What had changed, what sent shivers of worry sliding over her, was the way he stared into space when he thought she wasn't looking, a smile curving his lips, one she hadn't seen in many years, a smile she remembered from their first days together. A dopey, smitten smile of love. Lust she could have discounted but this was something else. She remembered the way he'd put her on a pedestal back then, how she could do nothing wrong in his eyes. He'd made her feel like a queen.

Now someone else had stolen her crown and stepped onto the pedestal she'd vacated at some point over the years.

But he was still with Susan. There was still a chance. She clung to that fine thread of hope until Saturday came around.

It was their routine to go to a local café for breakfast, buying the weekend newspapers on the way. They ordered the same things almost every week: a large fry-up for Mark, poached eggs on toast for Susan. Coffee for both. They pored over the newspapers as they ate, swopping titbits as they read, then swopping sections. They laughed at the crazy news, shook their heads at the state of the economy.

Usually, they had more coffee. Usually... no, always... so when he shook his head, and said, 'No, thanks, I won't have any more,' she stared at him in disbelief. This more than anything worried her and brought stinging tears to her eyes. She kept her head down and waited for the wave of sadness to pass.

Mark folded the sports section of the paper he was reading and put it down. 'Actually, I can't stay much longer. I need to go into the office for a couple of hours.'

It was rare rather than unheard of for him to need to work at the weekend. That he needed to that weekend was simply a coincidence. A week ago, she'd have thought nothing of it. She'd have happily stayed in the café on her own, having a second coffee, reading the newspaper. Thinking that all was right in her stupid, little, boring, dismal world.

'You don't mind, do you?'

'Of course not. I promised to call around to Jan this weekend, so that'll leave me free to do that today. I'll let her know.' She took out her mobile and tapped out a message. Not to Jan, who'd be surprised, even horrified, to see her on a Saturday when she'd be busy with her children, but to Ethan.

Mark says he has to go into the office today.

The response came almost immediately.

Don't worry. I'm on it.

He was on it? Startled, she looked around the busy café, expecting to see Ethan peering their direction. If he was there, perhaps in one of the booths that lined the walls, he wasn't visible. She supposed it was the point of surveillance but it unsettled her to think someone was watching, even if this was someone she'd paid.

Was he taking photos of them? The thought made her squirm. What would they show? A happily married couple, relaxing on a Saturday morning? How would the photos compare to ones he'd take with Mark and whatever woman he was spending time with? Perhaps Susan would look at them and see what was lacking between them. Because something had to be. Something had to be wrong. Otherwise Mark wouldn't be looking elsewhere. Something had to be wrong with her.

'Where are you meeting her?'

'What?'

Mark frowned. 'Jan. Isn't that who you said you were meeting?'

Susan's laugh was too hearty. Too fake. She was losing it. Maybe she already had. The way she'd lost Drew and Mark. 'Sorry, I was elsewhere. Trying to think what to cook for dinner.' She saw it then: his little sigh of disappointment, of regret. Maybe she should have said she was thinking about going to visit a gallery or booking to see something in the Hippodrome with one of her friends. Something interesting. 'Yes, Jan. I'm going to go around to hers.'

But he'd already lost interest, his eyes flicking over the news-

paper, scowling as he read something he didn't approve of, bad news about something or other.

'What time will you be home?'

He turned a page before answering. 'Not late.'

A non-answer that injected irritation into her misery. 'I might do fish, so I'll need a time, Mark.' Her voice was sharp enough to bring his face up from the paper in surprise at hearing his sad, passive wife grow tetchy.

'Fish'd be nice.' He folded the newspaper in half then in quarters. A sure sign he was done with it. 'How about I message you when I'm on the way home?' He smiled, obviously pleased he'd come up with an answer to her dilemma. 'That suit?'

Of course it didn't suit but what could she say? She'd really no desire to cook fish, hating the smell that lingered regardless of what she did. 'Yes, that's fine. But you won't be too late, will you?'

'No, I shouldn't be.' He pushed back his chair and got to his feet. 'You going to stay a bit longer or are you ready to go?'

His movement had rocked the table, dislodging the knife she had balanced on the plate. She reached for it to straighten it, then picked it up and looked at the sharp, curved edge, felt the weight of the handle in her hand, wondered about finishing it all then. How dramatic it would be.

Why didn't she?

Analysis paralysis.

She couldn't decide whether to stab him or herself.

SUSAN

Rather than moping around all afternoon, Susan decided to do something she'd wanted to do for a while. She'd mentioned it to Mark once. He'd laughed and said he wasn't interested, so she'd thought it was a silly thing to want to do. But now, on a sunny Saturday, she got a self-guided leaflet from the tourist information office in Bristol and visited all the Banksy artwork.

It was a lovely day, walking in the city was always enjoyable and there was nobody to rush her along. It allowed her to stand and stare at the artwork and exchange views with total strangers. She'd seen most of Banksy's work in some form or other over the years but seeing them in situ was as special as she'd expected.

She took photos of them all, thinking that she'd send them to Drew when she got home. The first few days after he'd left, she messaged him compulsively several times a day. She'd weaned herself off the need and restricted herself to once a day. Sometimes, he even answered.

The last Banksy to see was *Well Hung Lover*. It made her smile, the good mood lasting as she walked slowly to the bus station for the journey home. It faded as the bus chugged on its way. When it

reached her stop, she picked up her dismal mood like a coat she'd discarded earlier and slipped it back on, buttoning it tightly around her, feeling the thickness, the weight of it.

The house was sullenly quiet. She shut the front door behind her and stared down the hallway to the kitchen. Only then did she realise she'd bought nothing for dinner.

It was almost six before she had the message from Mark.

On my way. You can put the fish on now.

She looked at the words, trying to read between them to see the truth. It wasn't there. She brought up Ethan's number and tapped out a message.

Where did he go?

Her finger hovered over send, then with a grunt of irritation, she deleted it instead. Monday would be time enough to know the truth. Until then, she could cling to the fading, friable thread of hope.

* * *

She was in the living room when Mark returned. It had taken her a long time to set the stage, to ensure she looked relaxed, unconcerned, happy in her skin. She'd changed from the jeans and shirt she'd been wearing into her favourite pyjamas. A Christmas present from Drew the previous year, they were pink, brushed cotton, and patterned with penguins. She left her feet bare – she thought it made her look younger.

Usually, she read on her Kindle but a paperback looked better. She chose one at random from the bookshelf and settled herself

on the sofa, feet up, head resting on a cushion. Mostly, she stared at the words on the page without any recognition, turning a page now and then as if to convince herself she was actually reading. Sometimes, she shut her eyes, but when she did, it was to see Mark and some nameless hussy, cavorting together, their naked skin glistening in the light of numerous candles poised around a huge bed.

She heard the front door open, the leather soles of his shoes slap across the hallway to the kitchen, followed by silence. In her imagination, she saw him standing in the kitchen doorway, puzzled not to see her busy cooking something for his dinner. Slower steps then as he retraced his way to the living-room door, the click as he pressed on the handle.

Even then, she kept up the pretence, looking up startled when he called her name. 'Mark! Gosh, sorry, I didn't hear you come in.' She shut the book and rested it against her chest. 'Such a good book, I was completely lost in the story.'

'Right.'

She examined his face, his whole demeanour, for any clues. There was nothing she hadn't seen every working day for years. He looked slightly tired and a little distracted. Maybe this idea of an affair was all in her imagination? This stupid empty nest syndrome causing her to behave and think with an irrationality new to her. It was a straw she reached for, she grabbed hold of it, clung to it as it pulled her up, brightened her smile and her voice, almost put a bounce into her step as she got to her feet and crossed to him.

'I didn't get fish after all.' She placed a hand on his chest. Close to him, it was his usual scent that hit her, that woody aftershave he favoured. She pressed closer, sliding her hand to his face, leaning in to press a kiss against his lips. They tasted of the cherry-flavoured lip balm he'd used since goodness knows when.

Everything was as it always was. She wanted to do a twirl, dance down the hallway, skip over to the fridge and take out a bottle of wine to celebrate. Instead, she stayed with her hand resting against his cheek. 'I thought we'd get a takeaway for a change.' She wasn't surprised when he raised an eyebrow; over the years, she'd made her feelings about takeaways clear. She wasn't a fan. 'I thought I should join the twenty-first century,' she said, 'so I started a Just Eat account.'

He laughed, took her hand, and pressed a kiss on it. 'Good idea. Order whatever you like; I'm not fussed.' He stepped back and turned for the stairway. 'I'll just get out of my suit.'

Just like any day. Normal. Everything was as normal. She kept telling herself this, even when she heard the hum of the shower. He'd showered that morning. It wasn't a particularly hot day so why did he need a shower again? Was he washing away his shame?

The eggshell-thin façade of her optimism cracked. She tried to keep it in place with sticking plaster of hope, keeping herself busy by placing an order for an Indian meal, then taking out glasses, cutlery, and putting plates in the oven to warm. She wondered about setting the table in the conservatory. It would take only seconds to put out candles and light them; it'd be a nice surprise for when Mark came down.

There were new tea lights in a cupboard. She took out the packet, then searched for the matches. Unable to find the box she'd used recently – had she thrown it out? – she went into the hallway, and pulled open the drawer of the hall table. It was used as a general dumping ground for all kinds of bits and pieces. Despite constantly clearing it out, it had the ability to magically refill itself within days. If she was in luck, there might be a box of matches lurking inside. She had her hand on the handle of the drawer when she heard the faint trill of a voice drifting down the

stairs. Tilting her head, she strained to listen, then moved slowly towards the stairway and up, one careful step at a time.

On the landing, there was silence for so long, she thought she must have imagined it and raised her eyes to the ceiling at her stupidity. She had descended one step, when the sound came again. Closer to the source, it still took a few seconds to pinpoint exactly which room it was coming from. The bathroom.

She edged over to the door, pushed her hair back, and pressed her ear against it. Mark's voice. Stopping and starting. On his mobile. Having a conversation with someone. She had to hold her hand over her mouth when she heard the laugh that told her, in case there was the least doubt, that it wasn't a business call. It was one she recognised, the one he'd use after they'd made love, when they were lying wrapped in each other's sweaty arms, and they'd talk nonsense and he'd laugh that very same laugh he was now sharing with someone else.

As hard as she pressed against the door, she couldn't make out the words. It didn't matter. You didn't have to join all the dots to see the full picture.

She crept away, down the stairs, back to the conservatory. The packet of tea lights sat on the table, taunting her. She put them back into the cupboard, then slammed it shut, opened it, slammed it shut harder, then harder again and again till her ears rang with the noise.

The kitchen door burst open, Mark standing there in a pair of boxer shorts, wet hair on end, eyes wide in an emotion she'd no chance of identifying. The door was open, her fingers curled around the handle.

'What the hell, Susan?'

She didn't know how it happened, but suddenly, there was a knife in her hand. Mark looked at it, various emotions flitting across his face before settling on disbelief when she raised her hand and plunged the

blade into his chest, into the spot marked x where his heart used to be. The spurt of blood was startlingly cold; it gushed over her hand, then oddly, morphed into ice cubes that fell to the floor and smashed into red shards of glass that skittered across the floor.

She shut her eyes and the image vanished. When she opened them, she caught his dismissive eye roll and shut the door, gently this time. 'The catch was stuck.' She didn't wait to see or hear his reaction to her admittedly ridiculous explanation. Crossing to the kitchen, she opened a cupboard and took out wine glasses. 'You had a shower?' she said, putting the glasses on the counter.

Yes, I spent the afternoon with my mistress and was afraid you might smell the afterglow of the amazing sex we had. God, she's so hot, she drives me crazy.

'What?' She looked at him, startled.

Mark frowned. 'Are you okay? You seem distracted.' He pulled at the waistband of his shorts. 'I thought a shower might relax me after a tough day.'

'Yes, right.'

'It was working till I heard all the noise. I'll go and throw some clothes on. Is the food on its way? We could have it on a tray; there's a movie on tonight I'd fancy watching, okay?'

He smoothed a hand over his hair as he spoke. Water trickled down his neck. It lingered in the dip above his collarbone. She wanted to go to him, lick the water out, rub against him, mark him as hers. The longing was almost overwhelming. Her hands were wrapped around the wine glasses so tightly, she wondered they didn't snap, cut her, make her bleed. 'That sounds like a good idea,' she mumbled. She dragged her eyes from his body and her thoughts from memories of a time when she wouldn't have hesitated, when all it would have taken was a smile for him to know what she was thinking. That's all it would have taken. 'It should be here in a few minutes.' She released the glasses and turned to

open the fridge, keeping her face buried in it until she heard Mark's footsteps recede.

By the time he came down, ten minutes later, she'd assembled a good version of her face, widening her eyes, stretching her mouth into a semblance of a smile. She checked her reflection in the door of the eye-level microwave, startled by the face staring back. Light was coming from the window on one side. It illuminated half her face, leaving the other half in semi-darkness. As she stared, she had the crazy sensation that the darkness was creeping across, dousing the light or maybe it was simply the way she felt.

A sudden blast of sound made her gasp and turn away from her reflection.

'Sorry!' Mark shouted from the living room as the sound faded to a more acceptable level. If he wasn't wearing his glasses, he couldn't see the remote properly and frequently pressed the wrong button. Sometimes, he'd even be using the wrong controls. It used to amuse Susan, and made Drew roll his eyes in affectionate derision. Now Drew was gone, and nothing seemed funny any more.

The doorbell announced the arrival of the takeaway. 'I'll get it,' Mark shouted over the TV. The next few minutes were filled with the companionable unpacking of containers and non-verbal sounds of pleasure as lid after lid was removed. Susan took the plates from the oven, putting one on each tray.

'Careful, they're a bit hot,' she warned. She helped herself to a little of everything. It was more than she wanted, probably more than she'd eat, but she didn't want to give Mark a reason to ask if she was okay because if he did, she wasn't sure she'd be able to restrain herself. The words would burst out, a torrid flow of pain.

'This was a good idea,' he said, piling food on his plate. He balanced a garlic nan bread on top. 'This'll do me.'

He vanished into the living room, leaving Susan to put the lids back on the cartons. There was enough for tomorrow; it'd save her having to cook.

The movie, *The Godfather*, was one she'd seen many years before but Mark had somehow missed. 'You don't mind watching it again,' he said, pointing the remote at the TV to start the movie rolling.

'No, it's fine. It's good enough to watch again.'

It also meant she could drift away into her thoughts without worrying she'd miss something.

Anyway, wasn't it fitting... wasn't it so fucking, unbelievably perfect... that he'd want to watch a movie about a bunch of amoral, cheating, lying men.

28

SUSAN

The Godfather is a long movie. After an hour, the smell of congealing food on her plate was beginning to make Susan feel queasy. 'I need a toilet break,' she said, reaching for the remote.

'I'll do it.' He snapped it from her hand. As if she was incapable of pressing the button to stop the film without losing it. As if he were the king of the goddamn remote.

'Fine,' she said, getting to her feet. He'd left his tray on the floor. It took her only seconds to combine everything, the plates, cutlery and condiments, onto one tray. A lazy man's load. She noticed Mark didn't offer to help and frowned as she rested one end of the tray on a hip to free a hand to open the door. He used to, didn't he? Or was she looking back with thick, rose-coloured glasses?

In the kitchen, she scraped the uneaten lamb from her plate back into the container and put it into the fridge. The sombre voice of a newsreader drifted through the open doors from the living room. Mark would be content catching up with the news. There was no need to rush back. She took her time, putting the

covers on the various cartons, finding space in the fridge for everything, wondering once again what she was going to do with all the damn cheese she'd bought.

Maybe Mark was still hungry.

She stood in the living room doorway. 'You fancy some cheese and crackers?'

'Sure,' he said without looking at her.

So much cheese. She took out a handful of packets, using scissors to open the waxed paper. A few slices of each on a plate for Mark, a couple of thin slices on a separate plate for her. She opened the cupboard to take out a box of crackers, staring in confusion when she didn't see any. Maybe she'd put them in a different place to usual, challenging herself by doing things differently. A stupid thing to do, she thought with a shake of her head as she opened another cupboard, then another and another. Every cupboard was opened and searched, then opened and searched again. She was making such a racket, she was surprised Mark hadn't come to investigate.

Finally facing the truth, she leaned back against the counter. Cheese but no crackers. What an idiot she was. She thumped the side of her head, then remembered there was bread in the freezer. It would do fine.

Nobody ate bread except Drew and it was frozen into a block, resisting her efforts to free individual slices. She reached for a wide-bladed knife, inserting the sharp edge between the slices, and pressing down. It freed quicker than she'd expected, the metal hitting the granite worktop with a snap, the point of the knife scoring a line down her hand.

She stared as blood bubbled along the cut. Bizarrely, it reminded her of the water running down Mark's neck earlier. This time, she didn't resist and held the cut to her mouth, the

metallic taste on her tongue making her cry. Or maybe it was the sudden pain.

Opening a drawer, she took out a clean tea cloth and wrapped it around her hand. Blood had smudged across the slice of still-frozen bread. She turned on the tap, rinsed it away, patted the bread dry with the edge of the towel, then put the damp, frozen bread into the toaster.

'Here you go,' she said minutes later, putting the tray on the coffee table. If he noticed the band aid on her hand, he didn't comment.

He topped up her half-empty glass from the wine bottle on the floor beside him. It was, Susan noticed, almost empty. He poured the remainder into his glass. Without comment, he stood, left the room, and returned a moment later with a second bottle. It was unusual for them to finish one bottle in a night; she couldn't remember them ever opening a second bottle. Not when it was just the two of them. The way it was now.

The movie was playing. She sat back with the glass in one hand, a plate of toast and cheese on her lap that she nibbled now and then, washing it down with mouthfuls of wine, holding out her glass for a refill when it was empty. Maybe this was another change she could make. Hit the bottle. Drown her sorrows, anaesthetise her worries.

She glanced at Mark, who was engrossed in the movie. Or pretending to be. Was that why he was drinking? To deaden his worries, or to drown his guilt?

It was after ten before the movie ended. The second bottle of wine was gone, the plates empty. Normally, she'd fuss about, tidy everything away, restore order. That night, she stood, looked down at the plates and glasses and wondered why she bothered. Being a tidy housewife hadn't stopped Drew leaving home at the first

opportunity. It hadn't stopped Mark having an affair. 'I'll tidy up in the morning.'

She was halfway up the stairs before she heard him get to his feet. Through the open doorway, she saw him stagger alarmingly before resting a hand on his head and pressing down. Perhaps his demons were trying to escape.

She left him to it and continued up to their room. The routine of nightly preparation left too much space to think, and in the deathly quiet of the house, it seemed she could hear her heart beat. Once, it would beat in anticipation of the lovemaking that would lie ahead of her; now it was in fear.

Their sex life was good, although like many couples who'd been together a long time, they'd drifted into a comfortable, almost companionable coupling. A gentle waltz that was a long way from the tango they'd danced in their first days, months, years together, when they'd explored each other's body and experimented in what gave them pleasure.

Now, it was the missionary position, in bed, once a week on a Saturday night. On holidays, the frequency might increase to two or three times a week. Never more than once a night. Or not for many years anyway.

But always on a Saturday night.

That night.

The linen sheets were cool against her skin. She always slept naked so why did she feel so vulnerable? The consequence of facing the truth perhaps. No longer anticipating pleasure, but instead, the grim, stark reality with the expectation of pain.

She ran a finger over the dressing on her hand. It stung a little. Like most women who'd suffered badly from period pains in her youth, she considered herself to have a high pain threshold. Physical pain. It could be eased with over-the-counter pain relief. But

this pain drilling into her head, into her heart, there was no cure for that.

Unless acceptance made it easier. She wasn't sure it would. Even if it did, she wasn't there yet. There was still the hope that he was going to come into the room, climb into bed beside her and take her into his arms, as he had done every Saturday that she could remember. And they'd move in unison and it would be so good that she'd cry when she felt him inside her, where he belonged, where she needed him to be.

The bed moved as he slipped in beside her and she waited, bracing herself for his usual overtures, a hand slipping over her belly, up over her breast. She waited. When it didn't come, in desperation, she turned on her side, reversed the routine, moving her hand over his belly.

Different but it would be all right.

His hand closed over hers, stopping its downward momentum, squeezing it gently before lifting it upward to rest on his chest.

'Too much to drink, Sue. Plus, I'm wrecked.'

'Oh, right,' she said, as if it were nothing, as if this was something ordinary in their ordinary life. As if it wasn't something not in the slightest bit in any shape or form fucking ordinary.

'I'm sorry,' he said, squeezing her hand gently.

Then he let her hand go, turned over on his side, and moments later, she heard the heavy, regular breathing that told her he'd fallen asleep.

Was he dreaming of *her*, whoever she was? In that moment, Susan hated her with such passion she had to wedge her hand between her teeth and bite down painfully to contain it, to stop it exiting in a loud waft of vile, bitter words that would ricochet around the room, wake Mark, and have him stare at her in horror.

The pain as her teeth pressed into the flesh and bones of her hand focused her. It was a long time before her jaw relaxed,

releasing the bruised flesh. She rubbed it with her other hand, feeling the indents in her skin as she stared into the darkness and saw nothing but a long, bleak, empty future.

Unless she found this woman.

And got rid of her.

HANNAH

My relationship with Mark was developing nicely. I put no pressure on him, agreeing to meet whenever it suited him, for lunch, coffee or simply to talk. We didn't return to the hotel. He wanted to, of course he did, but experience had taught me it was better to keep a man wanting.

'I need to get home,' I said after coffee on our third meeting. 'Mother wants us to spend more time together. She's been so good to me; I don't like to let her down.'

'Tomorrow?'

'Yes, and maybe I could stay late then, if you'd like.'

'I would.' He reached across and grasped my hand in his.

But when the following day arrived, when he was almost panting with desire, I broke the bad news. 'I can't stay late.' I looked at the slim, gold watch that encircled my wrist, a present from an old boyfriend whose name was long forgotten. 'Mother is taking me out for dinner.' I reached for his hand, drawing my fingers gently over his skin. 'You know I'd prefer to be with you. You've saved me, you know.' I smiled, lifted his hand and pressed a kiss on it. 'When I returned, I'd hoped Mum would help me find

my feet again but it's been you, Mark; you've made me realise there is life after divorce.' I saw the conflict in his eyes. Thwarted desire and the pleasure my words had given him vied with a wide band of guilt that was narrowing and loosening each day. Soon, I'd be able to pull it off, throw it away. Soon, but I wasn't there yet.

He reached under the table to lay a hand on my knee, his fingers finding the edge of my dress, wriggling under, stretching over my skin. I almost changed my mind then and dragged him to the nearest hotel. But he was still wriggling on that hook; I needed him firmly caught.

'When I find somewhere suitable to rent, I'll have more freedom and you'll be able to come around now and then.' Keeping it easy, no pressure. Allowing him to believe the string he was on was completely elastic. That it would stretch as far as he wanted. The biggest fish were reeled in gently and slowly. And then they stayed caught.

* * *

I didn't want to commit to a long-term rental so it made sense to find an Airbnb apartment. There was plenty of choice and it didn't take me long to find exactly what I wanted. A two-bedroom, two-bathroom apartment on The Grove, a five-minute walk from Mark's office. Although it overlooked the car park, it was on the top floor, giving a view of the Floating Harbour from the tiny balcony. The kitchen was too small but then I hadn't planned on doing much cooking.

It was available from the Saturday, so I had a day to spare. I could sit around my mother's unfriendly house or drive to Ivan's to tackle the pile of laundry. No contest. It would give me the opportunity to pick up a few things to lend a stylish air to the Airbnb's rather bland décor too.

Rather than staying overnight in Windsor, I left Thornbury early. Ivan's home, which I'd shared for the length of our marriage, had been inherited from his parents. An eighteenth-century manor house, it was set in an acre of land with a winding driveway leading from the front gate to the front door. Originally, the house had been surrounded by hundreds of acres of park and farmland but over the years, inheritance tax and various other money woes had necessitated selling portions off until finally the house and the acre of garden was all that remained.

I arrived after a little more than an hour and a half's drive and pulled up to the gate. It was old and wasn't electrified. I'd nagged Ivan about having it changed but he'd looked at me in horror. 'That gate is over a hundred years old,' he'd said, as if I'd asked him to cut off one of his fingers.

Old, but not particularly attractive, and a blasted nuisance to open, especially in the light rain that had started to fall the last twenty minutes of my journey. Both sides of the gate needed to be opened before I could drive the car through. By the time I was back in the car, rain had drenched my light jacket, turned my hair into rats' tails, and seriously dented my mood. Leaving the gate open, I drove along the potholed, winding avenue to the house. The breeze had picked up, the rain changing to a thunderous deluge that, even at speed, the windscreen wipers battled to clear.

Luckily, I was able to pull up close to the front door. I still had my keys and they were in my hand as I climbed from the car and made a dash for the shelter of the porch.

'Shit,' I muttered as the wind-driven rain pelted my back. The lock, like the damn gate, was old, and I always struggled to turn the key.

'You're too impatient,' Ivan had insisted. 'Old things need a bit of finessing.'

He'd thought this was funny. In the beginning. But that was

before he began to blame my advanced years on my failure to become pregnant. It always struck me as ironic for two reasons – I was six years older than he thought, and he was thirty years older than me.

Finally, the key turned in the lock and I pushed the door open.

I shivered automatically as I stepped into the wood-panelled entrance hall and shut the door behind me on the belting rain. It was a chilly room even on the warmest day and always smelt damp. Now though, something nastier than dampness was making my nose crinkle.

An oak stairway rose to the bedroom floor. I'd tripped on the moth-eaten stair runner several times over the year I'd lived there. But it had been hand-loomed specially, sometime early in the previous century, so rather than pulling it up, throwing it out and replacing it with something nicer, it was sprayed on occasion to treat the bugs who feasted on it.

Fortunately, for my sanity, the plumbing had been improved over the years and the bathrooms were modern and well designed. As was the kitchen.

'Damn!' The holdall with my laundry was in the boot of the car. I looked up the stairs. I supposed it was only polite to go up and say hello to Ivan before using his facilities. If I was lucky, the rain would have stopped before I came back down.

My soon to be ex-husband – I hadn't exactly lied to Mark but we weren't quite divorced – was exactly where I expected to find him. I knocked gently on the door before opening it. 'Hi,' I said.

He stared at me, that silly smile he thought made him look sexy still on his lips. It didn't work on me then; it certainly didn't work on me now. Mark was my future. 'I need to pick up a few things, and I'd like to use the washing machine, if you don't mind.'

I spent as little time as possible chatting with him. He'd never been an entertaining conversationalist. Money was the only

vocabulary he thought he needed; he thought it bought everything. And for a while, he was right.

Back downstairs, when I opened the front door and looked out, the rain was still pelting down. The laundry wasn't going to come in on its own. I squealed on the mad dash to the boot, wrenching it open, water splashing into my eyes. I grabbed the bag, slammed the boot shut, then dashed back inside.

'Bloody weather!'

The washing machine was a massive one, Ivan labouring under the idea that big, like old, was better. Except, of course with women. Then it was young and slim. And sexy.

I shook him and his stupid ideas from my head and started the delicate cycle running.

It was going to take time, but I wasn't in a hurry. I made coffee and took out my phone to check my socials. I wasn't obsessive; once or twice a day was enough to catch up with the crap that most people posted. It helped pass the time.

The washing machine conveniently gave a countdown of time remaining. Ten minutes. I'd use the time to collect some things to prettify the apartment a little.

Ivan wouldn't come to check but anyway, there was no fear that I'd pinch any of his valuables. The old paintings on the walls, the porcelain figures that roamed the shelves and mantelpieces, the pots and vases. All suited this old mausoleum; they would look scarily out of place in the Airbnb or any place I saw myself living in the future. Mark's super modern home, for example. I smiled at that thought as I walked through the rooms searching for anything suitable.

I found a couple of candlesticks. Heavy glass, they were old, might even be antique, but they were nicely made, with a simplicity that was almost modern. Ivan wouldn't miss them. He had a fear of candles ever since Windsor Castle had been so badly

damaged in the fire of 1992 and wouldn't allow any to be used. It didn't matter that candles hadn't been responsible for that fire; he had it fixed in his head that it could happen to his precious house.

I'd resisted the temptation to tell him that it would have been the best thing to have happened to the ugly dump. Burn the whole lot down, build a big modern house. With a swimming pool, perhaps. And a home cinema. Maybe a home gym. I hadn't said it, hadn't even been tempted to set the pile alight myself. I might have done if I hadn't realised the marriage wasn't going to last much longer.

Back in the utility room, I put the damp clothes into the tumble drier, checked it was at the right temperature and set it going.

There wasn't much more I wanted to take. Some bed linen and towels. A bottle of whisky, one of vodka, a few bottles of wine. I wasn't a big drinker, but I'd noticed Mark liked a tipple. We could sit on the balcony, stare out over Bristol, and sip a whisky.

I left everything by the front door and was humming as I turned to go back to the kitchen. A bang from upstairs stopped me mid-stride. I'd never managed to get used to the old house's creaks and groans when I'd lived there; they'd come out of the blue, startlingly loud at times, making me yelp in fright. Ivan, used to the sounds it made, would laugh. In amusement in the early, love-flushed days, derisively, sneeringly later.

From where I stood, I could see the door to his bedroom. It was still shut. He wouldn't be coming to catch me filching his booze.

When there was nothing more worth taking, I returned to the kitchen and unpacked my clothes from the drier.

That was it. I checked the time. Almost midday. Plenty of time to get back home and pack up, ready for an early departure the following morning. The owner of the Airbnb had promised to be

ready with the keys at ten. Mark was calling around in the afternoon. No doubt we'd christen the apartment. Maybe even twice. After all, there were two bedrooms.

I went up to say goodbye to Ivan. 'Thanks for letting me do my laundry.' He didn't reply. An unpleasant odour made me beat a dignified retreat. He'd let himself go a little since I'd left. 'I'll call back in a week or so, see how you're doing.' And with a wave, I left.

It was still raining when I opened the front door. Instead of using the boot, I dumped everything onto the back seat of the car, swearing loudly as a trickle of water fell from a gutter overhead as I was shutting the door. It ran down my neck and between my breasts.

I was still swearing when I went to shut the front door. It was always more of a problem when it rained. According to Ivan, the wood swelled. To me, it made a clear argument for uPVC but he seemed to think it added to its charm.

There was nothing charming about me trying to get it to shut. I grabbed the doorknob and slammed it a couple of times, feeling the rain soak through my jacket again. My hand slipped when I tried to pull it shut again and it was sorely tempting to leave it ajar. To allow the rain to soak the entrance hall, drown the bloody house.

Luckily, it was third time's a charm and it closed as if it had been teasing me all along. It must have realised I was near the end of my limited availability of patience.

In the driver's seat, I peeled off the wet jacket, used a dry patch of it to rub through my hair and over my face, then started the engine and went back down the driveway. The heavy rain had filled the potholes, making them impossible to avoid and the car bumped and lurched as it hit one after the other. I hadn't secured the bottles on the back seat, and when I hit the third pothole, I

hear the distinct and ominous sound of one bottle cracking against another.

'Shit!' I stopped, undid my seat belt, and twisted to see the damage. Noise, but thankfully no damage. I separated the bottles so they wouldn't drive me crazy clinking together all the way home. Starting the car again, I barely slowed as I drove through the gates, leaving them wide open behind me.

Ivan would understand.

30

HANNAH

My darling mother was home that evening. I stayed in my room while I heard her pottering about in the kitchen, waiting for the silence before going down. She was sitting in the small, poky dining room, eating what she still insisted on referring to as her 'tea'. She no longer offered me anything. It was as if I wasn't really there. Just the way she liked it.

I stood with my hand on the door frame, looking at her as she sat hunched over her meal.

'I'll be moving out in the morning,' I said.

Mother merely nodded without bothering to look up. An unaccustomed ache hit me; the pain sharp enough to have me clasp an arm around my midriff. I'd have laughed, sneered maybe, if she'd asked me where I was going, I'd have lifted my chin and refused to give her the information. But she didn't ask. Didn't care. Glad to see the back of me. Because I was trouble. Always had been, always would be.

When she went back to her meal, I turned wordlessly, my arm still gripping my belly, my eyes filling with stupid tears.

I packed that night and, in the morning, I took everything

down to the hallway. To my surprise, Mother was already gone. No message to wish me luck, or to ask that I leave a forwarding address. I packed everything into the car, swearing loudly when I snagged a nail as I put the heavy case into the boot. I looked at it in dismay. If I didn't cut it off, it would catch in things all day, might break down further and hurt like hell. I had a manicure set, but it was packed into one of the cases.

I nibbled the broken piece, spat it out, then rubbed a finger along the rough surface. 'Damn it,' I muttered and went back into the house. Mother had a manicure set in a leather case she kept on top of her dressing table. I'd used it once but she'd caught me and taught me never to use it again.

I'd use it now; perhaps I'd take it with me. I smiled at the childish thought as I reached her bedroom and turned the knob to open the door, surprised to find it locked. It hadn't been while I lived there. She hadn't loved the child and didn't trust the adult.

I could have given up. It was only a snagged nail, but her decision to lock the room intrigued me. I took a step back and looked around. Putting the key above the door would have been too simple, but it was bound to be nearby.

The landing carpet was old, threadbare in parts. It took only a few seconds to find where she'd slipped the key under a corner of it. I picked it up and slotted it into the lock.

Her bedroom hadn't changed in all the years with its gaudy, floral wallpaper and the hideously clashing carpet. The same dull, gold-coloured eiderdown covered the double bed she'd shared with my father. I'd wondered why she brought it with us when we moved. Had she hoped he'd return even then?

A cricket bat was propped against the wall in the corner near the door. It had been my father's but had been kept, not for any sentimental reason, but for defence in case anyone broke into the house to steal any of the tat my mother prized.

Truth was, any of the local hooligans were wise enough to stay well clear of a woman who had a reputation for being menacingly mean.

I crossed to the dressing table where the manicure set had always been kept.

Only it wasn't there. I looked over the cluttered surface in annoyance. Where had she put it? There were three drawers each side of the kneehole space. It had to be in one of them. I pulled the first open. It was jammed with all sorts of stuff. To the right were letters and statements from a variety of financial institutions. I had no interest in her finances but still had a flick through, unsurprised to see she was quite well-to-do.

I had reached the back of the drawer and was about to shut it and try the next when I came upon something that made my eyes widen. When I took it out and looked at it, I was confused, then shocked, then numb. I slipped it into my jacket pocket, abandoned my search for the manicure set and left the room, leaving the drawer and the bedroom door open behind me.

It was still too early to go to the apartment. I couldn't risk leaving the car anywhere with suitcases on the back seat so I drove to the Grove car park and sat watching the Floating Harbour, my head spinning with thoughts of what I'd discovered.

At exactly ten, my mobile beeped with a message from the Airbnb owner to say he was there to let me in. When I replied to say I was in the car park, he came across to meet me, and kindly gave me a hand to bring everything up to the apartment. He was a thin, wiry man; I hoped he was stronger than he looked.

'They're heavy,' I warned him. Especially since I'd put all the bottles of booze into one of them.

He hefted one up, then nodded. 'You're right, I'll take them across to the lift one at a time. You stay here.'

Still trying to absorb the recent revelation, I was more than

happy to be organised. 'This the last?' he asked a few minutes later.

I reached into the car to grab a holdall and handbag. 'That's everything now.'

The lift opened across the corridor from the apartment, making the offloading of the cases easy. Minutes later, they were sitting in a pile in the living room. The owner handed me the keys, and a folder. 'Anything you need to know is in here,' he said, tapping the edge of it with a broken fingernail. 'My mobile number is there. If there's any problems, ring me. If I don't answer, leave a message and I'll get back to you tooty sweety.'

That made me smile. 'I'm sure everything is fine. Thank you for your help; you've been very kind.'

He nodded. 'If you don't mind me saying so, you look like you could do with a bit of kindness. You take care of yourself. Life can be tough.'

I was rarely taken aback, rarely surprised by people, but I was suddenly hit with the same ache that had struck me the evening before. Was that it? Were the words spoken to me by this stranger with the dirty, broken fingernails, the words I'd hoped my mother might have said to me? Silly to have expectations after all this time. Sillier in the face of what I'd discovered.

Best to be busy. Over the next couple of hours, I unpacked everything into the wardrobes and dressers in the two bedrooms. I unwrapped the glass candlesticks I'd recently acquired and placed them on one side of the mantelpiece over the fake fire.

Once the three suitcases were empty, they fitted one inside the other, like Russian dolls, and slid under the bed in the spare room.

The white wine went into the fridge, the other bottles of alcohol onto a shelf in the living room. I checked the cupboards to see what had been supplied, pleased to see there were decent

glasses. Nothing to eat obviously, but a quick check of the folder supplied me with the location of the nearest convenience store. I didn't intend to cook, but I'd need coffee and milk. Maybe some bread and butter. Some olives perhaps and other nibbles to go with the wine and whisky. Tonic water for the vodka. A list made in my head, I picked up my bag and jacket and headed out.

Of course, I bought more than I'd expected, tempted by packets of biscuits, some artisan bread rolls, and eggs – in case I'd need to provide breakfast one of these mornings. I couldn't do much, but I could fry an egg. I was unpacking my purchases when I heard my phone buzz.

I'm on my way.

Only four words but I could sense the excitement in them and it gave me a thrill. I hurried to prepare the stage and made up the bed in the main bedroom with the fine cotton sheets I'd taken from Ivan's. Then, because you just didn't know what life was going to throw your way, I made up the bed in the spare room too. I had just enough time to slip into something to gladden Mark's heart, when I heard the intercom buzz.

There was a video screen; I could see his face. He looked anxious. Or was it guilt that clouded his features? It seemed I hadn't caught him quite as firmly on my hook as I'd wanted. 'Hello,' I said, hoping my voice sounded suitably husky and inviting.

'Hannah?'

Maybe my voice came out so distorted that he didn't recognise me. After all, I wouldn't have recognised his tinny, weedy voice. 'Yes, it's me, come on up. Top floor.'

I waited until I heard the lift opening before opening the door a fraction to check he was alone, then pulled it wide open to show

me in all the glory of the black, lacy negligee that revealed more than it could possibly cover.

His open mouth and wide eyes were the reaction I expected. I stood back and waved him in, allowing my fingers to slide down his back as he passed. He was wearing a suit. I guessed, officially, he was in the office. His stupid schmuck of a wife would probably believe anything he'd tell her.

'It's a lovely apartment,' I said as I followed him through into the living room. 'And look,' I opened the door onto the balcony, 'we can sit outside and watch the world go by.'

'It's very nice.' He shook off his jacket, pulled off his tie and threw both onto the sofa. 'But you... you look stunning.'

It was gratifying, but I'd have preferred not to see that glimmer of guilt hiding in his eyes. Taking his hand, I led him to the bedroom where I could make him forget, and perhaps for a while too, put my shocking discovery from my head.

31

HANNAH

I suppose it was silly to hope Mark would stay with me into the evening. An even slimmer hope that he'd stay overnight and give me a chance to show off my skill in cracking an egg.

'You know I would if I could,' he said, buttoning his shirt wrong, swearing softly under his breath as he started again.

It would have been easy to have started one of those conversations that went round in circles. The one that said *you could if you wanted to, if you really wanted to* and ended by him screwing up his face and admitting that he didn't want to hurt his wife, that he needed time, that he loved me but... And the words would trail off, just like that. It was a conversation that was always destined to fail, so why start it? It was pointless making Mark feel more guilty for cheating on his wife and was shooting an own goal to make him guilty for upsetting me. 'I know you would, darling,' I said, climbing from the bed and moving closer to wrap my arms around his neck and press my naked body against him. This was the memory I wanted to leave him with. 'I'll be here when you come back.'

His hands swept down my back and lingered on the swell of

my buttocks. 'I really wish I didn't have to go,' he said. He pulled back, then kissed me so gently, it made me quiver. 'I'll work something out, I promise.'

Work something out? A step in the right direction perhaps, but we seemed to have reached a plateau. Perhaps I should have stayed with my mother for longer, ramped up his sympathy for my plight, denied him sex until he was ready to make a commitment to me.

I threw on a T-shirt and stood on the balcony watching as he walked down the street. I wondered if he'd call into his office, just so he could tell his wife he'd been there.

It was a little after five, a long evening lay ahead, hours of time and space to decide what I was going to do with what I'd learnt at my mother's. The balcony chairs weren't comfortable so I didn't linger there, getting to my feet and giving the view a final glance. I'd turned away before someone caught my eye. Not all the men I'd been with over the years had stuck in my mind, and even when their faces or bodies did, their names certainly didn't.

But this man I knew, and I frowned, immediately suspicious to see him there.

Coincidences happened, but this one stunk. And if something stinks, it's usually wise to smell a rat.

32

SUSAN

It was a Sunday tradition for Susan to cook breakfast. In the summer, they had it on the patio, when it got cooler, in the conservatory, and now with the first hint of winter in the air, they had it in the kitchen.

The rejection of the previous night seemed to confirm her fears that Mark was having an affair. It was strange to be acting as if everything was business as usual. And acting was exactly what it was, each of them skirting around the other, his voice conciliatory, hers brittle, a reflection of the way she felt, as if she'd already cracked into a million pieces and was simply waiting to fall apart.

On automatic, she cooked the same breakfast she'd cooked every Sunday for as long as she could remember. Stupidly, she cooked enough for three people, two of whom didn't seem in the mood to eat. Most of what she'd cooked ended up being thrown in the bin.

'I need to go into the office again today,' Mark said as he helped her clear the table. He didn't meet her eyes as he added, 'Just for a couple of hours. I won't be late.'

She should have said something then, should have asked him

if he thought she was stupid. The words were there, waiting, but she knew if she opened her mouth, it wouldn't be words that came out, it would be a long scream of desperation, of defeat, of stomach-churning sorrow.

Better to wait. To get the proof from the private investigator. To face Mark with it in a calm manner, not like a woman possessed. Maybe if she handled it properly, he'd confess he'd been stupidly led astray, apologise and beg forgiveness.

And maybe if he did, Susan wouldn't have to find where this woman lived. Find her and gouge her eyes out.

* * *

She couldn't face Mark again that evening, couldn't go through the same pretence. There was a portion of lasagne in the freezer. She took it out and left it on the counter with a note.

Bad migraine. I've gone to bed. Put this in the microwave for a while. See you in the morning.

He'd get the message. It wasn't subtle.

She did go to bed, resisting the temptation to lock the bedroom door, smiling at the thought of Mark smashing it down to get to her, the smile fading as she realised he was more likely to be relieved. He wouldn't have to bother showering either.

Propping herself up with a couple of pillows, she flicked the switch on her Kindle and opened a book she'd started a few days before. It was engrossing enough to keep her attention but not enough to stop her hearing Mark's arrival home. Later than he'd promised. He'd have seen the light in the bedroom as he came down the road, and when he read the note, he'd know her migraine tale was a lie. A frequent sufferer, her routine when she

had one was simple and hadn't changed over the years: medication, and a few hours in a darkened room.

He'd know it to be a lie, but in his relief not to have to explain his late return, he wouldn't come to investigate. What a kind wife she was to hand him a get out of jail free card.

For a while, she listened to the sounds he made getting on with his evening. The ping of the microwave, the snap of a cupboard door, the click as the living-room door shut behind him, then the rise and fall of voices on the TV. The noises seemed unnatural. Sound effects made for a radio play. A bad one where everyone sounded wooden and unreal.

It was far too early but she shut her Kindle down and switched out the light. Snuggling her head into the pillow, she prayed for sleep to come, for the weekend to be over. Tomorrow, Ethan would come with the evidence she needed to go forward.

She curled onto her side. The curtains were still open. It had been bright when she'd climbed into bed. It was dark now, and a moon had risen to hover above the house across the street. A *full* moon. Was it to blame for the unaccustomed violence that was seeping into her thoughts, the knives, the blood, the eye gouging?

It wasn't who she was.

But who was she?

Maybe tomorrow, she'd be able to join a club she'd never expected to be in. The wronged women's club.

She kept her eyes fixed on the moon. She'd never have considered herself to be a violent person but was that simply because she'd never had the need to be? Now, she could feel violence thrumming under her skin like a disease. To save what she had, she'd do whatever was needed.

33

SUSAN

She woke early. It was still dark, and there wasn't even the sound of Mark's breathing to disturb the silence. Strangely, she found she didn't miss it, or his arms and legs which always seemed to take up more than their fair share of space. It was, in fact, nice to be able to stretch out unencumbered by the worry of disturbing him while he slept because she'd always been such a considerate wife.

Being a considerate wife and a doting mother hadn't worked out so well for her. Bitterness... she could feel it twisting her face, etching deep lines that would spell out the words *discarded, unwanted, worthless.*

She turned to bury her face in the pillow, keeping it there until the desire to scream was lost, staying there as tears soaked into the pillowcase. When she finally turned, she grabbed the edge of the sheet, dried her eyes, and blew her nose. Worthless and disgusting. She threw back the covers, dragging the sheet with her as she moved. It was balled up and thrown into the laundry basket to be dealt with later. If only everything could be sorted so easily.

It was only five. Mark wouldn't stir for another hour at least.

She dragged a robe on, opened the door quietly, then tiptoed across the landing and down the stairs.

There had been other mornings over the years when she'd woken early and come down to sit drinking coffee as the day arrived with whatever it was bringing with it. She'd thought of it as *her* time. No husband, no son, nothing to do but flick through the previous day's newspapers or magazines she hadn't finished reading, sometimes a book that she was desperate to get back to. Or sometimes, she'd simply sit.

She'd wait till Mark or Drew drifted down, discuss their plans for the day, whether they'd be home for dinner that evening, what they'd like to eat. And she'd make them breakfast, pour juice, cereal, lift bowls, fill mugs, adding milk and sugar, the clink of spoons at work. A lovely dance of normality with intricate steps that came from knowledge, love, and compromise.

Some memories are so clear, they come with sound. Susan stood in the kitchen and shut her eyes, listening to the echoes of those mornings, Drew's laugh, Mark's morning-husky voice. It struck her that there always seemed to be laughter in her memories. She wondered when that had stopped.

She made coffee and sat in the conservatory. Too cold for comfort, she shivered and wrapped her hands around the mug, sipping now and then and staring at nothing. It wasn't till she heard footsteps on the floor above, signalling Mark was up and about, that she got to her feet. The cold had seeped through to her bones, making her stiff, her movements jerky.

It was warmer in the kitchen. She shut the door into the conservatory and switched out the lights. In the silence, she could hear the faint hum of the shower. Mark was in the bathroom; she had about thirty minutes before he arrived down. Plenty of time to make another coffee and get back to her bedroom. She'd no

intention of speaking to him until after she'd heard from Ethan. It was better that way.

She'd reached into the airing cupboard for a fresh sheet when she heard the sound of the bathroom door opening. There was no time to run to her room. Instinctively, she took a step inside the spacious cupboard and pulled the door shut. What if he opened the door in the search of a fresh towel? Unlikely but not impossible. She imagined his expression if he opened the door and found her standing there, and she started to giggle, the rising tide of hysteria threatening to expose her. She grabbed a towel and held it over her mouth as she tried to get back in control. It was a minute before she felt able to open the door and scoot across to the bedroom.

There, she giggled again before shaking her head and dressing the bed with the fresh sheet. A few minutes later, she heard footsteps on the landing. They stopped outside the door and she held her breath as conflicting emotions swept over her. She wanted him to open the door, come in and take her in his arms, reassure her of his love, but if he did, could she really believe him? It didn't matter; the footsteps moved away. He hadn't even peeked in to see if she was dead or alive.

She slipped under the duvet and wrapped her arms around the almost unbearable ache of hurt that seemed to be swallowing her.

He didn't look in on her before leaving the house either. If she was looking at it with a glass-half-full attitude, she'd have praised him for not disturbing her, but she hadn't been operating with that positivity for a while and saw his neglect for what it was: a reluctance to explain his late return the previous night. This way, he hadn't needed to lie to her again. They'd always been honest with each other. She knew him well enough to know that guilt

would be gnawing away at him. Guilt for having an affair, or guilt because he was planning on leaving her? Had it gone that far?

She pulled the duvet over her head. Ethan would be coming in a few hours and then she'd know for sure.

In the darkness of her bed, she was suddenly fearful of that knowledge. Because when she knew, she'd have to act, and she was suddenly afraid of what she might do with the violence that had been making her skin itch. But it was either know the truth, or stay in the dark, fearful and miserable.

* * *

Ethan had said ten o'clock. Susan remained hidden under the duvet till nine forty-five, growing hotter and sweatier as the minutes ticked by. When she could put it off no longer, she threw the covers back and scrambled from the bed to have a quick shower. She didn't give clothes much thought, simply pulling on whatever came to hand. Perhaps it was her subconscious that chose the black jeans and black jumper. They certainly suited her mood although they accentuated her pallor. In fact, looking in the mirror as she brushed her hair, she thought she looked like death.

She felt like the walking dead too. Fear curdled her gut, making her too worried to eat in case she'd do an *Exorcist* on it and hurl the contents of her belly at Ethan when he finally told her what she already knew.

Rather than coffee, she made a cup of herbal tea. Ginger in the hope it would settle her stomach. The scent was soothing and she sipped it as she watched the second hand of the kitchen clock sweep slowly around the face.

It was almost fifteen minutes past ten before the doorbell chimed. Susan, hunched over the remnants of the ginger infusion,

stared towards the door with wide eyes. Once she knew for sure, she could never go back, never unknow the truth.

She felt heavy as she got to her feet and plodded across the floor. It seemed a long way to the hallway, further than usual to the front door. The bell rang again before she reached it. Ethan was obviously as impatient to get rid of the bad news as she was reluctant to receive it.

'Hi,' she said, standing back to allow him in.

'Morning.' He came in and headed towards the kitchen without direction.

He was dressed more smartly. A dark suit, white shirt, and dark tie. Almost funereal. Maybe it was his go-to outfit for delivering bad news. But it was the slim attaché case he held that caught and held her gaze.

She shut the door and followed him, slightly annoyed to find him sitting without waiting to be asked. The case was lying flat on the white table. Bizarrely, from where she stood, it looked as if a black hole had opened up on the surface. Perhaps it was her recent thoughts about *The Exorcist* but it seemed to her that it was pulsating with dark matter. She imagined it spewing forth to cover her in filth, the stink embedding in her skin so she'd carry it with her forever.

Ethan was looking at her, curiosity in his dark eyes. 'You okay?'

Rather than answering, she turned away. 'I was going to make some coffee; would you like some?'

'That'd be great, ta. And if you'd anything to eat, that would be even better. I missed breakfast again this morning.'

Something to eat? There was all that damn cheese. She opened the fridge, looked at the packets, and took them all out. 'Here,' she said, dropping them in the centre of the table. 'I'll do you some toast to go with it.'

Five minutes later, Ethan was chomping on thick slices of

cheese on toast. He ate with his mouth open, crumbs flying carelessly to scatter on the surface of the table.

Susan couldn't help but notice that none appeared to land in the black hole. Or if they did, they were sucked into it to vanish. It would be nice to be able to do that. Jump in and vanish. Not have to face whatever was coming. She gripped the mug of coffee she'd made but didn't want and waited for the private investigator to stop eating and break the news to her.

'I needed that,' Ethan said, wiping a hand over his mouth and dislodging crumbs that had gathered in the corners of his mouth. He picked up his mug, slurped a mouthful, then put it down and nodded towards the tower of cheese packets. 'You like your cheese, don't you?'

'My son. I buy it for him.'

He looked surprised. Had she told him Drew had moved away? She couldn't remember, but anyway, she wasn't interested in getting into a conversation about the man who'd left her life voluntarily; she wanted to know about the one who was being stolen from her.

'I'm sure you're very busy,' she said, releasing one of her hands from the death grip it had on the mug to point to the black hole sucking the life from her. 'If you're finished eating, perhaps you could tell me what you found.'

He seemed immune to taking umbrage. Putting the coffee down, he reached for the case and unzipped it. Slowly. The sound ripping into her. She watched as he reached inside and withdrew a sheaf of paper. No, not paper: photographs. She fixed on them as he held them in his hands, trying to see through the plain, white reverse to the image that was going to cause her pain.

He started to fill her in on the hours he'd trailed after Mark, the times he'd spent waiting, the efforts he'd made to get the

information he held so tightly between his fingers. Making a good argument for the money he'd yet to demand.

She wanted to scream at him that she didn't care; that she'd pay him double if he would just shut the fuck up and tell her about the woman her husband preferred to spend his time with. In Susan's head, she was tall, slim, staggeringly beautiful, with long, thick, curly hair that she'd toss like those stupid women in shampoo adverts. Luckily, for her sanity, Ethan stopped talking and put the photos flat on the table.

'I took shots of him in various places as you can see from this selection.'

He slid them towards Susan. They sat taunting her. It took a concerted effort to peel her fingers from the mug, push it to one side, and reach for them. One after the other, she looked through the collection. Then again, peering closer, wondering if she'd developed some kind of weird eyesight problem because... 'There's nothing,' she said, putting them down and looking across the table to meet Ethan's eyes.

'Just your husband going to and from the office. Going out for coffee, sitting alone before heading back to work. In a pub with a couple of work colleagues.'

'But...' She'd been so sure. Now she didn't know what to think. Had she wanted to believe he was having an affair, preferring to blame a mysterious woman rather than believe he'd simply lost interest in her, had stopped loving her? Because that was so much worse, heartbreakingly, devastatingly worse. 'There's no woman?'

Ethan shook his head. 'As I said, I followed him everywhere he went and didn't see anything of any woman other than you.'

'Right.' She looked through the photos again, holding them up, desperate to see something she could pin her fears on. There was nothing. It was all her stupidity. 'Right,' she said again because she couldn't think of another word to use. 'Thank you.

This is good news.' Was it? She was confused, like a child who is convinced Santa Claus exists only to be told, on Christmas morning, that he doesn't. She needed to be alone to process this. 'Thank you. How much do I owe you?'

He mentioned a sum that made her blink. It seemed a lot to prove that nothing had been going on, a lot of money to prove she'd been a suspicious, stupid, stupid woman.

'If you could pay me by bank transfer, that would be best.' He took a card from an inside pocket and handed it to her.

When she didn't move, he smiled, an unpleasant twist of his mouth that made her look at him in a different light. 'I'm afraid,' he said quietly, 'it's policy that we're paid at the completion of a job.'

'Oh yes, of course.' She reached for her phone. It took longer than usual and she could feel the impatience that rolled across the table. It was the tears that filled her eyes, or the fog that seemed to have worked its way into her brain, dulling her thoughts, making every action a trial.

'That's it done,' she said finally.

'Do you mind if I...?' He reached for the phone.

She supposed suspicion came with the territory and she handed it to him. He looked at the screen, nodded in satisfaction and returned it. 'It was a pleasure doing business with you, Mrs Shepherd.' He waved to the photos. 'You want me to get rid of those for you?'

She'd picked up the photographs again. Her thumb was pressing a concave dent over Mark's face as if trying to obliterate him. Mark, who'd done nothing wrong. Blameless. She released her grip slightly and smoothed a finger across his face, trying to undo the harm she'd done. Perhaps she should keep the photographs to remind herself of what an idiot she'd been. 'No, that's okay, I'll hang on to them, thank you.'

'Fine,' he got to his feet. 'I'll be heading off then.'

She waited until she heard the front door shut before standing. The pile of cheese in the middle of the table was a sad testament to how incapable she was of thinking properly. She went to a cupboard, tore a refuse bag off a roll and snapped it open. Then she swept every trace of her visitor inside – the cheese, the two mugs, the crumbs, even those damn photographs. She knotted the bag twice, as if to make sure her shame wouldn't escape, then spent minutes undoing the knots to reach inside and take the photographs out again, dusting the crumbs off with one trembling hand.

Unable to think of anywhere else to put them, she took them upstairs and slid them under a pile of knickers in her underwear drawer. If she hadn't felt so numb, she might have smiled at the cliché.

What was wrong with her? She should be relieved.

Instead, she felt cheated, confused, bewildered.

34

HANNAH

When I had a call from Mark to say he'd like to call around after work, I was surprised, but I was taken aback and unaccustomedly lost for words when he said, 'And maybe it's time I stayed over. What d'you think?'

What did I think? I wanted to punch the air in excitement. I thought I'd blown it the previous night. He'd stayed later than he'd planned thanks to my artful seduction, but as he left, I saw a mask of guilt settle over his features. I wondered if I'd miscalculated and pushed him back into his wife's arms. Guilt is the mistress's biggest enemy.

But it looked as if I'd been lucky. Perhaps his wife had given him a hard time for arriving home late, had shouted at him for neglecting her, perhaps had even hinted that she'd had enough. Perhaps things had escalated and anger had succeeded in drowning the guilt. I neither knew nor cared. All I cared about was that my plan, which looked for a while as if it might have stalled, was suddenly shooting ahead. 'I think that would be absolutely amazing. I'll order in some food; you bring the wine.'

'I think I could do better than wine,' he laughed. 'It's definitely time for champagne.'

I hung up with a smile on my face. Well, who'd have expected this? I certainly hadn't. My smile faded. I hadn't expected it at all. I tapped my mobile against my chin.

I looked at the message I'd received earlier. I hadn't replied, but now I needed to get rid of the man who'd agreed to oblige me in return for a couple of nights of mediocre sex. It took a few tries, a few messages written and deleted before I settled on one that worked for me.

It's best if we don't meet again. You were a rebound lover. I need space to find what it is I want from life.

It was a nice blend of truth and lies... well it was mostly lies, but he wouldn't know that. He might guess, but he wasn't a fool; he'd move on. I read my message over once more and frowned. It needed something more. I added a sentence after *lover*:

I wasn't being fair on you.

That should do it. I pressed send, then forgot about him.

Hours later, the food I'd ordered was keeping warm in the oven, the champagne glasses were waiting, a carefully chosen sexy dress covered my curves, my hair washed and shining, my make-up perfectly applied. Everything was ready to make this first night we spent together so perfect that Mark would be able to relax knowing he'd done the right thing.

It was the way it should be.

Twenty years ago, I'd made a mistake. It was time to make it right.

When Mark arrived, he had a bottle of champagne in one

hand, an enormous bouquet of flowers in the other and his brief-case tucked under one arm. His briefcase – not a suitcase – that did give me a second's pause for thought but I brushed the slight concern away. It was all going to work out. I didn't feel a smidgeon of guilt for the wife. She'd only ever been a stopgap – okay, so a twenty-year one – but he was always destined to be mine.

He made a fuss about opening the champagne, laughing as the cork flew across the room and bubbles fizzed as he poured into the waiting glasses. It seemed to me that he was happy with the decision he'd made and I felt a glow inside where it had been cold for so long.

'Let's have it on the balcony,' he said, putting one of the glasses in my hand.

We sat there, side by side in the tiny space, the view ignored in favour of staring into each other's eyes. Mark was unusually serious as he touched his glass to mine. 'To our first night together.' He said it like it was a prayer, or was it a wish?

I wasn't shy about asking his intentions, but I was cautious about putting a foot wrong, my hope a brittle, fragile thing needing protection. There was also the issue of that briefcase preying on a tender part of my mind. 'The first of many?' It was the nearest I could bring myself to asking what was going to happen.

He swallowed his champagne and reached for the bottle to refill our glasses. I'd barely taken a sip of mine but he topped it up anyway. Maybe he was hoping my question would float away on the bubbles. He turned to stare out across to the water where it glinted as it caught the last rays of the sun.

I was good at waiting for what I wanted. After all this time, there was no point in rushing in where angels, or daemons, might fear to tread.

He took a few sips of his champagne before turning with a rueful smile. 'I wish I could say *every* night.'

I rejected the instinctive, *well, why don't you*, substituting the more considered, 'I wish you could too.' It seemed the perfect time for tears so I allowed them to come, brushing one away before it did too much damage to my make-up.

'Hannah!' He put his glass down and pulled me awkwardly and abruptly into his arms. Caught unawares, my still full glass tilted and before I could compensate, it emptied champagne over my breasts, the chill making me gasp. Mark, interpreting the sound as a reaction to his arms around me, tightened his hold so it was several seconds before I was able to free myself. The champagne had soaked into the fabric of my dress, making it like a second skin. I pulled at it and grimaced.

'I'm so sorry,' he looked appalled and brushed a hand over the wet patch as if his hand had magical drying powers.

'I'll go and change,' I said, getting to my feet. Irritation swept over me. Not for the ruination of my dress – did champagne stain silk? – but for the wasted opportunity. Tears, if overdone, lose their impact. 'Anyway, we should go in; the food's waiting.'

I was pleased to see he'd made himself useful when I returned and had removed the dishes from the oven and lined serving spoons up beside each. 'Perfect,' I said, picking up a plate and serving myself. I caught him staring at me. Rather than another dress, I'd slipped on a robe, the deep V of the neckline leaving little to the imagination. Tears, after all, weren't the only weapon I possessed.

'You are,' he said, running a hand over the curve of my bottom.

I planted a kiss on his cheek. 'Food first, I'm starving.' I *was* hungry and wasn't delaying my food for the dubious delights of a tumble in bed. If he was going to engage in sexual gymnastics, I

needed to eat first. I also wanted, and needed, to get the conversation back to what was happening next.

But it seemed as if Mark had been giving my question some thought while I was gone. He played with his fork before putting it down and resting his elbows on the table.

Definitely a prayer. I wondered if it would ruin the moment if I shovelled some lamb into my mouth while I waited for whatever he was going to say. He was obviously struggling to find the right words. Had he struggled as much when he told his wife? Had he told her?

'I want to be with you,' he said, 'you have to believe that.'

I could hear the 'but' coming and felt my features tighten, the corners of my upwardly curved lips freezing into place. It might look as if I was smiling. I was good at pretending.

'It's Susan. She doesn't know about us yet.'

I understood now why he hadn't brought a suitcase. Where did the poor fool of a wife think he was?

'She thinks I'm with a client,' he said as if I'd spoken aloud.

'She's not suspicious even though you've been late home and spent hours over the weekend with me?'

'I sometimes have demanding clients. It's a part of my job; she accepts that.'

'Food's getting cold,' I said, and picked up my fork again. The lamb was tender and fell apart in my mouth. But as I smacked my lips and swallowed, it was the unexpected bitterness of guilt I tasted. It was an unaccustomed emotion for me; my façade was of platinum... or at least it had been until I discovered... no, I wasn't going there. I wished I'd never gone into my mother's bedroom, never opened that damn drawer.

Anyway, I thought, trying to force my thoughts back to the present, I wanted Mark because he was one of the few men who'd

been good to me, who'd made me happy. Wasn't it ironic how he'd also been inherently decent – until I came back into his life.

So, of course his stupid wife wasn't suspicious. He'd never given her reason to be until now. I brushed away the guilt. I'd made a mistake; he was always destined to be mine. I was simply rewriting history.

My lamb might be tasteless but it was evident from the little mewling sounds of pleasure Mark was making that he was enjoying his. I tried a little more, washing the tasteless piece of meat down with a mouthful of champagne. Pushing the plate to one side, I reached for the garlic nan bread and tore a piece from it, relieved to find it tasted sufficiently garlicky.

'You haven't brought any things. How will you explain going into work tomorrow looking a little dishevelled?'

He reached for the nan bread, tore a piece off and ran it through the sauce on his plate before popping it into his mouth. 'I've told them I'll be working from home.' My face must have registered surprise because he suddenly looked worried. 'That's okay, isn't it?'

Was it? I wasn't sure I liked being backed into a corner. It was quite a leap from the odd few stolen hours to a full night, and now a day. I should be thrilled, shouldn't I? 'We could go out somewhere. I'll check the weather; we might go for a drive, maybe to the coast. Walk along the beach or something.' It would be great.

'No, I'm not going to have time for that; I really do have to work.' He nodded to where his briefcase was sagged in the corner. 'I have my laptop with me.'

'Right.' So what was I expected to do while he was working? Housework? 'Maybe we could go out for lunch. You have to eat.'

Another piece of nan bread was dragged through the sauce before he answered. 'If I'm supposed to be working from home, I can't afford to be seen around here; it's a bit too close to the office.'

He put the sauce-soaked bread in his mouth, chewed and swallowed before smiling across the table. 'We could have some mid-afternoon fun here though.'

I kept a neutral, fairly pleasant expression parked on my face. I was expected to lounge around doing nothing to be available for a bit of rumpy pumpy when he was free. Be careful what you ask for, wasn't that what they said? But I hadn't asked for this. 'Actually, if you're going to be working, I might take a trip to Windsor. I didn't manage to pick up everything the last time I was there.'

I was pleased to see Mark's forehead crease with concern. 'Your ex-husband doesn't mind you popping back?'

'Ivan doesn't mind me calling in as often as I like. Actually, he's not an ex as yet.' I thought it was time to make that little confession. 'You know what paperwork is like.' I waited for that to sink in. 'You'll be gone by the time I get back.'

'Yes.'

'And...?'

He ran a hand over his hair before downing the contents of his glass in two mouthfuls. 'I'll talk to Susan, I promise. Just give me a little more time.'

It was a dance. I knew the steps; I just had to teach him. 'We have tonight, and the morning.' I got to my feet and held out my hand. 'Let's make the most of it.'

35

SUSAN

She stood for a long time staring at the message Mark had sent her. There weren't many words. There was no ambiguity. She wished there was. Wished there was something between the lines, some secret code.

> The same client causing me problems. Not going to get home tonight. Sorry. See you tomorrow.

There had been times, years before, when he'd had to stay away, but he'd ring and speak to her, reassure her, explain, tell her he loved her and would miss her. Had there been text messages back then? She shook her head; maybe not, she couldn't remember. It didn't matter. Back then, he'd have rung, and he'd have whispered words of love at the end. Not this cold, almost impersonal message.

In all their years together, he'd never given her reason to doubt his fidelity. She wasn't sure why, recently, it had been called into doubt in her head. A crazy link with Drew's departure perhaps. A deep-rooted fear that she might lose both the men she

loved. Her imagination looking to fill her boring life with excitement. *But the phone call she'd heard him take where he'd laughed that laugh, and the receipt for the Prosecco?*

She brushed both aside.

That private investigator had proved her suspicions weren't valid. There *wasn't* another woman. Just the same cigar-smoking, demanding client. Poor Mark. He was too conscientious for his own good. He'd be irritated but trying hard not to show it, even to her. He liked to be seen to be in control. It was why he hadn't rung; he'd have known she'd have guessed his annoyance. It was a relief to get that clear in her head.

A long evening stretched ahead. She was tempted to ring Drew, but if she was searching for a friendly voice, he mightn't be the best person to ring. Instead, she sent a brief, friendly message, telling him how busy she'd been, how unusually warm it had been recently, and ended by telling him about all the cheese she'd bought, forgetting he wouldn't be there to eat it. That should make him smile. It took huge effort not to ask how he was, if he was eating properly, looking after himself.

She was in a WhatsApp group with her sisters, but when she rang and neither answered, she gave up and put the phone down. There were a couple of friends she might have phoned, and her finger hovered over one after the other. But she gave up without ringing either when she realised she'd nothing to say.

To fill the time, she spent the next hour making a lasagne, finding the preparation relaxing. When it was done, all bubbly and crispy, she smiled at the memory of Drew devouring a huge helping before asking for seconds. She cut a small portion for herself, then divided the rest and put it into containers. They'd go into the freezer when cool.

Mark would insist on a glass of red when they had lasagne. Susan was as happy with a glass of water. She took a tray with her

into the living room and put it on the coffee table while she switched on the TV and flicked through the channels to find something to watch. An old episode of *Morse* was a perfect choice.

Kicking off her shoes, she stretched out on the sofa with her tray on her lap. The lasagne was the best she'd ever made, *Morse* as good as she remembered. She should have been able to relax, enjoy a pleasant, quiet evening with nobody making demands on her.

As soon as she'd scraped the last morsel of pasta from the plate, she put the tray on the floor and got to her feet. John Thaw was speaking, his deep, unmistakable voice following her as she left the room and headed up the stairs.

There was something bothering her. Niggling. Perhaps she shouldn't have watched *Morse*, after all. He had a habit of seeing behind the obvious. The obvious... she crossed her bedroom to the chest of drawers and pulled out the top one. Sliding a hand under her underwear, there was a gut-churning moment of panic when she thought the photographs had gone, vanished, a figment of her imagination, just like Mark's mistress. It was a relief when her fingers felt the edge of the envelope.

She sat on the edge of the bed and tapped the photographs out, spreading them out with her hand. A montage of Mark. Coming out of the office on Queen Square. Sitting in a café. Standing in the doorway of a building she didn't recognise. Walking down a street, his briefcase hanging from one hand.

Behind the obvious... she picked up each image and stared at it, much as she had earlier. But then, she'd been looking for something that *wasn't* there, this time it *was* what was there that she was interested in examining.

Mark's face. She knew it better than her own, the curve of his cheek, the deep grooves between his eyebrows, the tiny scar under his ear from where a schoolfriend had thrown a stone when he

was seven, the slightly crooked nose, neat ears. Every feature was familiar.

So what was bothering her?

She picked up the photo of him exiting some unknown building. His tie was slightly askew, his hair a little tousled. It made her smile. When he was stressed, he did have a habit of playing with the knot of his tie and running his fingers through his hair. She held the photo up to the light. She could see now what was niggling. His head was turned slightly to one side, his lips parted as if he was speaking to someone. But there was nobody there.

Placing the photo down, she picked up the one where he was sitting in a café. Only one cup on the table, indicating he was there on his own. But the niggle made her look more closely and question two things – why was he out drinking coffee on his own during the day? They'd a perfectly good coffee maker in his office; he'd frequently mentioned it was so good, he drank too much of it. And the second question, the one that made her grip the image so tightly that it crumpled in her hand: if he was there on his own, who the fuck was he smiling at?

And smiling in that particular way. As if he was looking at someone he found attractive. She remembered he used to smile at her in just that way. Once upon a time, a long, long time ago.

One after the other, she went through the photographs. Disbelief shimmied into irritation before exploding into anger that sent the photographs flying into the air, swirling and falling to the bed and floor. She left them there and paced the room.

She'd paid that investigator, and he'd lied to her. She'd seen apps advertised on Facebook and elsewhere that allowed you to delete unwanted people from photographs. It wasn't, the adverts said, difficult to do. With all the money she'd given Ethan, he could have afforded to buy the best software. The question was – why?

There was only one reason.

Mark had found out, somehow, and had paid the two-timing bastard to lie to her. And there was only one reason her husband would do such a thing. He *was* having an affair. And it was serious.

36

SUSAN

She sank on the bed under the weight of a deluge of emotions. Relief that she had been right all along, anger at Mark for having an affair. Fury at the private investigator she'd hired and paid in good faith. Staggering disbelief that she'd been cheated by both. Tears came, hot tears of self-pity to find herself in such a mess, of breathtaking sorrow, and then of soul-corroding anger.

It was anger that remained when exhaustion doused the other emotions. She flopped back on the bed and let it simmer in her head. What had she thought days before? That if she discovered she was right, she'd fight for him, do whatever it took? She remembered the knife she'd felt in her hand, the feeling of warm blood, the smell.

She'd never have considered herself to be a violent woman, but she'd never have considered herself to be the other woman either.

The other woman.

No, that was wrong. She was the wife. It was this intruder who was the other, wasn't it?

She flung her arm across her face, shutting out the light. So

many lies. She guessed Mark hadn't been in the office over the weekend, wasn't dealing with a difficult client that night. She wondered where they were. A hotel, perhaps. She rolled onto her side and sat up, searching the photographs that were scattered around the room, searching for one. Mark coming out of a building. When she found it, she peered at it, searching for something familiar.

There wasn't anything, but the pillars on either side of the door were distinctive. Bringing the photo with her, she went downstairs, took her laptop from under the sofa and switched it on.

Pulling up Google Maps, she worked out in a circle from Mark's office, stopping at every hotel, bringing up a photo of the entrance door and comparing it to the photograph. 'Bingo,' she said when she brought up the fifth, the Floating Harbour Hotel.

'A five-star, boutique hotel,' she read, her lips twisting in a sneer. Is that where they were, my husband and this other woman? 'His mistress.' The word felt strange on her lips, incomprehensible. She shut the laptop with a snap. Now what?

Her mobile was in the other room; she went through, picked it up and ordered an Uber. She had no plan. All she knew was that she wasn't going to sit around while her husband entertained his floozie in a five-star hotel.

Ten minutes later, she was sitting in a taxi, heading into Bristol. All she'd done was slip on a pair of shoes, grab a jacket and a bag. She hadn't brushed her hair, or even slicked lipstick over her lips. There didn't seem to be much point. She'd no idea who this woman her husband was fucking looked like but there was no doubt she'd be gorgeous, beautiful, younger – of course – no lines, laughter or otherwise.

As the taxi negotiated the always busy roads of Bristol, she'd time to wonder if she'd lost her marbles. Just what did she hope to

achieve by accosting them in their hotel room? Would she find them naked together, point with a loud gasp, and hold a hand over her forehead like some sad Victorian lady having a fit of the vapours?

When the taxi stopped outside the hotel, she stared at the entrance, pictured Mark standing there with a stunning woman at his side. She'd been air-brushed from the photograph. Susan suddenly knew what that felt like. It was as if the edges of her body were shimmering, becoming transparent, blending in with the surroundings. Soon, she'd be invisible, wiped from Mark's life.

The anger she'd felt earlier had faded as the image of Mark and this woman solidified. For all Susan's brave talk about dealing with her, for all the violent thoughts of knives and blood, she knew there was nothing she could do except try to stop the damage as she was tossed aside, discarded, an empty crisp packet swirling along the street to get caught in barbed wire or stamped on by careless feet.

'You getting out?'

She stared at the back of the driver's head. Was she? She should go home. This had been a crazy idea. Crazy, she thought again as she pushed open the door and climbed out.

Since she was there, she might as well make a complete idiot of herself. She climbed to the top step of the entrance, and turned, imagining Mark beside her, smiling at her the way he'd smiled at that woman. She tried to dip back into the well of anger, but it seemed to have run dry.

The lobby was small with a reception desk angled diagonally in one corner to make the most of the space. A woman stood behind it, frowning at a computer screen. As the automatic door slid open, she looked up but the frown didn't fade into something more welcoming.

Susan wasn't surprised. She didn't present a five-star, boutique

hotel appearance. Fuck's sake, she hadn't even brushed her hair. Anger returned, and for the first time, it was directed solely at Mark rather than being shared with the unknown woman he was with. He'd done this to her. Turned her into this mess. This discarded, unwanted, redundant mess.

'Can I help you?'

The tone of the words wasn't particularly encouraging. Susan gripped her bag tighter and approached. She was there, she might as well find out the worst. Close up, the receptionist was just the kind of woman Susan found both fascinating and intimidating. Perfectly applied make-up, glossy hair pinned back in a neat bun with only a couple of strands artfully curling under the curve of her chin, the pussy-bow blouse she wore startlingly white. This wasn't a woman who was going to help.

Susan felt the edges of the photograph in her pocket. Were they upstairs in one of the fancy bedrooms, the woman with her mouth pressed to the scar under Mark's ear? It was that incredibly intimate image that made her pull the photograph from her pocket and slap it on the desk with such force, the receptionist's heavily made-up eyes widened, and her hand moved along the edge of the desk. Perhaps there was an alarm there. Maybe it would sound throughout the hotel triggering an evacuation. That would be perfect. To see Mark and his floozie run out, clothes hastily pulled on to cover their shame.

It could also be an alarm connected to a police station and she'd find herself being arrested. The thought made her hold a hand up. 'I'm sorry, please, listen.'

Obviously deciding she was crazy rather than dangerous, the receptionist nodded. Her hand, however, remained where it was.

Deciding she'd nothing to lose, Susan went with the truth. 'This is my husband. I think he's having an affair.' She pushed the photograph further across the desk. 'This was taken outside. The

woman has been airbrushed out, but I know she was with him. I think they're here tonight.' She watched the woman's expression. It didn't change. Maybe it couldn't, Susan thought, allowing the catty thought to cross her mind. 'Right, it looks as if I'll have to wait and see, doesn't it?' She nodded towards where the receptionist's hand still lingered. 'You can get me thrown out, true, but you can't stop me standing across the street to wait. It'll be a long night. I'm that desperate.'

The beautifully painted mouth pursed, then parted to allow a sigh to escape. 'I do recognise him. And yes, he has been here with a woman, but they're not staying tonight.'

Susan clutched the edge of the desk. 'You're sure?'

'Positive.'

She'd been so sure she'd find them there, she felt suddenly lost. Bereft. It was a feeling she'd have to become accustomed to. 'I was so sure.' She reached for the photograph. 'I'm not even sure what I was going to do, you know. I thought...' she shrugged and put the photo back into her pocket. 'I don't know what I thought. Maybe to shame them into breaking up so he'd come back to me.' Was that what she thought? It didn't matter; they weren't there. It had all been a waste of time. 'I don't suppose you could give me her name, could you?' She knew the answer before the receptionist shook her head.

'It's against hotel policy to give out information about customers, I'm afraid. I've told you more than I should have really.'

'Yes, I understand. Thank you.' At least Susan knew she wasn't going completely crazy. Mark had stayed there with a woman. The same one who'd been airbrushed from the photograph. 'It's just hard. I know I should confront him about it but I'm afraid if I do that it'll be just the push he needs to leave me.' She gave a shaky smile. What was she doing? How sad and pathetic to be

standing in a hotel lobby, spilling her heart to a woman she didn't know and who couldn't possibly care. One who'd already turned away and was back in work mode, tapping away on her keyboard.

The automatic door slid open. Susan stared out to the step where Mark had stood with his mistress. She wondered what they'd talked about.

'Excuse me!'

She sighed and turned with a hand raised in apology. 'I'm going.'

'You should take this with you,' the receptionist said, holding her hand out.

Puzzled, Susan re-turned and took it from her. It was a flyer for the hotel.

'You might want to stay here sometime.'

Once again, violent thoughts crashed in Susan's head. *She crumpled the flyer in her hand, then reached across, grabbed the receptionist by those stupid, curling strands of hair, dragged her over the desk and rammed it between her narrow painted lips until she choked on it.* 'Thank you,' she said, putting the leaflet into her pocket.

Outside, she was lucky and flagged down a passing taxi. She sat back and took a deep breath that shuddered on a gulp. Where were they? That they'd had to go to a hotel for their sexual gymnastics indicated the floozie didn't live nearby. Maybe that had changed. Maybe... Susan felt her heart swell with sadness... maybe they'd rented an apartment together.

Or maybe the bedrooms in the hotel didn't live up to their boutique hotel description and they'd gone elsewhere. She reached into her pocket for the flyer the receptionist had given her. It was good quality as befitting a posh, expensive hotel, a nice shot of the hotel on the front, making it look grander than reality. Inside, there was a photo of the dining room, and one of the bedrooms. Mark would have hated the silly cushions piled on the

bed. He could never see the point and removing them was the first thing Susan did when they went away. Did his floozie do that for him, or were they so lost in passion that he didn't even notice them?

She sighed, folded the flyer shut, then bent it in half. That's when she saw it. Written in small, neat writing above the directions and social media information on the back of the flyer.

A name.

Hannah Parker.

37

SUSAN

Hannah Parker. It was a name Susan knew. When she'd met Mark first, he'd been standoffish, happy to go out with the gang of friends but reluctant for anything more. Susan heard on the grapevine that he'd been in a relationship that had ended badly. A brooding guy with movie-star looks, she hadn't been the only woman who'd been interested in nursing him back to health.

It hadn't been luck that had led to her sitting beside him at a friend's barbeque. She'd filled her plate, then stood and waited till she saw him do the same, watching as he scanned the huge garden for somewhere to sit. He'd ignored the women patting the seats beside them and headed to a bench slightly cut off from the melee.

As soon as he sat, Susan wandered over, trying not to run, keeping her eyes open for anyone who might beat her to the prize. But by then, most of the women had given him up as a bad cause.

'D'you mind if I sit?'

His mouth was full of burger so he merely nodded.

They'd been mixing with the same group of friends for weeks so he knew her name and she, of course, knew his and more: the

university he'd been to, the law school he was attending, where he was from. And of course about his last disastrous relationship.

'What was she like?'

He took another bite of his burger and spoke with his mouth full. 'Who?'

She'd nothing to lose. 'This woman who everyone says has ruined your life forever and a day.'

'Forever and a day?' He wiped a hand over his mouth and turned to look at her – really looked, seeing her for the first time. 'Who the fuck said that?'

She waved a hand around the assembled group. 'Take your pick.' She speared a sausage with the plastic fork she was holding, lifted it like a trophy and waved it at him before taking a bite. 'So tell me about her.'

He seemed amused. 'What do you want to know?'

'Her name for starters.'

'Hannah... Hannah Parker.'

'Nice name. What was she like?' He looked off into the distance and she didn't think he was going to answer. 'It helps to talk sometimes.'

It wasn't till he'd cleared his plate and finished his bottle of Bud that he spoke again. 'She's beautiful, exotic almost. Made me laugh and do crazy things.'

'Like?'

'Like...' He smiled, then laughed out loud. 'Like once, we went to visit an aunt of mine in Hawkesbury. I took her for a walk to show her the area and into the church. It was open, and you can go up to see the bells, but she insisted we climb the tower and get out at the top so we could admire the view. The door out is only about three foot high. She's slim, agile, got out without any problem and egged me on to follow. I managed with great difficulty and the view was fabulous.' He laughed again, longer,

louder, drawing curious glances. 'It was getting back down that was the problem. I thought we'd have to ring for help when I got stuck in the doorway.'

I imagined the almost six-foot man trying to manoeuvre through a three-foot-high door and laughed too.

Story after story he told. Things Hannah had done, things she'd said, how funny she was, how much better his life had been with her in it, how stunned he'd been when she'd dumped him, out of the blue. Leaving him gutted.

'You did ask,' he said finally.

Maybe she'd looked stunned. She probably was. How could any woman compete with such a goddess? 'I did.' She put a hand on his bare arm. 'And thank you for sharing.' She felt the muscles in his arm tense, then relax.

'You were right, it does make it easier.'

That was it really. Next time she was out with the group, he made his way to her side. 'Can I get you a drink?'

She'd put her empty glass down only moments before. She'd been drinking water. But water-drinking earthlings had no hope of competing with goddesses. 'Thank you. Prosecco please.'

It was impossible to compete with the vision that was Hannah, so Susan didn't try. She wasn't beautiful or exotic, but she was pretty and dependable. Maybe even boring. She wondered later, when they were a couple, if it was this that had appealed to Mark. The fact that she was so different. A contrast. The absolute opposite.

Hannah had left the area. It should have made it easier but there were times when they'd be out somewhere and she'd notice the faraway look in Mark's eyes. She didn't need to ask where he'd gone, knowing immediately that something had triggered a memory of Hannah. Competing with a memory was difficult.

Feeling second best was painful. She might have given up if she hadn't come to realise that he needed her.

'What are you planning to do when you finish law school?' she asked him one night, when she lay in his arms.

'Haven't given it much thought.'

She pushed up on one elbow, rested her hand on his chest and looked down at his face, expecting to see him smile. He wasn't, his eyes were shut, his breathing deep and relaxed. 'You need to start,' she said. But he was already asleep. It was in that moment that she realised he was handsome and kind but weak. He needed a strong woman. Not a beautiful, exotic, flighty one. He needed someone like Susan.

A year later, when Mark asked her to marry him, although she wasn't sure she loved him, she'd no hesitation about saying yes. The love had come, and it had lasted because they were made for one another. His good looks, charm and education, her strength, get up and go, her pure determination.

When he made partner, the pinnacle of his career, she relaxed.

Perhaps she shouldn't have done... Maybe a rich successful, handsome man like Mark, at the top of his career, needed someone dazzling on his arm. Susan had been pretty enough in her day. Recently, she'd heard herself described as a nice-looking woman. *Nice.*

Pretty hadn't compared to beautiful and exotic all those years before. Hannah would have aged, of course, but maybe she'd retained that certain something that had made Mark so crazy about her.

Perhaps she still had it.

And now she was back.

38

SUSAN

The first thing she did when she got home was to switch on her laptop and do a search for Hannah Parker. She'd never seen the woman – Mark had destroyed any photos of her before they'd met – so how could she possibly know what she looked like today? Plus there was no guarantee she was still using the same surname; she might have married. Neither stopped Susan from looking. There were several Hannah Parkers on Facebook but none looked to be likely candidates. What had Susan hoped – that she'd find a Facebook page called *Hannah the Husband Stealer*?

Time vanished as she searched through every social media platform she knew, staring at thumbnail photos of women, wondering if they could possibly be the floozie. It was a waste of time, she knew it was, but she couldn't stop looking at woman after woman. Comparing herself to each, diminishing herself with every comparison.

It was after two before she shut the laptop and slumped back on the sofa. She should get up, go upstairs, try to get some sleep. Instead, she kicked off her shoes and stretched out where she was.

Her dreams were haunted by visions of hundreds of beautiful

women, sharp knives dripping with blood, Susan's face crumpled with age, lined and haggard, mouth wide open, calling Mark's name as he got smaller and smaller until he vanished.

She woke with a cramp in her leg and an ache in her neck. Struggling to her feet, she felt as old as the woman in her dream. The room was pitch dark, the heavy curtains she'd drawn earlier shutting out the light from the streetlamps outside. Blindly, hands patting the air in front as she moved, she hobbled from the room, up the stairs and into her bedroom. There didn't seem to be any point in undressing so she slipped under the duvet, swaddled herself in it, and made believe it was Mark's arms holding her. Maybe her imagination was that good, or she was simply that tired, but she felt the warmth of his hands, his soft breath brushing her shoulder, and she drifted away.

When she woke again, it was daylight. The house was unnaturally quiet. She'd wondered if Mark would come home to change before going into the office. Maybe he'd managed to squeeze a fresh shirt and razor into his briefcase or maybe the floozie had provided him with new clothes and toiletries.

There seemed to be no reason to get out of bed. Nothing to do. Nobody to do anything for. Apathy, perhaps edging towards depression. She'd thought she had everything. It seemed a mirage now. There was nothing wrong with wallowing for a while. She'd reason to after all. But she wasn't a woman given to self-pity usually, nor to lying in bed doing nothing. Throwing the duvet back, she climbed from the bed. Somewhere during her hours asleep, she'd opened her jeans, pulled off her shirt and the straps of her bra. Perhaps she'd tried and failed to unhook it because it lay around her waist.

She took everything off and had a shower. A firm believer in the positive power of running water, she stayed under the spray for a long time, washing her hair, using her favourite shower gel.

Feeling a little better, she dressed in fresh jeans and shirt and used a band to tie her wet hair back in a ponytail.

It was only nine. The whole day was ahead of her, waiting to be filled. She could make coffee, have breakfast, maybe watch TV. Pass the hours doing nothing. Worse, spend the day wondering where Mark had spent the night, imagining him with Hannah, their naked limbs entwining. She could sit and drive herself crazy.

A bowl of cereal was half-eaten, a mug of coffee clasped between her hands, and she was lost in thought when the doorbell rang. She looked up in surprise. It was too early for their postman to make an appearance and she wasn't expecting a delivery.

Nothing to do didn't mean she wanted to deal with tradespeople, or someone collecting for something, or someone proselytising. She'd answered the door to them a few times, clean-cut, young men in suits, with kind, sincere faces, and she was always polite when she told them she wasn't interested, but that day, she'd probably tell them to fuck off. Better not to answer – they'd go away eventually.

But they didn't. The doorbell rang, then rang again, then whoever was there kept their finger pressed to it. Susan looked at the wooden block holding the knives. Her hand was shaking as she dragged fingers over her face as if trying to wipe away the image of blood that had popped into her head.

The doorbell was still ringing. 'Fuck's sake,' she growled, getting to her feet, marching into the hallway and down to the front door. She threw it open, ready to yell at whoever was there, her mouth shutting with a jaw-grating snap when she saw who it was. 'You!'

'Can I come in, please?'

'Why, so you can lie to me some more?' She folded her arms across her chest and lifted her chin. 'Yes, you might well look

surprised. I know you lied to me. My husband is having an affair. He paid you to airbrush those photos. Very clever, weren't you? Money from him, money from me. What a nice little earner for you I was.' What a fool she'd been. How stupidly trusting. Her hand was resting on the edge of the door, she pushed it shut, yelping in shock when a hand stopped her and the private investigator, a man who'd already proven he couldn't be trusted, pushed into the house, and shut the door behind him.

HANNAH

It was a good night; I made sure of it, showing Mark exactly what I could do for him. He had an unfortunate habit of wanting to hold me afterwards, wrapping his sweaty arms around me and pulling me into his even sweatier chest. It was obviously something he did with his wife. Maybe she liked it. Me, I liked a bit of space after sexual gymnastics. Rather than rocking his boat, I waited till he fell asleep before sliding from his embrace and shuffling towards the cool edge of the bed.

He was ready for more in the morning. 'I can't get enough of you,' he whispered, shimming over to me, running a hand over my belly, down between my legs.

I groaned. It seemed the appropriate response although morning sex never had been my cuppa. He, however, was ready, willing, and obviously able, so I did my part with as much gusto as I could muster when all I really wanted to do was sleep for another hour or two.

He was far more romantic than I remembered. His wife's influence, I supposed. When he suggested we shower together, it seemed

like he'd learned a script from a bad chick-lit novel and I had to bite my tongue to ask if his wife read them. I had to bite harder to stop myself telling him not to be so stupid. 'No, you go ahead; you have me so exhausted, I'm just going to doze for a few minutes.'

When he made a move towards the bed, I quickly shut my eyes and let my head flop ever so slightly, hoping he'd get the hint. He must have done, and I must have been as exhausted as I claimed because my pretence of falling asleep became reality. When I woke, the silence and the cold, white, unadorned walls of the bedroom were disorientating, and I wondered where I was. It hadn't been the first time I'd woken in a strange bedroom over the years. Only when the silence was punctured by the distinct rumble of a man's voice, did I relax. My new apartment... and Mark was here with me.

I should have felt happy. My plan was working. But my thoughts kept returning to what I'd found in Mother's bedroom. The implications of it were so staggering that I couldn't take them in. Not yet... perhaps never... because if I was right, my whole life had been a lie.

It was a terrifying thought. I scrambled from the bed, dragging the sheet with me and fled the room to search for Mark, wanting his presence now as much as I hadn't wanted it earlier.

He was sitting at the small table I'd set in front of the floor-to-ceiling window. His mobile was clamped to his ear and as he listened, he nodded in agreement to whatever was being said.

'Not a problem,' he said, 'I can have that for you today.' Another nod and he cut the connection and put the phone down. His loud sigh stirred the leaves on a plant in the corner of the low windowsill.

'Bad news?' I'd have liked for him to turn and tell me it was his wife, that she was upset, and he needed to go to her. I'd have liked

a reason to be angry, to feel any emotion rather than the fear that was still reaching for me.

He turned and reached a hand out to me, his expression relaxed. I'm guessing it hadn't been his wife.

'Just work stuff. Paperwork I need to get done.'

'You can take a break though, can't you?' I tugged at his hand. If I couldn't stir up some anger to rid me of the daemons, I'd do what I'd done for so many years; I'd wipe them away with the closeness, the heat, the connection that sex brought. A temporary release, but it would do.

Fifteen minutes later, Mark was back at work, and I was still strangely restless. His assumption that I was simply going to sit around and wait for him to be free was irritating me too. Leaving him to it seemed to be the best idea.

I packed an overnight bag and dropped it at the front door. My jacket was draped over the back of a chair. I pulled it on, patted the pocket, but refused to dwell on what it held. Instead, I crept up behind Mark. A kiss on his cheek startled him, his fingers hitting a series of letters that sent lines of gibberish flying across the screen. 'Blast,' he said, carefully deleting before turning to me. 'Sorry, you startled me.' He nodded toward the monitor. 'I really need to get this done.'

'I'll leave you to it,' I said coolly. 'I'm going to head to Ivan's. I think I'll stay for a night, maybe two. It'll give you a chance to have a word with your wife.'

He was on his feet, stumbling in his haste to reach me and drag me into his arms. 'A night or two? I thought...' He opened and shut his mouth, as if suddenly realising he'd no right to the words he was going to say.

I knew exactly what they'd be. He'd thought that once I had an apartment, that he could come and go as he pleased. That I'd be there waiting for him whenever he could tear himself away

from his wife. He never really believed he'd have to make a decision. 'Right,' he said, letting me go. 'I will speak to Susan, I promise. Let me know when you get back; we can meet. I'll take you for dinner and we can talk. Okay?'

I'd used the lash, now it was time for the velvet glove. I stepped closer, put my hand on his cheek and looked into his eyes. 'I'll be thinking of you every moment I'm away, remembering the wonderful lover you are, how good you make me feel.' And then I kissed him, a long, slow, sensual kiss that aroused him as I knew it would. Always leave them wanting more. I stepped away with a smile, then turned, picked up my bag and left.

40

HANNAH

It was a miserable day, rain-heavy, low clouds making it feel like early evening rather than mid-morning. The kind of day I'd have been happy to remain curled under my duvet with a good book rather than driving to Windsor. Mark and his self-serving idea to work from home – my home – had made that impossible.

Going away for a while would give him time to reflect. I'd planned one night; maybe I should stay for a few. It wasn't as if Ivan was going to complain. The idea made me snigger. I turned the volume of the radio up and let out a long breath. The earlier fear that had almost swamped me had receded. I refused to give credence to the notion that I felt better away from Mark. He was perfect for me and made me happy.

My life would be good from now on. I lifted my hand from the steering wheel and patted my pocket almost obsessively, then turned the volume up higher, desperate to drown out my thoughts. It didn't work. All it succeeded in doing was giving me a headache that was throbbing as I pulled into the driveway of Ivan's house grateful to find the gate had been left open.

The promised rain had arrived. I parked as near to the door as

possible, grabbed my bag and made a dash for shelter. The key turned easily in the lock for a change, and I was inside, shaking off the few drops that had managed to sneak up on me.

The smell I'd noticed on my last visit, only days before, was more intense, more nauseatingly stomach-churning. It seemed a wise move to go to my bedroom and open all the windows wide. Granted, rain would come in, soak the curtains and Ivan's precious Persian rugs, but more importantly, the stink would have a way out. If I was going to spend a night or two, I had to be able to breathe.

It took a couple of hours before the rank smell faded to an acceptable level. It necessitated opening windows, not only in the bedroom, but in the lounge and kitchen and propping open the front door to provide a through draught. The house was old, and creaked its age but with so many windows open, it developed an ominous rattle. A wind had picked up; it sent the curtains dancing at every open window until sufficient rain was lashed through to wet them and make them too weighted to more than flap noisily.

I kept my jacket on and made myself a cup of coffee. I should have thought about bringing some food. A glance in the freezer made me sigh. I wasn't hungry, but I might be later. Ivan had never been keen on takeaways so we'd never ordered one while I lived there but I had no doubt I'd find someone willing to deliver. It was that or drive out in the belting rain to the nearest supermarket. I looked out the window at the dark sky and the trees swaying madly in the wind, and shook my head. I wasn't going out in that.

I sipped the coffee slowly, putting off the inevitable, then dropped the empty mug in the sink and headed up the stairs.

Ivan's bedroom door was slightly ajar. As I got closer, my nose crinkled in defence as the offensive odour increased. It stank of body waste, of death, of hopelessness. I didn't need to go further

than the doorway and didn't. 'Hello, Ivan. I'm staying for a couple of nights. Hope that's okay with you. I won't be in your way.'

He didn't reply. Not that I expected him too. It was my duty done. I stepped back into the corridor and closed the door over.

I was suddenly tired. The previous night's shenanigans had taken their toll. I think I was getting too old for all-night sexual gymnastics. When Mark and I were married, that would be the first thing that would go.

Back in my bedroom, the air smelt fresher, but the wind was making the open windows rattle and the now-wet curtains slap noisily against the wall. I shut them over and hoped the stink wouldn't creep under the door and choke me while I slept.

The bed was comfortable. So were the pillows, far more comfortable than the ones in the apartment. They'd come with me when I left. On that positive note, surprisingly relaxed, I drifted off to sleep.

A deep sleep filled with dreams of stinking, rotting corpses and thick, foul-smelling effluent that came down like rain to pour in the windows. It grew legs and tramped through the house, leaving a rancid stink in its wake. And there were bells tolling, warning everyone of the ghoulish creature that approached. Loud bells but the people ignored them and instead of running, reached for the ghoul to shake his hand, their expressions changing to horror when the limb came away as they shook.

I felt the soft, putrid mass in my hand and threw it away with a cry of disgust. It was enough to take me out of the dream and jerk upward, checking my hands, half-afraid there would be something rotten clinging to my fingers.

I wiped my hands together. The sensation had been so strong.

'Hello.'

For a second, I thought I was still asleep, then the word came again, louder, firmer.

'Hello.'

I was still searching my body for any evidence of the ghoul in my dream, but at this second salutation, I looked up, peering across the darkened room. There was something by the door. A hazy form whose body and limbs blended into the dark wall behind. Only the pale face stood out, strangely bright as if all the light in the room were concentrated in that single oval. Perhaps I was still asleep and my ghoul was taking human shape.

'You're Hannah Parker?'

A nightmarish ghoul who knew my name? Slouched on the bed, I felt at a distinct disadvantage. What or whoever this intruder was, it seemed better to confront it on my feet. I stood and reached for the bedside light, all the while keeping my eyes on the figure still standing near the door. The lamp didn't lend much illumination; on the contrary, it threw up more shadows, making the scene scarily unreal. I needed the main light on, but the switch was by the door and would mean approaching the figure. I'd always considered myself a brave woman; I'd had to be, after all. But that was facing reality, this... well, I wasn't sure what this was.

Maybe the intruder felt the same, because suddenly, it moved and the light came on and I was facing a woman. Just a normal woman.

Mark's wife.

SUSAN

She was terrified when Ethan pushed his way into her house. With the exit blocked by him, she turned to run for the back door, hoping she'd left the key in the lock, not hanging on the hook in the cupboard where Mark insisted it should be kept.

With her thoughts in a tangle, it was a few seconds before she registered Ethan's voice begging her to listen.

'Please, take it easy,' he said, holding his hands out, palms first. 'I'm not going to hurt you; I just need you to listen to what I have to say.'

She glanced through the doorway. The key wasn't in the lock; there was no escape.

'Please, just listen,' Ethan said.

He sounded dejected rather than dangerous. She turned back to him, her fear ebbing a little. 'You haven't left me much choice, have you?' She went into the kitchen, leaving him to follow.

He sat at the table; in the same seat he'd sat in days before when she thought she could trust him. She reached into the cupboard, took out the key and inserted it into the back door lock. Turning it, she checked the door could open before relaxing.

Then, with her arms folded defensively, she glared at him. 'Forcing your way into someone's house isn't the best way of having them trust you, you know.'

'I do know, and I'm sorry.'

He did look sorry. Dejected, sorry and stupidly sad. She knew that expression; she'd seen it in the mirror that morning. 'You want some coffee?'

'That'd be good. I haven't slept and I'll need to mainline it to keep awake.'

If he was hoping for sympathy, he'd come to the wrong house. She frowned. What was he doing there anyway? She made the coffee and put a mug in front of him. 'Right, now, what do you want? If you've come to tell me you'd lied about Mark and another woman, it's too late; I already know.'

He slurped the coffee and put the mug down. 'How did you find out?'

'Mark rang yesterday to say he wouldn't be home, that a difficult client needed a bit of handholding. I believed him. After all, I'd been told he wasn't having an affair.' She stirred sugar into her coffee, fixing her eyes on the swirling liquid. Inside her brain felt very much the same. 'Maybe I didn't really believe you.' She shrugged. 'I don't know, but something made me take out those photographs again and look more closely. I noticed what I'd missed the first time. Mark was smiling *at* someone; his head was turned to look *at* someone. But there was nobody there.' She had no reason to trust this man, but it was good to have someone to talk to. 'I guessed the building he was standing outside was a hotel. It didn't take me long to do a search on the net and find out which hotel it was. Then I went there.'

Ethan snorted. 'You went to the hotel?'

Her husband might be cheating on her, she might have been discarded like yesterday's newspaper, but she was damned if she

was going to be sneered at by this little shit. 'I've discovered, if I want something done, I'm far better doing it myself than trusting anyone else. So yes, I went to the hotel. And no, I can see by your expression that you know I didn't find them there, and you'd be right, I didn't, but I did discover that Mark had been there with a woman, and I found out her name. Hannah Parker.' As she spoke, it struck her that she'd been courageous and had found out the information she'd wanted. She hadn't needed anyone. For the first time in a long time, she felt a weight lift off her shoulders and the spine she'd forgotten she had, straightened.

'Impressive,' Ethan said. 'If you're ever in need of a job, you should come and see us.' He picked up his mug, sipped, put it down, curled his hands around it, played with the handle. All the while avoiding Susan's eyes.

He reminded her of Drew when he'd done something wrong. She'd learned in dealing with her son, that if she gave him enough rope, he'd eventually hang himself by confessing. It wasn't as if she'd anything else to do. Having Hannah's name was one step. Susan had no idea what to do next. She was trying to think of anything she could do when she saw Ethan reach into his jacket pocket. He put an envelope on the table and pushed it towards her.

The undoctored photographs. It was exactly as she'd guessed. Mark was smiling at the woman sitting opposite, talking to the woman who walked beside him, looking into her eyes. Susan had guessed the floozie would be beautiful and had assumed she'd be young. She'd been wrong on both counts. The woman in the photograph was around her age, maybe even a year or two older, and she wasn't beautiful; she was stunning. Susan held the photo up, peering with envy at the high cheekbones, the glossy, dark hair that curled around her shoulders, the full lips. There was

something exotic about her, a voluptuous sexuality that screamed she'd be a savage in bed.

'So this is Hannah? She's stunning, isn't she?' When he didn't answer, Susan looked at him, surprised to see his mouth clamped in a thin line. Suddenly, she knew she'd been wrong here too. It hadn't been her husband who'd paid off Ethan; it had been Hannah. 'She paid you to doctor the photographs. I'm right, aren't I? Why would she do such a thing; surely it was in her interest for me to find out about their tacky affair and throw Mark out, right into her grubby little hands.'

'She didn't pay me.'

Susan looked from him back to the photograph. No, why use anything as sordid as money when you had everything else. 'I think you'd better tell me everything.' She put the photo on the table, face down. 'If you want to keep your job that is.'

He ran a hand over his unshaven face. Susan listened to the rasp of his bristle and thought what a suitable sound effect it was for the lying snake. An idea had come to her. She'd let him keep his job, she'd even let him keep the money, but she wanted something in return. First, she'd listen to his story.

'I met Hannah, maybe fifteen years ago. I was in a pub one night and saw her having a bit of a barney with an older geezer. When he hit her, I stepped in, showed him my warrant card, told him to do one.' He laughed and shook his head. 'Typical bully, he scarpered as fast as his little legs would carry him.'

'Leaving you with Hannah.'

'Yes.' He reached for his mug and found it empty. He kept it between his hands, rolling it back and forth. 'She was the most beautiful woman I'd ever seen. Sexy with it.' He fanned his face with his hand. 'Blisteringly hot.'

'And grateful to you for rescuing her?'

He laughed at that. 'She said she was. Fluttered her eyelashes,

played the damsel in distress, making me feel like a hero. She's a brilliant actress.'

'Ah.' This is what she needed to hear. Something she could use.

'I was under no illusions. The guy I'd chased off was a bully, but a filthy rich one. She was never going to be interested in someone like me, someone who had to work hard to make a halfway decent wage.'

When he stopped, Susan waited impatiently, then gave him a nudge. 'But you were together for a while?'

'A few weeks. Long enough to discover Hannah was as hard as she was beautiful. She knew exactly what she wanted and someone like me wasn't it.'

'She broke up with you?'

'Broke up?' He tossed a lock of greasy hair back with a jerk of his head. 'Nothing as kind as that, she simply vanished from my orbit. Scarpered from her apartment without giving notice or leaving a forwarding address. She simply dropped her keys into the landlord's letter box with a note saying she was off. I couldn't believe she'd left, just like that. Without saying goodbye.' There was something pitiful in those last few words; he seemed to realise it and met Susan's gaze with a wry smile. 'I was so besotted with her that I haunted the places where we'd been together, where she'd seemed to be a regular, but she never showed up. Nobody had seen her and within days, the ripple she'd caused had vanished as if she'd never existed. I never saw her again.'

'Until you followed Mark?'

'Yes.' He reached for his empty mug. 'Could I have some more, d'you think?'

She wanted to tell him to get on with it, but she recognised the sadness in his voice, the same tone of worthlessness she heard in her own these days. Perhaps they had much in common.

Once the mug of coffee was in front of him, he took a sip and continued with his story. 'I've done surveillance for a long time. The priority is getting a clear shot of the target. I take the photos, check they're in focus, but that's it; I don't pore over them. Apart from being aware your husband was with a good-looking woman, I didn't give her much attention, so I hadn't recognised Hannah.

'I followed your husband to an apartment in Bristol, not far from Queen Square. A few minutes later, he appeared on one of the balconies with her.' He indicated the envelope. 'The photo is there. They disappeared from the balcony after a bit, then a couple of hours later, he left. I guessed he'd be heading home to you so didn't bother following him. I was leaning against my car having a smoke when Hannah came out. She waved and ran towards me. For a second, I was sure she was going to punch me, but then...' he smiled. 'Then I recognised her. She squealed and threw her hands around me, as if we'd only seen each other the day before, as if she hadn't simply vanished all those years before.'

Susan could clearly imagine the scene: the besotted man, the conniving, manipulative, stunningly beautiful woman.

'She invited me up to her apartment, poured me a drink, told me how sorry she was for having left me without a word.' He wrapped his hands around the mug.

Susan stared at his fingers, at the whitening knuckles. Was he imagining choking Hannah? Maybe he had. She knew nothing about him. Her eyes flicked nervously to the back door, relieved she'd unlocked it. 'What happened?'

'She was coming on to me so strong that I remember thinking she must have finished with your husband. That it had simply been a fling. Alcohol makes fools of us all, and I'm no exception. When she asked why I'd been hanging around outside, I decided to be honest. After all,' he sneered, 'isn't that what relationships are built on? Honesty.'

'So you told her?'

'Yes. Everything. About you, the photos I'd taken outside the hotel, in the café. That I was meeting you on Monday to give you the proof you'd wanted. I expected her to look horrified, embarrassed even, but she simply shrugged and said it had been a mistake and it was over.'

Over? Hope made Susan's heart leap.

'She said there was no point in upsetting you over what she called a "silly little fling", that I should tell you that I hadn't seen him with anyone.' He reached out and tapped the envelope. 'I have an app; it's easy to delete a person.'

Susan was still struggling with the concept of the *silly little fling* that had almost destroyed her marriage, but she was puzzled. 'Why didn't you simply tell me you hadn't seen him with anyone? Wouldn't that have made more sense?'

'I thought the photos of him on his own were more convincing.'

She remembered the crazy money she had paid him and guessed the truth. 'You had to justify your invoice, didn't you?' She held up a hand to stop any argument he might make. She didn't care about the money. 'She persuaded you to do this for my good?' Maybe Hannah the heartbreaker of men had a compassionate streak after all.

'That's what she said.'

Hope was a fragile state of mind. She could feel it crack and tinkle as it collapsed around her. 'She didn't mean it though, did she? She said it so you'd doctor those photographs.'

He had the grace to look embarrassed. 'I should have known better but she's so convincing, even better than when I first met her. We had a wild couple of nights; she'd learned some tricks since our time together.' He licked his lips as the memory came to him. 'She talked about taking me to places that she knew I'd love.

Places it would take weeks, months to visit. She made me believe...' He stopped abruptly. 'Then I had a message from her yesterday afternoon to say it had been a mistake. I was gutted. I messaged her but got no reply.'

'She'd used you.'

He was staring into his mug. With a sigh, he looked up and nodded. 'I felt so stupid. What's that old saw; *fool me once, shame on you, fool me twice, shame on me...* well, that's me, a fool. I went around to the apartment, kept watch, wasn't a bit surprised to see your husband arrive. I stayed all night, waiting for him to leave so I could go and confront her but he didn't leave.'

They were still there. Together. Susan's eyes flicked to the knife block. She could almost feel the handle of the larger knife in her hand. Perhaps it was time to make her dream come true.

'Hannah did, though,' Ethan said.

Susan was still staring at the knives. She turned to look at him. 'What?'

'Hannah, she left. She took me by surprise, so I didn't get a chance to talk to her before she jumped into her car and pulled away. She was carrying an overnight bag, so I'm guessing she'll be away for a while.'

'But Mark is still there? And he's all right?'

The anxiety in her voice must have struck Ethan as amusing because he laughed. 'You're afraid she might have killed him off, eh? It wouldn't be of any benefit to her; she wasn't married to him. She's capable, though.' His expression turned ugly. 'More than capable.' He caught Susan's horror-widened eyes and shook his head. 'Relax, he's okay. He came to the balcony to wave her off.'

'So where's she gone?'

'I thought she might be going back to her mother's and followed, hoping to get a chance to talk to her, but when she took the turn for the M4, I knew I'd been wrong.'

'The M4? So where's she going?' She wasn't sure he was going

to answer. He looked shifty, sly. Could she trust a word he said? That any man said. She pictured Mark in that apartment, maybe sitting on the balcony relaxing. Had he given her one thought? He'd said he'd be home that evening but how could she face him knowing what she knew now? She was still waiting for Ethan to answer. 'Well,' she nudged. 'It's obvious you know, so why don't you tell me.'

'I don't know precisely,' he prevaricated. 'But I had a chance to do a bit of snooping while Hannah was asleep on Sunday.' He shrugged off any guilt. 'Call it an occupational hazard; I like to snoop. Because she'd recently moved, everything was neat and tidy, so it made it easy. I found her husband's address—'

'Husband!'

'Yes,' he frowned. 'She lied to me. Surprise, surprise. Said she'd never been married. But I found a copy of a will which referred to her as the wife of an Ivan Butler. When I got home, I searched for him. He's a wealthy landowner who's made himself even richer by some astute financial dealings.'

'Is she planning to divorce him to be with Mark?'

Ethan looked around the room. 'I don't mean to be rude, but you're not exactly rich, are you?' He shot her an apologetic look. 'I'd categorise you as very comfortable, but Hannah is a high-maintenance woman; comfortable won't get her what she's used to.'

'I don't mean to be rude either,' Susan said, 'but you thought you had a chance with her and I'd say you're a few steps below comfortable myself.'

'Yea, well I'm fucking good at fooling myself, aren't I?' He got to his feet, then sat again heavily, the feet of the chair scraping on the tiled floor. 'I knew I never had a chance with her.' He looked at Susan. 'She wants Mark, though, I'm guessing, and didn't want you throwing a spanner in the works before she was sure of him.'

Sadly, that made sense. She wanted to make sure he wouldn't wriggle free. 'But as you said, we're not rich.'

'No.' He tapped a fingernail on the table. 'Her husband is, though, and he's a lot older than she is. Maybe she's hoping he'll croak and she'll have his money.'

He laughed, a cynical, bitter sound that was painful to hear. A wave of weariness swept over Susan. It was all too much.

'Hell,' Ethan said, 'I wouldn't put it past her to help him on his way.'

It was a measure of how she was feeling that this didn't shock Susan. How could it when she'd imagined going around to that apartment with a knife. 'You really think she'd do that: kill him?'

'If she hasn't already done so. He's retired and they live in an old, detached house; he could be lying there dead, how would anyone know?'

It was a horrible thought. Surely, Hannah couldn't be as bad as he was painting her. Mark wouldn't have fallen for a monster. He liked nice, quiet women. Didn't he? Or was Susan fooling herself, just as much as the man sitting opposite had done? What idiots people could be for love. 'You make her sound like some kind of black widow or something.'

'Look.' He leaned across the table, his face creased in frustration. 'I only know that she's a manipulative woman who gets what she wants, and doesn't care what she has to do to get it.' He got to his feet again, and this time took a step away. 'I've done what I came for. Told you the truth. Apologised. That's it.'

'That's it!' Susan stood and faced up to him. 'You walk away and leave me worrying about what the fuck is going on. Is that really it?'

He held his hands up. 'That's really it.'

'Where does the husband live?'

'I don't know. Near Windsor somewhere.'

Susan felt a rage building. If she'd been able to reach a knife right then, she'd have taught this man not to treat her like a fool. She didn't know who she was any more, this angry woman full of violence. A deep breath helped. 'Listen,' she said, keeping her voice calm. 'I'll cut a deal with you. Give me the man's address and I won't go to your boss, tell him what you did. Give it to me and you can walk away with the money. And you'll never hear from me again.' She held his gaze, waiting to see him recognise the sense it would make to give her what she needed. There was never any doubt in her mind that he knew exactly where Ivan Butler lived.

'You fucking women,' he muttered, 'I'll be glad to be shot of the lot of you.' He reached into the pocket of his cargo pants and pulled out a notebook and pen. Leaning on the table, he scribbled the address on a page, tore it out, and handed it to her.

She quickly scanned it and nodded. 'Thank you.'

He stuffed pen and notebook back into the pocket and turned for the door. Curiosity stopped him, and he looked back. 'What're you going to do – go there?'

What was she going to do? When she'd asked for the address, she had a vague notion of looking at it on Google Maps. Maybe even going into Street View to get a closer look. But what would that achieve? Absolutely nothing. But if she went there, she could do two things. Confront the woman, beg her to leave Mark alone, and find out if there was any truth in Ethan's words that she might have harmed her husband, because if there was, Mark might be in danger, and despite his cheating, she'd risk anything for him.

'I don't think you've left me with much choice.' She folded the address and shoved it into her jeans' pocket. 'If you're worried, you could come with me.' She wished he would. She'd a vague idea that her courage, like her violence, was a transient thing, and

would probably vanish as soon as she knocked on Ivan Butler's door.

But Ethan shook his head. 'I'm sorry. I'm not sure I could survive a third round with Hannah Parker. Take my advice: stay well clear. If she wants your husband, she'll get him. I'd give up now if I were you.' And with that, he was gone, the front door slamming and echoing in the silence he'd left behind.

43

SUSAN

There didn't seem to be any point in hanging about. She looked down at the shirt and jeans she was wearing, wondered if she should change into something smarter, something more expensive. Then she laughed, the sound slicing through the quiet. She could dress in her very finest, and she still couldn't compete with Hannah. Unwilling to waste her time on a pointless exercise, she went to the coat stand and took down the first jacket, a worn, scruffy one she usually wore doing the gardening. It had pockets spacious enough to take her purse, keys and phone.

The journey took longer than she expected, heavy rain slowing the traffic, reducing visibility at times so she was forced to peer through the rain-washed windscreen as the wipers battled to clear the downpour.

To give her aching brain a rest, she slipped an ABBA CD into the drive and made herself sing along to all the songs. By the time she reached her destination, her throat was hoarse but rather than feeling calmer, she could feel anxiety sizzling through her veins as she looked through the open gate to the old house.

Susan hesitated only a moment before turning into the short

driveway. A car was parked directly in front of the entrance, another parked to one side. She pulled in beside this one and switched off the engine.

Climbing out, she leaned on the roof of the car and stared at the house. It was very pretty and, unlike the entrance gate, had been well-maintained over the years. The paintwork was fresh, the driveway around the house, weed-free. Someone loved the place.

Ivan Butler. Not Hannah, who only loved herself.

Despite the cars, there was no obvious sign of life. The rain had eased to a soft drizzle. It was a bit silly to be standing there getting wet when she could be inside finding out if Hannah was there. If not, she'd have a word with Ivan Butler, throw herself on his mercy. He might have something she could use as leverage to pry Hannah away from Mark.

Assuming Ivan was still alive. The drive had given Susan time to put Ethan's cruel assessment of Hannah into perspective. He'd had his fingers burnt for the second time, he was hardly going to sing her praises, so Susan would take what he'd said with a pinch of salt.

Edging around the smart, red BMW, Susan reached the front door and looked for a doorbell. With none to be seen, she stepped closer to the door and put a hand out to lift the knocker but as she touched it, the door swung open.

Already on edge, she gave a nervous giggle, stepped back and waited for someone to appear in the increasing gap. The drizzle had morphed back into heavy rain. There was little shelter in the doorway; the jacket she was wearing, the fabric thin with age, provided little protection and she was soon wet to the skin. That's what had her shivering. Nothing to do with the crack of thunder that rolled in the distance, or the black chasm that lay before her.

She looked over the roof of the car to where hers sat. She

could run back to it, drive away. To a café where she could get warm before heading home and forgetting about this ridiculous idea.

Or she could go inside. Do a bit of exploring. Be brave.

She had nothing, so what did she have to lose?

A gust of wind-driven rain at her back made it easier to decide, and she hurried forward and through the door. She pushed it shut after her, the click as the catch engaged sounding loud. With her hand still on it, she looked around. The entrance hall with its oak-panelled walls was a grim space. Light would have come from the window on the stairway return had dark clouds not been hanging over the house like a bad omen.

Susan, her hand still on the door, felt a dart of fear colour the anxiety that had solidified over the last few hours. This had been a very bad idea. She shivered again. The darkness was bad enough, but it was the smell that made her gut twist and her hand clutch the catch on the door. It was the faint stink of meat that had gone off, the unmistakable odour of decay.

Ethan might have been biased, but was it possible he was right? That Hannah had killed her husband? That his body was in a room somewhere, rotting away.

Her free hand closed over her mobile. She should ring the police and tell them... tell them what? That she'd pushed her way into the house of a man she didn't know and was afraid he was dead? Even with the hairs on the back of her neck standing to attention and that throat-catching stink making her feel nauseous, she had to acknowledge she sounded ridiculous.

It *was* ridiculous. She'd let Ethan's bitter words colour her thoughts. The stench might have a more reasonable explanation. Bad drains or something. It was an old house. It was possible. She wasn't sure she believed the reassurances her inner self was trying to sell but she took her hand away from the door and walked

forward. There were rooms off the hallway on both sides. Their doors ajar, it was easy to see they were in darkness. Guessing a kitchen would be situated to the back, she crossed to a doorway under the curve of the staircase and pushed it open. Windows overlooking the rear garden allowed some light through. The room was empty but when she crossed to a kettle and rested her hand lightly against it, it was warm.

There was someone in the house. It was simply a matter of finding them.

Back in the hallway, she put a foot on the first step of the stairway and looked up. Everything was in shadow. The torch on her mobile was powerful. She switched it on and directed the beam upward, relieved when it showed nothing scarier than a few dubious landscape paintings.

Step by step, stopping each time to listen, to look up, then to peer down over the banister, it took a couple of minutes to reach the landing. There were windows open somewhere, she could hear the wind whistling through the gaps but it did little to disperse the stink, stronger, more offensive here. *Ethan was right.* Susan could be in danger; she should get out of there.

Instead, she stood looking down the corridor that stretched in both directions. The beam of light from her mobile picked out doorways but there were no lines of light seeping from under any of the doors to indicate a room was in use. She stood swinging the beam to and fro for several seconds before grunting in frustration and heading down the corridor to her right.

The first door she came to opened into a large bedroom. It was empty. She slid a hand along the wall, found a switch and pressed it to fill the room with light. It was a pretty room, nicely furnished. A window had been opened far enough to allow the rain to batter the net curtain. It flapped wetly between the wall and the glass.

Her house-proud fingers itched to cross and shut it. Then she

remembered the stench and nodded. Maybe opening the windows had been a good idea.

The next door led into a spacious and surprisingly modern bathroom. Her hand rested on the pile of fluffy white towels. There had been no expense spared here.

Her anxiety level increased as she walked further along to reach the next room. She rested her hand on the handle and took a deep breath before pushing it open.

The room was in darkness, but although she couldn't see anyone, she immediately knew she wasn't alone. The beam from her mobile phone torch was pointing towards the floor. She raised it slowly and shone it around the room. It was furnished in a similar way to the first bedroom but there was one dramatic difference. Here, there was a body stretched out on the bed.

Suddenly, startling her, it sat up. Keeping the beam low, Susan stared at the woman she recognised from the photographs. Hannah Parker. She was rubbing her hands together and staring at her as if she'd seen a ghost. 'Hello,' Susan said, because she couldn't think of anything else to say.

When Hannah didn't reply or acknowledge her, she cleared her throat and tried again, louder, more firmly. 'Hello.'

Rather than replying, Hannah reached for the bedside lamp and switched it on, immediately throwing half her face into relief.

She looked like the devil. Panic shot through Susan as she turned the torch towards the wall and scrabbled to find a light switch.

44

HANNAH

I recognised Mark's wife, of course, although she seemed even more dull and plain than I remembered. But I'd only seen her that one time. It had been as much as I'd needed to see. Enough to tell me she was no competition.

I recognised her, but I couldn't figure out what she was doing there or how she'd known where to find me. Maybe I'd underestimated her. No, I groaned as I shuffled to the side of the bed and swung my feet to the floor. It wasn't her I'd underestimated; it was that stupid prick, Ethan. He'd obviously snooped while I'd slept, found out more about me than I'd ever shared.

I thought I'd dropped him gently so wasn't expecting him to be vindictive, but obviously, I was wrong.

'What are you doing here?'

Her mouth opened and shut like a gormless goldfish. Seriously, why had a man as gorgeous and intelligent as Mark stayed with this moron for so long. I slipped my feet into the shoes I'd kicked off a few hours before and combed fingers through my hair. No doubt I looked a sight, but even then, I'd leave this mess of a woman in the shade. 'Well?' I was losing patience.

'I want you to leave Mark alone.'

The poor fool. 'That's not what Mark wants.'

'We were happy before you turned up flashing your...'

She seemed to be lost for words so I decided to help her out. 'My tits?'

More mouth opening and closing as if she was offended by the word. 'Your somewhat obvious attributes,' she said. 'Some of which I'm guessing you weren't born with and some of which are beginning to look a little ridiculous on a woman of your years.'

My years! I was almost forty, although I only ever admitted to thirty-six to new acquaintances. But Susan spoke as if a woman had to stop trying to look her best after a certain age and as if it was a crime to get a little helping hand when it was necessary. No wonder Mark had been so easy to reel in. I almost felt sorry for her. But only almost. 'Perhaps if you'd made more of your some-what meagre attributes, Mark wouldn't have felt the need to look elsewhere. Have you thought of that?'

'I love him and know he loves me. If you'd go away, we'd be all right. I know it.'

I wasn't sure if she was trying to convince me or herself. It didn't matter; I was bored with her. I wanted her to go so I could order a takeaway, have something to eat and relax. 'Well, I'm sorry. I'm not going away. Mark spent last night with me. He's promised to tell you that he's leaving you.' Almost promised. A day or two missing me would have swung it for me. What I didn't need was a whining wife to stir up his guilt and to make him think twice. That damn Ethan, I had misjudged badly there.

'Please, don't take him just because you can.'

Had she just quoted a Dolly Parton song at me? 'My name's not Jolene.' She looked puzzled and I brushed it away. 'Listen, go home. You'll be okay. You'll find some other more suitable sap to

spend your boring days with. Mark has always been mine. I let him go twenty years ago and it was a mistake.'

'You let him go. I don't intend on doing the same.'

I looked her up and down, allowing my eyes to linger on the scruffy jacket, her rat-tail hair, the jeans that were all the wrong shape for her figure. My sniff was disparaging, dismissive. 'Yes, well he's not here, so why don't you bugger off back to the suburbs where your type belongs.' I suppose I didn't really believe she was going to leave that easily. If she'd come all the way from Bristol in this bloody awful weather, she must have had a plan. Or something more interesting to say than leave my husband be. I waited expectantly, but when she did speak, when she came out with her great plan, my jaw dropped. 'What?'

'You heard me. I know you killed your husband.'

It was almost amusing to see Hannah's face fall as it hit her that her secret was out. How arrogant, how stupid she'd been not to ensure the house was secure. Anyone could have wandered in the front door as Susan had done and they'd have reached the same conclusion as she had. How could they not; the house stank of death. A sliver of worry pierced a tiny hole in her satisfaction. Nobody knew she was there and this woman had already killed; what was to stop her doing so again? As soon as Susan had realised Hannah was asleep, she should have left to search for the proof, taken a photo, then scarpered.

Oddly, although she was worried, she wasn't scared. In fact, to her surprise, she hadn't felt so alive in a long time. Perhaps her sisters were right. She'd needed to get out there and do something rather than moping around the house. A vague idea that her sisters hadn't meant confronting a husband-stealing murderer in an isolated house miles from home, was brushed aside.

She wasn't scared, nor was she stupid. 'Don't worry, I'm not planning on going to the police. I should, of course, but that would keep me entangled in your life and that isn't what I want at

all. So, I'll tell you what I'm going to do, shall I?' Unsurprisingly, Hannah didn't reply. It was good to be in control, to have the power, to stop being so damn weak. 'I'm going to take a photo of the poor man, then I'm going to leave.' Susan saw surprise flicker across the woman's face. Yes, she wasn't expecting that, was she? 'You're surprised. You shouldn't be. All I want from you is my husband. So, it's going to be an exchange, okay. I keep your crime a secret; you leave my husband alone.'

'My crime.' Hannah shook her head. 'You've no idea. No clue.'

She suddenly looked older, less exotic. More like me, Susan thought, surprised. Or maybe it was simply that the balance of power had shifted away from Hannah and it was that power that had made her seem something special. Or maybe she was simply as weary of everything as Susan was. Maybe... and this struck her as a possibility... being with Mark hadn't proved to be the magic spell that Hannah had hoped.

'No, perhaps not. But d' y'know something, I don't care. All I want is my life back the way it was before you came barrelling in.'

Hannah snorted. 'Because it was so perfect? Mark said you were moping about the house like a wet rag fretting about your son. It sounds like the boy moved as far away as he could to escape the smothering hold you had on him. He wanted out. Mark wants out. You think I could have lured your husband away had he been happy?'

Once more, Susan was filled with a desire to unleash the violence that seemed to be constantly on a simmer just waiting for someone to turn up the heat. She could do it, grab this woman by her stupidly glossy hair, smash her face against the wall. Punish her for... for what, wanting what she had? For not only wanting it, but for having the balls to go after it. Who was really at fault here? 'Happiness needs to be worked at. Like marriage. I love Mark, but I'm not blind to his faults. He's a weak man, easily swayed. It's

thanks to me that he's been as successful as he has. If I'm not making him happy today, I did yesterday, and I will tomorrow. You're like the perfume they spray on test strips in department stores; you take a sniff, think it's fabulous, then you throw it away and forget about it. That's the way it'll be for Mark.'

'You think?' Hannah looked amused.

'I know.' Susan opened the door and pointed. 'I could search every room for your poor husband's body but the sooner I'm gone, the better. Before I leave, I'll want you to send Mark a message telling him it was all a mistake and you won't be seeing him again.'

'I'm beginning to like you, you know; you're very amusing.' Hannah didn't sound at all amused but when Susan pointed again, a jagged jabbing of her finger through the doorway, she huffed a noisy, resigned sigh and walked from the room. 'Right, I'll take you to the body, but not till I've had some coffee.' She didn't wait to see if Susan agreed or not, striding purposefully towards the stairway and descending two steps at a time.

Susan hurried to follow, a half-formed thought that the woman was going to try to make a run for it fading when Hannah turned for the kitchen.

46

HANNAH

I headed down the stairs and into the kitchen. If Susan followed me, fine; if she ran screaming from the house, even better. I wasn't surprised to turn around to find her standing there. I'd come to discover she was irritatingly persistent. I was curious though. 'Who told you I'd killed Ivan?'

She hesitated for only a moment before giving a shrug. 'I suppose there's no harm in telling you. It was Ethan. He said you were dangerous. That you always had a thing for rich, older men. Called you a black widow.'

Ethan! He'd got his revenge for the way I'd treated him. I had to give him credit for that. 'I need coffee,' I said, crossing to the kettle. I gave it a shake, judged there was enough water in it for a couple of cups and switched it on. Susan was hovering. 'Oh for goodness' sake, sit; I'm not going anywhere.' I grabbed two mugs and the jar of coffee. 'It'll have to be black; there's no milk.'

She dragged a chair noisily from under the table. 'Fine.'

Sitting, she folded her arms across her chest. Perhaps she was trying to look tough, but I could see the whisper of fear in her eyes, the slight quiver in her lower lip when she forgot to keep

them pressed firmly together. I'd dismissed her as being of no account; I'd been wrong and once more felt a stirring of regret for what I'd done to her.

The kettle seemed to take forever to boil, giving me too much time for self-reflection. Before it reached boil, I flicked the switch. It was hot enough.

'Here you go,' I said, placing a mug on the table before her and taking the seat opposite with mine. 'There's nothing to eat, I'm afraid. No biscuits or anything.'

'This isn't a social event! I don't want any bloody biscuits.'

Her hand was wrapped around the mug. For a moment, I thought she was going to throw the contents at me. I leaned back in my chair to put more distance between us, only relaxing when I saw her grip ease.

'I just want what I came here for, and then I'll be gone and you'll be out of our lives forever. Okay?'

What she came for. Proof that I had murdered my husband. I shivered and slid my hands around the cooling coffee, trying to absorb some of its heat. 'It's not that easy.' Then, because I decided I owed this odd woman, I said, 'Let me tell you a story...'

I'm not sure that I had the right words to paint a clear picture of what Ivan had done to me, or if words even existed that would convey those minutes of vicious terror. 'Ivan discovered I was taking the contraceptive pill. He decided to make his displeasure felt with his fists. And his feet.' I saw her expression change from accusatory to shocked. 'He was a lot older than me, but a big man and he was determined to make his message clear. Apart from the multiple bruises, I had three broken ribs on one side, one on the other, and kidney damage that had me peeing red for days. I was lucky, the doctors said, because I was fit and had good all-over muscle tone. The kidney damage, luckily, was reversible but I have to have regular blood tests to keep a check.' The sympathy in

the eyes opposite had changed to pity. It wasn't something I appreciated. 'I find myself obsessively checking the toilet bowl when I wee,' I said, adding a laugh to lighten the mood.

There was no responding smile. I wondered vaguely if Susan had a sense of humour, then remembered that Mark didn't have much of a one and realised, probably for the first time, how well suited they were. 'As I lay in hospital, the only thing that kept me going was planning how I was going to make the bastard pay for what he'd done to me.'

I could have told her more, how finding that photo of me and Mark in that old book had pulled me out of the deep fug I'd been in since Ivan's brutal attack. That it had given me hope that there were good men out there. Mark had been a good man, and what had I made of him?

I could tell her much more. Explain why I was drawn, despite everything, to much older men.

My jacket was hanging on the back of a chair, the outline of what I'd removed from the drawer in my mother's bedroom clearly defined by the thin fabric. I stared at it, still trying to come to terms with the hideous lie I'd been told. Perhaps this was the story I should tell Susan: the one that had made me who I was.

47

SUSAN

Hearing Hannah's story made Susan sympathise a little but not enough to change her from the course of action she'd decided upon. Anyway, it wasn't as if she was going to go to the police. She'd meant what she'd said; she just wanted Mark.

She pushed her chair back. 'If you've finished your coffee, can we get on with this?' Perhaps Hannah had expected her sad story to have more of an impact because for a moment, she didn't move. 'Now,' Susan said, getting to her feet, relieved to see the other woman following suit, afraid she'd have to use force, not quite sure she'd be capable.

There was silence as the two-person procession moved up the stairs and along the long corridor towards rooms Susan hadn't investigated. The stink of death was stronger here, catching in her throat, making her blink rapidly.

Hannah stopped outside a door. She kicked a large, yellow bag that was slouched on the floor beside it. 'Bastard,' she muttered before turning to glare at Susan. 'You're sure you want to see this?'

Susan gulped. The stink was nauseating. She could feel her insides squirm. She didn't *want* to see a dead body. Hannah had

forced her into this unbelievable situation. 'Positive,' she said, swallowing convulsively. Dead bodies couldn't hurt her. In fact, this particular dead body was going to be of help. Blackmail of sorts. She'd take the photograph, wait till Hannah sent a message to Mark before leaving this hideous place and putting this whole sordid mess behind her. That's the way it would go. And her life would go back to normal... back to being fucking happy. It was anger rather than violence that surged this time. Anger at Mark who, instead of supporting her through a difficult time, had simply raided the sweetie jar. 'Let's get on with it, shall we?' she bit out.

Hannah shrugged and pushed the door open.

The large room was in semi-darkness. Oddly, the smell that was so intense outside was barely noticeable here. A line of sunshine peeked over heavy curtains that hung on the bay window. The only other light came from an Anglepoise lamp in a corner of the room, its beam directed onto the pages of a book held by a person lounging in a comfortable-looking, leather chair. He didn't get up or raise a head to acknowledge their entry.

But he was definitely alive. In the lamplight, his white uniform tunic glowed a startling white. When Susan glanced at the woman beside her and saw her face wreathed in malevolent amusement, she knew she'd got it all wrong.

Ignoring the seated man, Hannah nodded towards the hospital bed that had been pushed against the back wall. 'Come and say hello to my beloved husband. They say he can understand everything. Tell him that you thought I'd murdered him. He'll enjoy that; it might give him a laugh.'

Susan crossed to the end of the bed and stared at the gruesome sight of the cachectic man propped up against the pillows. Even in the dim light, his skin had an unhealthy grey tinge. His thin, white hair had been combed back from a high forehead,

making his face look unnaturally long. With his sunken cheeks, he bore more than a passing resemblance to the agonised face in *The Scream*.

'He's not dead yet, but he's dying,' Hannah said, not bothering to lower her voice. 'The stink is simply him rotting away. It's just a matter of time, then I'll be the Widow Butler and inherit quite a lot of money.' She reached down to pat the man's cheek. 'I don't visit often, but when I do, I like to thank him for leaving me so well off, and to tell him how much I'm going to enjoy spending every single penny.' She'd patted his cheek with every word, increasing the strength until, on the final three words, they were hard enough to send the man's head bouncing on the pillow.

'Stop!' Susan was horrified. She looked to the man seated in the armchair for support but finding none, turned back. 'You can't hit him. He's dying, for pity's sake!'

'Not fast enough.' But Hannah withdrew her hand. There was a tub of wipes on a nearby table, she pulled one from it, wiped her hands and tossed the used wipe into a bin. 'Right, let's get out of here.'

Susan wanted to say something to the man. Some reassuring, socially acceptable, empty words. But then she thought of the beating he'd given Hannah. Maybe this end was simply karma. She turned away without a word and followed the other woman from the room.

48

HANNAH

I didn't know what Susan was going to do now. Perhaps it had been cruel to string her along, to allow her to believe I'd killed Ivan, but I liked to think she deserved it for believing I was capable.

I went back to the kitchen and sat at the table. I half-expected her to leave, and raised an eyebrow when she came into the room. Since she was there, I might as well get the answer to something that was puzzling me. 'Ethan didn't actually say I'd killed Ivan, did he?' She had the grace to look embarrassed. Or maybe she was annoyed. Her ridiculously crazy plan to blackmail me into giving up her husband had backfired. 'I'm guessing by your silence that he didn't. Ethan's a bit of an idiot, but he's not that stupid.' I stood, crossed to the back door, and pushed it open. Behind me, I heard the scrape of a chair being pulled from under the table, and a loud sigh as my unwanted visitor sat. It seemed I wasn't getting rid of her that easily.

'I don't understand... what's causing that awful smell?'

I took another breath of the clean, fresh air before turning. 'I

was only half joking about him rotting away, you know; he has pressure sores. One on his arse, one on each heel.'

'You've twenty-four-hour nursing care?'

'Oh yes.' Hannah smiled as she returned to her seat. 'I'm not giving his relatives any reason to complain I neglected him in his final days. Twenty-four-hour nursing, the best care money can buy. There's plenty of it; I don't begrudge spending some to make sure he goes in comfort, as long as he goes.'

'The nurse...' Susan frowned. 'He didn't say a word. Is he always like that?'

Hannah sniffed. 'He's good at what he does, and reliable, but he's a pig. A few weeks ago, when the smell wasn't nearly as bad as it is now, I complained about it and asked him to tie the top of that yellow bag that's outside the bedroom door. He never does. It's only taken away once a week by a specialised clinical waste company. That's why the place stinks so badly.'

'But not inside the bedroom, isn't that strange?'

'You probably didn't notice but there are odour neutralisers on almost every surface in his room; they're very effective.'

She still looked puzzled. 'But if the nurse doesn't speak to you, how do you know how Ivan is doing?'

I thought I'd made it crystal clear. Obviously not. 'Ivan is dying. It's not a matter of if, it's a matter of *when*. I don't need a report from the nurses. They're paid to do the job, that's all I want from them.'

'Right.' She was still frowning. 'I know what Ivan did to you, but he is dying; should you speak to him the way you did? And hitting him... that's not really right, is it?'

Miss High and Mighty with her middle-class mores, her conservative, boring lifestyle, her suburban home and tired marriage was daring to criticise me? Without knowing a thing

about me. Maybe I was tired of it all, of being the baddie in everyone's story. Of being the baddie in mine. I was tired too of trying to decide what to do with what I'd found in that drawer. Susan was waiting for an answer; I felt her eyes boring into my bowed head. There was a set of knives on the counter. Sharp ones – I'd cut my finger the first time I'd used them. I wanted to stand, grab one and chase this irritating woman from the house. Instead, I sighed and lifted my head to look at her. 'Do you know why he has pressure sores?' Of course she didn't. Mrs Suburbia knew nothing. I leaned an elbow on the table and looked her in the eye.

She shuffled in her chair, looking uncomfortable, as if I'd mentioned something disgusting.

Pressure sores. They were disgusting, often screaming neglect and poor care. 'Let me explain what happened.' I settled back in the chair, folding my arms, making myself comfortable. 'I told you about him beating the crap out of me, didn't I?' I waited until she gave a reluctant nod before continuing. 'It seems it took a lot out of the old bastard. He had a stroke. A big one. And you know what all these adverts say about getting treatment as soon as possible? Well, unfortunately for him, the only person available to help was lying unconscious on the floor above. It was the following day before I managed to get down the stairs and found him.' I pointed to the floor under where she was sitting. She looked suitably horrified and I was amused to see her shuffling the chair away from the spot as if Ivan was still lying there.

'He'd been there for around twelve hours, give or take an hour, unable to move. By the time the ambulance arrived to take him to hospital, tissue damage had already occurred to all the pressure points.' I lifted my hand to my head. 'The only one that healed was the nasty one to the back of his head. The rest...' I shrugged. 'Well, you saw for yourself.'

'There's nothing they can do?'

This made me smile. 'People think because it's the twenty-first century, there's a cure for everything. There isn't. Ivan was in hospital for a couple of weeks. He had extensive assessments by a variety of people and they all came to the same conclusion. There was no chance of rehabilitation. As next of kin, I had a meeting with the team looking after him and they explained in great detail that in view of his advanced age, they were recommending letting nature take its course, and asked if I agreed.'

'Which of course you did.'

'I wanted to ask if they could simply euthanise the bastard, but I guessed that wouldn't go down well.'

For the first time, Susan laughed. 'No, that would have set warning bells ringing all right.'

'Indeed, and I was very careful not to give Ivan's relatives any ammo. Hence, the twenty-four-hour nurse, and everything money can buy.' I sighed. 'I didn't expect the old bastard to last this long, though.'

'I'm no expert but I wouldn't have thought it would be much longer.'

'But as you say, you're no expert.' My voice was sharper than I'd intended and I saw her flinch. I pushed back the chair, the feet scraping noisily to fill the sudden uncomfortable silence. 'I need a drink; you want one?'

She shook her head so adamantly that her thin hair whipped her face. 'I'm driving, I'd better not.'

I did an eye roll. 'I meant tea or more coffee. A glass of water maybe.'

Colour flushed her cheeks. Embarrassment or a hot flush. I neither knew nor cared.

'A glass of water would be good.'

I filled a glass for her and switched on the kettle to make more coffee for myself. I could feel her eyes on me, weighing up every-

thing I'd told her. I wondered if she believed me. I could show her the photographs I'd taken of my bruising, but I couldn't see any point. It didn't matter if she believed me or not. Would I have believed her had our positions been reversed? Probably not, but then I didn't trust anyone.

49

SUSAN

She sipped the water and tried to process all she'd heard and seen. There was no disguising Ivan's terminal state, but had he really beaten Hannah so badly? Was any of her story true? She looked across the table to where the woman was sitting, like her, lost in thought. Was she wondering how much Susan had swallowed? Did it matter?

If Hannah had been trying to drum up some sympathy, it had worked for a while. She had painted a horrific picture of abuse, but there was something in her eyes and her expression that said she wasn't to be trusted. It was difficult; Susan tended to trust everyone. Like an affectionate Labrador, her sisters often said.

But even the most affectionate animal could turn given just cause – she'd read *Cujo*. She'd come here to fight for Mark, but plan A had failed and she didn't have a plan B. Not a realistic one. Not one a sane, rational woman would think was a good idea. She'd spotted the knife block as soon as she'd come into the kitchen. Similar to her own, it sat innocently on the corner of the counter, brushed, stainless steel handles standing to attention.

They looked more expensive than hers. The blades would be sharp.

Nobody knew Susan was there. That nurse wouldn't be able to describe her since he'd barely glanced her direction. There was nobody to connect Susan to Hannah – apart from Ethan. She considered him for all of a second before dismissing him. A man with his morals didn't count.

Hannah didn't look up when Susan got to her feet. Why would she? Everyone dismissed Susan so easily. As if what she did was seldom important. Perhaps they were right. It would help, wouldn't it? Nobody would ever think her capable of what she was about to do. 'I'm just going to get a refill,' she said, nodding towards the kitchen sink. 'I'll help myself.' She had to clamp her mouth shut to stop talking. Nerves, that was all, she'd never done anything so horrendous, so unbelievable before.

But she hadn't done it yet.

She glanced over at Hannah, whose arm was moving rhythmically as she swirled the contents of her mug around and around. She seemed mesmerised by whatever she was seeing, her face down, eyes fixed.

Susan turned on the tap and held her glass under the flow of water until it was full, then turned the tap off and took a sip, as if she was tasting the damn stuff. The knife block was within hand's reach. Bigger knives lined up at the back, shorter ones to the front. The middle back one would be a wide blade, a cleaver. Would that be the best option? Or would a long, slimmer blade be best? She'd liked to have taken them all out one at a time to compare, but she guessed that might alert the woman still hunched over her coffee that something wasn't quite right.

In a minute, there is time for decisions and revisions which a minute will reverse. There was no time. She placed the glass gently

in the sink and, without turning, reached for the cleaver. It slid out with an expensive whisper. Sun breaking through the heavy cloud streamed through the window and hit the blade; it sparkled and for a moment, Susan was enthralled.

It looked pretty rather than lethal.

SUSAN

She held the cleaver tight against her chest. The handle was well designed and fit comfortably in her hand, the blade long enough so that the point sat slightly under her chin. When she turned, Hannah was seated exactly as she had been in the lifetime before Susan had decided that murdering the woman was the only way out.

Over the years, the ones when Drew was sleeping, or Mark was working, and then when Drew was studying, she'd learned the art of moving quietly, of being virtually unseen, unnoticed. It had become part of who she was. It was good to use the few skills she had to get her out of the predicament she was in.

Hannah didn't move as Susan glided across the floor and behind her. Nor did she move as her hair was gathered in one hand, and the knife was slid oh-so quietly across her throat. The blood was warm, thicker than Susan would have expected, and there was so much of it. It spurted forward over the table and dripped from the edges of it to the floor, it soaked into the shirt Hannah wore, flattening the fabric to her skin.

Blood dripped from the end of the knife when Susan held it up.

There was nothing pretty about the blade now.

51

HANNAH

Movement to my right made me turn my head. Susan. I'd forgotten about her. 'You okay?'

'I needed some more water.'

Hannah blinked. Her hands were curled around her mug; it was barely warm. How long had she been lost in her thoughts? She shook her head. Too many things were confusing these days. 'I'm sorry, I've been a bit distracted.'

'So have I,' Susan said, returning to her seat. 'Life used to be more simple.'

I squeezed out a laugh. 'Not mine, I'm afraid.' I slid the mug away and leaned both arms on the table, leaning forward a little, closer to the sad-faced woman sitting opposite. 'I'm sorry. About Mark.' There was no change in her expression. 'I'll send him a message, telling him it was all a big mistake, okay?' Still no acknowledgement. I didn't want praise, but I needed to know she understood that I was doing the right thing. Maybe I wanted absolution. 'Susan? Did you hear what I said?'

Finally, Susan stirred and anger sparked from her eyes. 'Was it a game to you? Was that it? Find an old boyfriend, see if you can

make him fall in love with you again. It didn't matter that he was married.' The anger vanished as fast as it had appeared and her face sagged in misery. 'And now that you're tired of him, you're giving him back and you think that's all okay.'

Suddenly, I wanted to make her understand, to make her believe I wasn't all bad. Because I wasn't, was I? 'I made a mistake,' I said, searching for words that might help to explain what I'd done. 'I was in hospital for a few days after Ivan beat me up, then I returned here to recuperate. I was still in pain, still shook up. I'm no saint, I'll be the first to admit that, but I'm not a violent person and the level of violence he inflicted on me...' I pressed my lips together to stop them trembling. Even months later, I still found it difficult to think of what he'd done to me without becoming distressed. 'I didn't do much during those days. Slept a lot. Watched rubbish TV, or read. I was searching for a book to read among those I'd added to the bookshelves next door, ones I'd already read and enjoyed, and wanted to read again. When I picked out one that I hadn't read for several years, I found a photo of me and Mark. I'd used it as a bookmark and forgotten about it.' I remember the instant feeling of calm when I'd seen it. 'He'd loved me, we'd been happy, and right at that moment, I wanted that feeling back.'

Susan snorted a laugh. 'Look at you! You're beautiful, you could have whoever you wanted. Why did you have to fixate on him? He's nothing special really. Kind, gentle, averagely handsome. If you knew him better, you'd also find that he's a bit weak and a little dull. I don't understand why you wanted him so badly.'

'I didn't want him!' The words coming out on a cry surprised me as much as her. I pushed to my feet, the chair toppling to the floor behind me with a crash. I turned away, but it wasn't that easy to get away from her critical eyes. Her reflection in the window was clear. I wrapped my arms around myself and turned back.

'When I saw the photograph, I remembered how much he'd loved me, how good he'd made me feel. I didn't want Mark, not really; I wanted to recapture that feeling of happiness.'

Susan got to her feet to face me, hands flat on the table as she leaned towards me, her face scrunched in anger. 'Happiness! You're kidding me! It doesn't come that easily. Ethan said you'd moved in with your mother when you came back to Bristol. Why wasn't that enough for you? She'd have kept you safe from Ivan. You'd have been happy enough there, wouldn't you?'

I pushed my fingers into my hair. 'You couldn't possibly understand.'

She straightened and folded her arms across her chest. Looking almost militant. 'Contrary to what you might think, I'm not the least bit stupid, so why don't you try me.'

52

HANNAH

Anger bristled between us. Oddly, right at that moment, I realised we had a lot in common. We'd both been let down by the people who were supposed to love and protect us.

I reached down and picked up the chair. 'You might as well sit. It's a long story.'

'Another one,' Susan said with heavy sarcasm.

She looked towards the door and for a moment, I thought she was going to leave. It suddenly seemed important that she knew everything. That she believed me. I reached for my phone, turned it on, and opened my photographs. 'Here,' I said holding it out to her. 'I know you're not sure if I was telling you the truth about what Ivan did to me. I took photos.' When she didn't take it, I reached forward, slid a finger across the screen to bring up one after the other of the shots I'd taken that day. 'What the camera doesn't show is how painful all this was.'

Finally, she took it from me, her thumb sliding across the screen, eyes narrowing as she peered at each image. It was a good phone; they'd come out well.

'The last few were taken a couple of days later when the bruises had turned more colourful.'

'Right,' she said, handing it back to me. 'So you told me the truth about what he did.'

I put the phone down and sat. 'I told you the truth. I told the police, the doctors and nurses in the hospital that I'd fallen down the stairs. I don't think they believed me but I stuck to my story.'

'For goodness' sake, why didn't you tell them the truth?'

I sighed. 'For the same reason that many victims of domestic violence don't tell; I was ashamed, embarrassed. Anyway, I'd already been told he was in a bad state so it seemed a bit pointless to have him prosecuted.' There was no reason to tell her that I'd been determined to get my revenge but had been beaten to it by fate. 'Anyway, now that you've seen the proof, you believe me. And maybe you'll believe the rest of my story.' I swallowed the lump in my throat, the one that appeared automatically whenever I thought about those days. 'I adored my father. He was a gentle, sweet man.' I smiled, remembering. 'He'd lift me up on his shoulders and run up and down our long back garden, jumping over the vegetable beds, ducking under the boughs of the fruit trees.' Laughter and sunshine. A magical world.

'He was the one who'd read me a bedtime story. I slept in a single bed and I remember I had to press against the wall to give him space to sit beside me.' I wasn't sure why I was telling Susan about him. Maybe I was simply working it out in my head and she was a good listener. 'Then he was gone.'

'Gone? He died?'

Everything was so black and white in her world. I thought it had been in mine. 'Mother broke the news the following morning. Told me he'd gone off with some tart to Thailand. I was ten and didn't understand how he could simply leave that way. No good-

bye, no explanation, no attempt to contact me in all the years that followed. This man who'd said he loved me.'

Maybe the poker-face I'd always prided myself on wearing had slipped, or perhaps Susan was more empathetic than I'd given her credit for, because she suddenly stretched a hand across the table and took hold of mine. Her hand was warm, her grip stronger than I'd expected as if she was trying to share some of her strength, to infuse me with it.

'I'm sorry,' she said, her voice quiet, calm, motherly. 'As it happens, my father left too. But I was older and I had my sisters. Being alone, that must have been hard.'

Her kindness brought stupid tears to my eyes. Reluctant to pull my hands away from the comforting warmth of hers, they soon trickled unhindered down my cheeks and plopped to the table.

It was Susan who finally took her hand back. She stood and moved away. I heard cupboard doors opening and shutting before she returned and placed a handful of kitchen roll into my hands. She let me sob for a few minutes, waited while I blew my nose, cleared my throat, then I met her eyes. 'Thank you. I'm not usually such a wuss.'

'You were ten and abandoned by a man who was supposed to have loved you. I think the damage he caused left you stuck in a self-destruct cycle.'

'You mean getting involved with older men who treat me badly, then pay me well.' I smiled. 'Psychobabble but possibly true.'

Susan didn't take offence. 'I have to admit, all the psychology I know comes from self-help books but I think I'm right. I think you went looking for a father figure, but then wanted to punish them for what your father had done in the only way you knew how. Making them pay.'

'You make it sound like I'd prostituted myself,' I said, pulling a few more sheets off the roll to blow my nose. I really hadn't seen it like that. All the money, all the *things*... the jewellery, handbags, clothes... I'd taken them as my due. Making them all pay for what my father had done. I was determined no man was going to abandon me again. I was the one going to do the running away. 'Mark was so crazy about me, kept telling me how much he loved me.' I looked up and met her eyes with a grimace. 'Loved me! I'd been there. Men who say they love you, leave. I wasn't waiting around to be hurt again, so I did what I'd always done. Finished it first.' I got to my feet and crossed to where my jacket was still hanging on the back of the chair and reached into the pocket. When I sat again, I looked at what I held, then put it on the table and slid it across, keeping my hand flat on top.

'My darling mother's god is respectability. She moved us from the house we lived in to the one she lives in now and told the neighbours my father had died. I was slapped if I didn't remember the lie. Slapped if I cried and said I missed him. Slapped if I forgot.' I managed a shaky smile. 'My mother was proud of her slap.' I lifted a hand and brushed it over my head. 'She was careful and aimed for my head, not my cheeks. God forbid the neighbours would see a bruise.'

'How could she be so cruel!'

'Not all mothers are like you.' I lifted my hand slowly to expose what I was hiding. 'See what you make of this.'

SUSAN

She picked up the burgundy-red passport and looked at it. Seemed like an ordinary passport to her, but she saw the gleam of expectation in Hannah's eyes so she guessed there was more to it. Flicking to the photo page, she slanted it to look at the image. It was a typical passport shot, unsmiling, but there was no disputing that this was a good looking, pleasant-faced man. There was something about his eyes that said he smiled easily.

'James Parker,' she read, then looked up. 'Your father. You take after him. Maybe it's why she hated you so much. You reminded her of the man who abandoned her.'

'Hated me!' Hannah looked surprised for a moment. 'Yes. Do you know, I never really thought of that. Oh, I know she didn't have any affection for me, but hate... but yes, I think you're right.' She reached out and tapped the back of the passport. 'But for the wrong reason. Look again.'

The wrong reason? Perhaps Susan was tired, weary, her head over-filled with her own problems, but she didn't know what Hannah was talking about. She could see disappointment in her eyes, and looked at the photo again, trying to understand. Then it

came to her. A bit like the photos that idiot investigator had originally given her, but this time, it wasn't what she *wasn't* seeing that was the issue; it was what she *was* seeing. The passport. Because if James Parker had gone to Thailand, how could it be there? She checked the dates, then nodded and looked up. 'Your father never went to Thailand.' She shut the passport. 'He didn't go anywhere.'

'He always seemed like a magical person to me, but not even he could have crossed international borders without documentation.'

'So he's still in the UK.' The disappointed expression had returned. Susan wanted to shout at Hannah, to tell her she'd had enough. That she didn't care, that all she wanted was Mark.

Hannah reached for the passport, opened it, and stared at the photograph of her father. 'You don't get it, do you?' She snapped the passport shut. 'I don't think he ever left our home in Yorkshire.'

Susan was weary and befuddled, not stupid. She looked at Hannah in horror. 'You think she killed him?' It seemed to be a huge leap to her but then she remembered how the mother had slapped the grieving child, how she'd forced her to lie. Susan had never met a woman like that. She was possibly capable of anything.

'I think it happened that last night, in their bed.' Hannah spoke calmly in a matter-of-fact way, but Susan could see the struggle it was for her as she dabbed tears away roughly with the balled-up tissue in her hand. 'I always wondered why she'd brought it with us when we moved. She left everything else behind.' She snorted a laugh. 'Would you believe I thought it was because she hoped he'd come back. What a fool I was.'

'You were ten!'

'Ten,' she nodded agreement. 'And since then, for thirty years, I've hated him for leaving me, for never saying goodbye. And now

I know it wasn't true, and I feel...' She snuffled noisily, '...bereft and angry. I could have been a different person, a good person.'

Susan could have said she was, but it was too late for more lies. 'What are you going to do?'

It was a long time before Hannah looked up, her fingers almost caressing the cover of the passport. Susan wanted to ask her what she was thinking, but she wasn't sure she wanted to know. Not really. Her thoughts might be even darker than the ones rattling around Susan's head.

'Do?' Hannah rubbed the tissue over her eyes, then snuffled again. 'All these years believing he'd abandoned me. All these years searching for...' She looked at Susan, her eyes focused and sharp. 'What the fuck was I looking for all these years, eh? You were right. A daddy complex. And all this time...' She took a deep breath and straightened in her seat. 'There's only one thing to do really. Make my bitch of a mother pay.'

Her face was twisted and angry, her fists clenched. Maybe she'd learned something about violence from Ivan. Susan reached a hand across the table towards her. 'Don't do something you'll regret.'

Hannah looked at the hand for a moment before sitting back and folding her arms across her chest. 'You thought I'd killed Ivan; now you think I'm going to what? Kill my mother?'

Susan felt colour flood her cheeks. It had been exactly what she'd thought. 'I'm sorry.'

Hannah blew her nose and dropped the tissue onto the pile that was building up on the floor beside her chair. 'Don't be. I would kill her if I could, but despite everything, despite what you saw–' She pointed towards the ceiling. '–I'm really *not* a violent person. What I'm going to do is take the passport into my local nick and tell my story to the police. I'll give them the passport, tell them how swiftly we moved from Yorkshire, and about the

vegetable plots at the end of our garden there. Mother was always digging. I guess that's where they'll find him.'

How far Susan had come, when she didn't think it was strange to be sitting at a table opposite her husband's mistress discussing whether or not her father was buried in the vegetable patch. She was about to say that she'd heard Hannah was a great actress, had opened her mouth to say she didn't believe a word of her story, when Hannah spoke again, silencing her.

'When I do, then at last, I might finally be able to write my own narrative.'

It was such an odd thing to say, Susan gave a gruff laugh. 'What does that mean, write your own narrative?'

'Doesn't it sound better than getting a life?'

Actually, Susan had to admit, it did. 'Much better. My sisters, Mark, even my damn son, they're always telling me I should get a life. Writing my own narrative sounds far better.'

'Why don't you?'

Susan wasn't sure if Hannah genuinely wanted to know or just keen to switch the conversation away from herself. It was no harm to give her a little space. 'Write my own narrative?' Why didn't she? She thought of all the excuses she'd used over the years. Her sisters, Mark, Drew, no time, too much to do. 'Ruts, they're dangerous traps. You stick your head over the parapet, it looks scary out there, so you duck back down where it's safe. Stay there nice and cosy.' She shook her head as the truth hit her. 'I'd wanted to go to university when I left school. I couldn't then but I could have in the years that followed. Damn it, I could go now.'

Hannah smiled. 'You're around the same age as me, aren't you? Forty-ish?'

'Forty-one.'

'Not too late then, is it?'

'Not for you either.' Susan watched as Hannah's smile was

replaced by an expression of defeated sadness. It had probably been there all along, buried under the exotic layer of glamour she'd kept in place for years. 'What's stopping you?'

Hannah took a deep breath. 'I'm afraid.'

The voice was light, almost childish. The voice of that little ten-year-old girl finally being able to admit that she was frightened. Susan did what came naturally: she got to her feet, went to Hannah, and put an arm around her shoulder. 'You can do it, go to the police, get justice for your father. And then do that writing your own narrative stuff.' She gave a final squeeze, then straightened. 'What about Mark?' As if they were going to discuss custody of her husband. The situation was getting more ridiculous. She wanted to leave, to get away from this stinking house, this damaged woman, but she couldn't leave until she knew where she stood.

Hannah pulled her mobile from her pocket. 'He'd never have been happy with me, you know, not long term.' She tapped out a message. 'There,' she said, turning the screen towards Susan, who leaned forward and squinted to read it.

This was a mistake. I was trying to recapture what we'd had. It wasn't working. Goodbye.

'He won't hear from me again,' Hannah said. 'You've been kind to me, it is much appreciated, and to show how much, you won't hear from me, or see me again.'

Susan looked at her. Not one word of apology for what she'd been put through. The words sounded sincere and were matched by the expression on her beautiful face but could she really believe she'd gone to all this trouble to get Mark, then drop him when she had him? *She's a brilliant actress.* Ethan's words echoed

in her head. But then he'd been a liar too. There was nobody to trust. 'I'd better get going. You going to be okay?'

'Yes.' Hannah picked up the passport and got to her feet. 'I'll say goodbye to Ivan, then head to the police station in Thornbury.'

'Right.' There didn't seem a lot else to say. They weren't friends. Susan shivered at the thought. She'd done what she'd set out to do, even if the journey to getting there was far different to what she'd planned. 'Good luck,' she said, then nodded towards the door. 'I'll get going.'

She felt Hannah's eyes following her and was suddenly conscious of the knives sitting only a few feet away. What if she grabbed a knife and killed Susan? Nobody knew she was there. If the story about her father was true, it could be a case of like mother like daughter. There were probably vegetable plots nearby. Susan would be fertiliser. She was about to break into a run for the door when she heard Hannah speak again.

'Drive carefully.'

Two simple words, but there was a hint of malicious glee in them as if Hannah had known exactly what Susan was thinking. She didn't turn, but simply raised a hand in a last farewell, and walked quickly to the front door, pulling it open on a sigh of relief. Then she was outside, in the rain, breathing cool, fresh, clean air.

Susan pulled the door shut behind her and crunched across the gravel driveway to her car.

It was time to go home.

54

SUSAN

To Susan's surprise, it was only a little after five thirty when she pulled into the driveway of their home. It had been such a strange day, her head was still buzzing trying to slot everything into place. An impossible task – lies and truths were inextricably tangled. She'd seen the message Hannah had sent to Mark, so perhaps regardless of her suspicions, she'd been telling the truth about that.

Such a strange day. She felt different to the woman who'd gone pell-mell to Windsor only hours before. Good different, though. Hannah's notion of *writing her own narrative* had intrigued her, occupying her mind for the journey home, pushing both Drew and Mark outside.

The house was quiet. Whereas before, she'd seen it as an absence... no son, no husband... now, she saw it as a haven of peace. She dropped her bag on the bottom step of the stair, went into the kitchen and stood looking out over the garden.

It was the buzz of her phone that finally broke the silence. She reached for it, looked at the screen and shook her head. Drew.

She pressed to answer. 'Hi.'

'Mum, hello. Is everything okay?'

She frowned. Mark hadn't said anything, had he? Hadn't told their son that she was losing the plot. Worse, hadn't told their son that he'd met someone and was leaving. 'Of course, why wouldn't it be?'

'It's just that...' A long sigh came down the line. 'Well, I haven't heard from you in a couple of days, that's all. So, I was worried.'

He was worried about her! 'I've just been busy; everything is fine.'

'Right, that's okay then. I was thinking I might come home for a weekend. Just a quick visit. I miss you.'

Susan wanted to laugh, or cry; she wasn't sure what the appropriate emotion was. If Drew had rung her a few days before, she'd have cried from happiness. But now... all the one-word answers to her messages, all the phone calls where she was left talking to herself because of that mysterious black spot, all the heartache he'd caused her in the last couple of months when all she'd wanted was the little shit to reply to her messages with a bit more detail than *I'm fine*.

This, her only son, who'd gone to the best schools, only wore designer clothes and only had the best sports' gear. This darling boy who was given a more than healthy allowance so he could enjoy university life without having to worry. A polite boy, everyone said, and he was, but thoughtless too. Perhaps it was time he learnt to be kind as well as polite.

'That would be lovely, Drew. What weekend are you thinking of coming?'

'I'm not sure yet, maybe next, or the one after. Does it matter?'

And there it was. Susan the doormat. Wipe your feet on it. Use it when you wanted to. Hop over it if you didn't and carry the muck into the house with you. 'Well, actually, yes it does. As I said, I've been very busy recently and may not be free. Actually, I

need to go now. Lovely speaking to you, darling. Give me a buzz or better yet, message me when you're thinking of coming home, and I'll see if it suits.' And she hung up before he had a chance to reply.

She immediately felt guilty and quickly tapped out a message.

I miss you too.

Nothing more. Not the *come home whenever you like, I'll be here waiting* he'd probably expected. She gave a quick laugh. Perhaps she should have told him that she was busy writing her own narrative.

And on that note, with more energy than she'd felt in a while, she went upstairs. She'd spent the drive from Windsor rethinking her life, all that had happened that day and the days and weeks before.

It took less time than she'd expected to pack two suitcases, and by the time she heard the front door open, she was finished. She shut them and with one dragging down each arm, headed down the stairs. Mark was still in the hallway, a briefcase in one hand, his other flicking through the post she'd left in a pile on the hall table. He gave a puzzled glance upwards as she descended with one suitcase shushing against the wall, the other tapping a rhythm against the oak uprights of the banister.

She dropped them on the floor near the door and turned to look at him. What a strange emotion love was... She'd loved this man for so long, still did, but now that love was shadowed with disappointment and edged with pain. He looked pale. Had Hannah's message left him feeling desolate or relieved? Desolate perhaps, but not for long. He was a man now, not a callow boy, and if Hannah stayed away as she'd promised she would, he'd soon realise he'd been trying to recapture a slice of his youth and

be relieved the affair was over. Relieved too that his darling, faithful doormat of a wife knew nothing about his transgression. Love and hate... how odd to feel both emotions so strongly at the same time.

Mark eyed the cases with vague curiosity. 'What's happening? Are you going somewhere?'

'Not really.' She gave a faint smile. 'Someone told me I should write my own narrative, so I thought I'd start today.'

'Okay,' he dragged the word out. 'I've no idea what that means. Where are you going?'

'Ah,' she said, pushing the nearest case with the toe of her shoe so hard, it rocked and wobbled before settling. 'I'm not going anywhere. You are. I've packed all you should need for a while. We can come to some arrangement about you coming back to collect the rest of your stuff another time.' She held out a hand. 'I'll have the house keys from you now though, thanks.' When he simply stood there looking stunned, she shook her head. 'Did you think I wouldn't find out about her, Mark? Do you really think I'm that stupid?'

'How...' The briefcase dropped from his hand, hit the floor with a clunk and fell over. His already pale face took on a grey tinge. 'I'm sorry.' He took a step towards her, stopping when she took a step away and held her hands up. 'It's over,' he said. 'Honest. It was a mistake.'

'Yes,' she agreed. 'A big one. When Drew left, I needed you and you bailed on me. I'm not sure I can forgive that.'

He stretched a hand towards her. 'I'm sorry, I was stupid, it was...' He shook his head, as if right at that moment, he wasn't sure what it was. 'I do love you.'

Yes, she thought, he really did, but he'd broken them, betrayed her, and demeaned himself. A weak man. She loved him anyway. She stood back and watched as he gathered his briefcase under

one arm, and picked up both suitcases, then stood helplessly looking at the shut door as if expecting it to miraculously open. Afraid he was going to cry, and that she'd weaken and beg him to stay, she hurried over to open it.

'I'm sorry,' he said again.

Then he was gone. She shut the door and listened to the sound of him opening and closing the boot of his car. She moved then, hurrying through to the living room to peep around the edge of the curtain, her heart aching to see the shine of tears on his face. The lump in her throat refused to shift until anger pushed it down. He'd done this to them.

She wondered where he'd go. Back to Hannah's apartment to appeal for yet another chance? He'd said it was over, but it hadn't been his choice. Maybe he'd beg. If he did, would she forget the promise she'd made to Susan and take him back?

She pressed her forehead to the cool glass. If she did, this time, Susan wouldn't hesitate. This time, she'd kill the bitch.

55

HANNAH

I didn't move for a long time after I heard the door slam shut, then I pulled the chair out and sat. The passport was in my hand; I opened it, looked at the photograph of my father. He was just as I remembered. I smoothed a finger over his face. Such a good man. If he had lived, my life would have been so different.

Maybe I would have stayed with Mark all those years before and built a different kind of life. I might have turned out like Susan. A snort escaped. No, I couldn't imagine ever being that gullible. The stupid woman had swallowed the lie.

Not about Mark, though. I hadn't lied about that. Learning the truth about my father had changed everything. I knew what I needed to do, and when I was done, I'd need to get away. There was no longer any room for Mark in my future.

I swallowed the lump in my throat. It didn't matter. Happiness was vastly overrated.

The wind had picked up outside, driving rain against the window, a rhythmic pitter patter that should have been soothing. It wasn't. Everything was irritating me. It was the waiting. I'd

never been good at it. Delayed gratification had never seemed much fun.

But there was no point in leaving yet.

* * *

It was two hours later before I manoeuvred the BMW through the gates and headed back to Thornbury. I wondered what Susan was doing. Such a doormat as she was, I pictured her rushing about, making Mark his favourite dinner, lighting candles, putting fresh sheets on the bed. Relieved to have him all to herself again. Stupid woman. She wasn't brave enough to confront him so he'd believe he got away with it. He'd miss me for a while, miss the great sex. Then he'd be relieved. And then, when he realised he was back in the same old rut, he'd look around for excitement.

Poor Susan. Poor, sad doormat. Someone else was always going to write her narrative.

My narrative, however – drive to the police station, tell them my theory, hand over the proof in the shape of the passport, have my mother arrested, my father's body exhumed and buried with the dignity he deserved – despite what I'd told Susan, that wasn't how it was going to be written.

The law might punish Mother for killing my father, but they'd never make her atone for what she'd done to me: depriving me of my father, setting me on a path to self-destruction. Vengeance was mine and I intended to take it.

I glanced at the cleaver that lay diagonally across the passenger seat then back at the speedometer. It was tipping at ninety. I eased off the accelerator. It wasn't a night to be stopped for speeding.

By the time I reached Mother's house, it was nearly eleven. I

drove slowly past, relieved to see the rim of light around the curtains on her bedroom window.

She'd have taken a sleeping tablet. She always did. I remember her telling the doctor she hadn't been able to sleep since my father died. Grief, he'd said. Now I knew better. Guilt, even deeply subconscious guilt, does not make a good bedfellow.

She'd take the pill, climb into bed, and switch out the light. Once asleep, it was almost impossible to wake her. I remembered trying over the years. The night I got my first period, waking in pain, my eyes wide in horror to find blood on my sheet. I knew what it was, of course, I'd been to the talks in school, but the reality was more shocking. I wanted comfort. There wasn't any.

It wasn't safe to park there in the valley of the squinting windows so I drove a few streets away, found a parking space and walked back.

I still had the spare key she'd given me; sliding it home, I opened the door quietly. Not because I thought she'd wake, but because the neighbours might hear and look out in curtain-twitching curiosity. I held the cleaver hanging down and tight against my leg for the same reason. Then I was inside and could relax. I had no fear for what I was about to do. It seemed rather apt that my mother should die in the bed where she'd killed my father.

The stair carpet was worn smooth and my feet glided on it as I climbed one step at a time to the small landing. The door to my old bedroom was shut. I guessed she'd have already stripped the bed, desperate to remove any trace of the daughter she disliked... no, hated, I had to get that clear in my head. Susan had been right; Mother hated me. Remembering that would make what I was about to do easier.

Her door was shut. The key gone from the lock. What had she thought when she'd seen her door open? And the drawer? Had

she known immediately that I'd found the passport and knew the truth about what had happened to my father?

Of course, she would have done. My mother might have been many things, but she wasn't stupid.

I reached for the door handle and pressed down ever so slowly, afraid, despite my mother's medicated slumber, a squeak might wake her. But the handle moved quietly and the door opened with a shush against the thicker bedroom carpet.

Perhaps violence was in my blood, because I felt no fear as I moved towards the bed. The room was in darkness, but enough light leaked around the edges of the ill-fitting curtains from the streetlamps outside to show me the bulge under the covers.

Had she done the same with my father? Waited until he was helplessly asleep before plunging a knife into his big, gorgeous heart. I moved closer. I could do this. Ivan had shown me how easy it was to inflict harm. The cleaver blade was broad. One thrust should do it. Sever a vital organ. Kill her.

I shifted the handle in my hand, then raised it and brought it down with such force that the whole blade vanished into her. Expecting some resistance – muscle or bone – I was caught off-guard when there was none and fell forward onto the soft mound of duvet.

The light came on, allowing me to see what I'd missed. Mother wasn't there.

'You always thought you were so clever, didn't you?' The voice came from behind me. 'You and your father, two of a kind. Both of you thought you could get the better of me.'

I pushed up from the bed, but before I had a chance to recover, I heard a swish and felt a draught as something came barrelling through the air towards me. I learnt some interesting things in those last seconds. That you can still think after your skull has been shattered; that for a few microseconds, as you

watch globules of your brain spattering in front of your eyes, you're alive and capable of rational thought.

I would have killed my mother, she *had* killed me, it seemed we were more alike than I'd realised. Or was it a case of nurture versus nature? Too late for that particular debate.

Too late too for a theological debate on heaven and hell – if they existed, I knew where I'd be going. I had time for a twinge of regret that I wouldn't see my father again. If there was a heaven, that's where he'd be.

A final thought slithered through what remained of my brain as my life faded: I wondered if I'd beat Ivan to hell.

ACKNOWLEDGEMENTS

I'm lucky to be published with one of the best publishers, Boldwood Books, and owe a huge thanks to all the staff, but especially to my wonderful, supportive editor, Emily Ruston.

Grateful thanks to all those who read, review and blog about my books, and for those who shout about them whenever they can – it's always worrying to name names as there are so many who are owed thanks, but deserving of a special mention are Sarah Westfield and Jade Potter – thanks ladies, you're both special.

Thanks to the usual bunch of people who keep me sane – Jenny O'Brien, Anita Waller, Judith Baker, Keri Beevis, Pam Lecky, and Lynda Checkley.

Last, but never least, thanks to my lovely husband, Robert, my siblings, extended family and to Fatty Arbuckle for purring so nicely.

I have a habit of memorising quotations, and like to make use of them when appropriate – I've used two in this book so for anyone who is curious about them, here they are:

'Would he have made of me a saint, or I of him a sinner?' attributed to St Augustine of Hippo, a 4th century Roman theologian.

'In a minute there is time for decisions and revisions which a minute will reverse.' From 'The Love Song of J. Alfred Prufrock' by T.S. Eliot.

I love to hear from readers. Overleaf you will find a number of ways to get in touch with me.

ABOUT THE AUTHOR

Valerie Keogh is the internationally bestselling author of several psychological thrillers and crime series. She originally comes from Dublin but now lives in Wiltshire and worked as a nurse for many years.

Sign up to Valerie Keogh's mailing list here for news, competitions and updates on future books.

Follow Valerie on social media:

 facebook.com/valeriekeoghnovels

 x.com/ValerieKeogh1

 instagram.com/valeriekeogh2

 bookbub.com/authors/valerie-keogh

ALSO BY VALERIE KEOGH

The Lodger

The Widow

The Trophy Wife

The Librarian

The Nurse

The Lawyer

The House Keeper

The Mistress

THE

Murder

LIST

THE MURDER LIST IS A NEWSLETTER DEDICATED TO SPINE-CHILLING FICTION AND GRIPPING PAGE-TURNERS!

SIGN UP TO MAKE SURE YOU'RE ON OUR HIT LIST FOR EXCLUSIVE DEALS, AUTHOR CONTENT, AND COMPETITIONS.

SIGN UP TO OUR
NEWSLETTER

BIT.LY/THEMURDERLISTNEWS